**"Listen. I hate to do t[...]
there's a lot on my mi[...]**

"Maybe we should do this another—"

"Nope," Everett said.

Kaya jerked her head back. "I'm sorry. 'Nope'?"

"That's right," he said with a decisive bob of his head. "Nope."

"You don't want me tonight, Everett."

He didn't miss a beat. "I beg to differ, sweetheart."

"I'm distracted. I'm tired. I'm a little cranky. I'm more than a little sore..."

"I'll take you any way I can get you. Distracted, tired, cranky... If you're hurting, I'll carry you."

"Oh, that's nice."

"As for the sore part, I plan to buy a large bottle of wine for our table when we get to the restaurant for our reservation in..." he checked his big silver watch "...a half hour. And I'm not waiting another three months for you to decide that this is right again, so get your bag because otherwise, I'm hauling you over my shoulder and we're leaving without it."

"I'd like a word with whichever barnyard animal raised you."

"Can't," he said. "We sold it for beef a while ago."

Dear Reader,

As a kid, I had vivid, exciting dreams of teleporting to interesting places. That's why I fell so deeply in love with reading and storytelling.

Eaton Edge and Fuego, New Mexico, are fictional places, but they are tangible to me. I feel like I've walked (sometimes run) alongside these characters. I've lovingly prepared authentic meals with Paloma in her kitchen. I've jumped canyon walls with Wolfe and galloped through a snowstorm with Ellis. Like Eveline and Luella, I've come home.

So when I tell you how bittersweet it is to see this trilogy come to a close, believe me. I've known exactly how I wanted it to end...but it's still hard to say goodbye.

I have anticipated writing Everett's book since his steely introduction in *Coldero Ridge Cowboy*. I fell in love with the grumpy, exasperating cattle baron in *Ollero Creek Conspiracy*. One thing I did not anticipate was how soft this uncompromising man would become when confronted with a strong, powerful heroine like Kaya Altaha.

I give you *Close Range Cattleman*!

Happy reading, as always,

Amber

P.S. If you like Kaya and Everett's story, visit www.amberleighwilliams.com for some exciting extras—including deleted scenes, after-HEA episodes and recipes from Paloma's kitchen!

CLOSE RANGE CATTLEMAN

AMBER LEIGH WILLIAMS

HARLEQUIN

ROMANTIC
SUSPENSE

HARLEQUIN®
ROMANTIC SUSPENSE™

Recycling programs
for this product may
not exist in your area.

ISBN-13: 978-1-335-59404-4

Close Range Cattleman

Copyright © 2024 by Amber Leigh Williams

All rights reserved. No part of this book may be used or reproduced in any manner whatsoever without written permission except in the case of brief quotations embodied in critical articles and reviews.

This is a work of fiction. Names, characters, places and incidents are either the product of the author's imagination or are used fictitiously. Any resemblance to actual persons, living or dead, businesses, companies, events or locales is entirely coincidental.

For questions and comments about the quality of this book, please contact us at CustomerService@Harlequin.com.

TM and ® are trademarks of Harlequin Enterprises ULC.

Harlequin Enterprises ULC
22 Adelaide St. West, 41st Floor
Toronto, Ontario M5H 4E3, Canada
www.Harlequin.com

Printed in U.S.A.

Amber Leigh Williams is an author, wife, mother of two and dog mom. She has been writing sexy small-town romance with memorable characters since 2006. Her Harlequin romance miniseries is set in her charming hometown of Fairhope, Alabama. She lives on the Alabama Gulf Coast, where she loves being outdoors with her family and a good book. Visit her on the web at www.amberleighwilliams.com!

Books by Amber Leigh Williams

Harlequin Romantic Suspense

Hunted on the Bay

Fuego, New Mexico

Coldero Ridge Cowboy
Ollero Creek Conspiracy
Close Range Cattleman

Harlequin Superromance

Navy SEAL's Match
Navy SEAL Promise
Wooing the Wedding Planner
His Rebel Heart
Married One Night
A Place with Briar

Visit the Author Profile page
at Harlequin.com for more titles.

As this is my tenth Harlequin romance and the ten-year anniversary of my Harlequin debut, I dedicate this book to you, reader.

Thank you for turning the page.

Chapter 1

"Hell's bells," Everett Eaton groaned as he crouched in the sagebrush.

Over his shoulder, his newest ranch hand, Lucas, bounced on the heels of his roughed-up Ariats and cursed vividly. "Jesus, boss," he hissed. "Jesus Christ."

"Calm your britches," Everett said as he examined the blood trail in the red dirt of his high desert country homeland. Among the signs of struggle, he saw the telltale teardrop-shaped prints with no discernible claw marks. He lifted his fingers, tilted his head and squinted, following the drag lines in the soil. "He went off thataway."

"Taking Number 23's calf with him," Javier Rivera, Everett's lead wrangler, added.

Everett swapped the wad of gum from one side of his mouth to the other. Standing, he shifted his feet and placed his hands on his hips. The trail disappeared over the next ridge, into the thicket of trees that surrounded Wapusa River, the lifeblood of his family's fourteen-hundred-acre cattle ranch, Eaton Edge and the sandstone cliffs that served as its natural border to the north. He nodded toward the mountain that straddled the river. "I reckon 23 dropped the calf during the night and the damn thing was lying in wait."

"Or smelled the afterbirth and came running," Javier guessed.

"He could have been out stalking and got lucky," Everett weighed. "Either way, he took it up Ol' Whalebones, ate what he wanted and covered up the rest."

"How do you know he's up there?" Lucas asked. His bronze cheeks contrasted with the paleness around the area of his mouth. His head swiveled in all directions as he tried looking everywhere at once. "He could be anywhere."

Everett eyed the back side of the mountain. It curved toward the bright blue sky. "You can hear him in winter. He's most active then. He doesn't go into torpor, like the bear. When Ellis and I rode out to check fences once the snow cleared after Christmas, we could hear his screams echoing off everything and nothing."

"Ah, hell," Lucas moaned. He gave an involuntary shudder.

Javier clapped him on the back. "You stay sharp."

"Watch your mount when you're up in these parts," Everett told him. "And make sure you're strapped. Got it?"

Lucas nodded jerkily. "Geez. Shouldn't the bastard have died like five, ten years ago or something? Ellis figures Tombs is eighteen. Mountain lions aren't supposed to live that long. Are they?"

"Not in the wild," Javier considered. He swapped his rifle from his left hand to his right, following the river with dark eyes. "Twelve years is a long life for a cougar. Could be another cat, moving into Tombstone's territory. Right, boss?"

"Maybe." Everett scanned the sagebrush, the canyons and the sandstone and couldn't chase the eerie sensation creeping along his spine.

Someone…or something was watching. "Mount up. I told the sheriff we'd meet near the falls."

Lucas sighed as they approached the three horses knotted together near the river's edge. "Sure wish we were riding in the other direction."

Everett laid his hand on his red mare's flank. Crazy Alice had been restless approaching Ol' Whalebones, tossing her head and the reins. She'd sensed that something was off long before he had. He patted her, then seated his rifle into the sleeve on the saddle and swung up into position with the ease of someone who'd spent a lifetime there. As he waited for the others to do the same, he knuckled his ten-gallon hat up an inch on his brow to get a better look at the canyon.

Tombstone was a legend and had been for as long as he could remember. Everett had first seen the mountain lion while camping with his brother, Ellis. Tombstone had watched them around their fire for the better part of the night. No one had slept. Everett remembered how the cat's eyes had tossed the firelight back at them. It was then he'd first seen what distinguished Tombstone from other cats— a missing eye.

His behavior, too, set him apart. Mountain lions shied away from human activity. It was why so little was known about them. In the last hundred years, only twenty-seven fatal cougar attacks had been reported. It was the rattlesnake they had to worry about most on the high desert plain.

But Everett had known that night what it was to be prey. He hadn't cared for it.

He'd seen Tombstone again off and on through the years. Males were territorial and Tombs ruled Eaton Edge's northern quarter and the surrounding hunting grounds.

Everett didn't believe in omens, but even he had to admit that it was strange how every time he or Ellis or their father, Hammond, had spotted Tombs high in the hills, trouble had followed. Hammond's first heart attack, the deaths of Everett's mother, Josephine Coldero, and his half sister, Angel, his sister Eveline's car accident...

Over the last year, Everett had convinced himself the animal was dead...until his father's death over the summer and a ride into the high country where he had seen Tombs take down a small elk.

Everett may be chief of operations at Eaton Edge, but it was Tombs who was king in these parts—and Everett reluctantly gave him his due.

He clicked his tongue at Crazy Alice, urging her to walk on.

"What's the sheriff and deputies think they're going to find up here?" Lucas asked as his neck mimicked a barred owl, rotating at an impressive angle so he could scan the shadows cast by boulders.

"Hiker," Everett grunted.

"Just one?" Javier asked.

"Yep. Kid thought he'd livestream his ascent," Everett said.

"He didn't make it?" Lucas asked. "Seems easy enough."

"The climb's intermediate," Javier noted.

"The broadcast cut off before he reached the top," Everett said. "No one's seen or heard from him in three days. Parents in San Gabriel are worried."

"How old?" Javier asked.

"Sixteen," Everett noted.

Javier made a pitying noise. "Same age as my Armand."

"Shouldn't he be in school?" Lucas asked.

Everett raised a brow. "Shouldn't you?"

"I got kicked out," Lucas informed him. "Didn't my mom tell you?"

Everett pursed his lips. "Your mama told me you were too much to handle and thought I could do something about it."

"How's that coming, *amigo*?" Javier asked, with a sly grin under the shade of his hat.

Everett shook his head. "I have a habit of inheriting problems of monumental proportions."

"Sure wish you had your dogs with you," Lucas told Everett as they crossed a stream. "They'd be able to smell a lion. They'd warn us, wouldn't they?"

Everett scowled, thinking of the three cattle dogs he'd raised from pups. "I'm not keen on putting any of them on Tombs' menu."

"He wouldn't attack them. Any animal would run from their baying. Even a predator."

Everett couldn't predict what Tombs would do, but he had trained the dogs for protection as much as herding. If they scented danger, they'd go looking for it. Everett couldn't think of any circumstance where Bones, Boomer and Boaz meeting Tombs wouldn't end in at least one of them maimed or killed.

"You've got a hot date tonight," Lucas recalled.

"What do you know about it?" Everett barked.

Lucas scrambled. "I heard it."

"From?"

"Mateo. Spencer told him. Spencer heard it from the house. Nobody knows who you're going out with."

Lucas was baiting him, and Everett wasn't willing to share any of his plans for the evening. He gnawed at the wad of gum in his mouth. "What've my plans got to do with anything?"

"We won't make it back to headquarters by sundown,"

Lucas considered. "I figure you'd have sent Ellis in your place to find the guy."

"Kid went missing," Everett reminded him. "If he's camped out somewhere on the Edge, I aim to find him."

The horses climbed to the mouth of a natural arch where the river sluiced and gurgled busily from the mouth of a cave. Water flowed freely now that the snow had melted in the Sangre de Cristo Mountains.

This was the lifeblood of Eaton Edge. The river fed the grass that made cattle ranching in the high desert of New Mexico possible.

As they neared the falls, Everett tugged on Crazy Alice's reins. A smile transformed the grim set of his mouth. The loss of 23's calf had unsettled him. But the sight ahead made the trouble slink back to the corners of his mind. "Howdy, Sheriff," he called. He took off his hat.

The Jicarilla-Apache Native American woman was five feet three inches at the crest of her uniformed hat. Under the two-toned, neutral threads that suited her position, she was built solid. Everett couldn't help but let his gaze travel over the hips under her weapons belt or the swell of her breast underneath her gold badge and name plate.

Sheriff Kaya Altaha's black-lensed aviators hid eyes as dark as unexplored canyons. If she'd take them off, he'd see the usual assemblage of amusement and exasperation that greeted him under most circumstances. She addressed him. "You're late, cattle baron."

"We set out at dawn, like I promised," he assured her, dismounting. He flicked the reins over Alice's ears and led the horse the rest of the way. "Ran into a snag a quarter of a mile south of here."

Her frown quickened. "Trouble?"

"Heifer dropped a calf before dawn," he said, fitting the hat back to his crown. "Something carried it off."

Kaya's frown deepened. "Did you find any remains?"

"Other than a blood trail…" He shook his head. "Cat took off in this direction."

"You think it was lion."

"I know it was. Normally, we don't keep the heifers this far north when the mountain's waking up for spring, especially not during calving season. 23's a wily one— makes a habit of slipping through fences. The big cats are more likely to carry off pronghorn, small deer, rabbit…" He wished she'd take her hair down for once. She kept it knotted in a thick braid at the nape of her neck.

Everett would love to see it free. He'd bet money it was as dense as plateau nights and as soft as the Wapusa between his fingers when it ran down from the mountain.

Something tugged just beneath his navel—a long, low pull that snagged his breath for a second or two.

That wasn't new, either.

Everett had had to come to terms with the fact that he had the hots for the new sheriff of Fuego County. He'd been wallowing in that understanding for some time—since the shoot-out at Eaton Edge over Christmas that had led to her being shot in the leg and, after some recovery, promoted to the high office she held now.

Everett knew what he wanted, always, and he chased it relentlessly. But the last eight months of his life had changed him. He'd been shot, too, in a standoff between a cutthroat backwoodsman and his family. He'd nearly died. Recovery had been a long mental process with PTSD playing cat and mouse with him. He'd found himself in therapy at the behest of Ellis and their housekeeper turned adoptive mother, Paloma Coldero. He'd set aside his chief of operations duties until doctors had given him the go-ahead to continue.

He had hated the hiatus. He'd worked since he was a boy—to the bone. He'd quit high school his senior year to help his father manage the Edge. Everett had never *not* worked.

After Hammond had died in July, work had felt vital. If he wasn't working, he was thinking about the state of his family and the grief he still hardly knew how to handle, even after all his months sitting across from a head doctor in San Gabriel.

Kaya Altaha had been a bright spot. The then-deputy had saved his life in the box canyon last July. Not only that—she'd checked in on him regularly. She'd worked to clear the name of Ellis's soon-to-be wife, Luella Decker.

The first time he'd smiled during his recovery, it'd been with her.

He hadn't known there were feelings attached…until Christmastime, when he'd seen her blood in the hay of his barn. He'd smelled it over the stench of cattle and gunpowder. To say he'd been worried was a damned lie—he'd gone over the flippin' edge.

She tucked her full lower lip underneath the white edge of her teeth, nibbling as she looked beyond him into the hills that tumbled off south. "Anyone get a look at the predator?" she asked.

He had to school himself to keep from rubbing his lips together. "Happened before dawn, as I said. Blood was dry."

"I'm sorry to hear about the calf," she said sincerely.

He could feel her eyes through the shades. He felt them from tip to tail. "I'm not looking forward to telling my nieces. They love the little ones come spring."

She studied him a moment before the professional line of her mouth fell away and a slow smile took over.

He darted a look at the two deputies roving around the space between the falls and the arch walls before he brought himself a touch closer, the toes of his thick-skinned boots nearly overlapping hers. He lowered his voice. "You can't be doing that."

"What am I doing?" Her jaw flared wide from its stubborn point when she smiled.

He'd thought about kissing that point…and a good many things south of it. "Flashing secret smiles at me and pretending I'm not going to do anything about it."

"I don't play games."

"You know what that mess does to me," he said, "and you're betting on me not doing anything about it."

"You wouldn't," she said.

"Why d'you figure that, Sheriff Sweetheart?" he asked with a laugh.

The smile turned smug. "Because I know the only things Everett Eaton fears in this life are bullets and bars. Not the honky-tonk kind—the ones that hem him in and keep him away from…all this." She gestured widely. "Despite how much we both know you like a challenge." She tossed him back a step with the brunt of her hand and raised her voice to be heard by the others. "Hiker's name is Miller Higgins. He's sixteen years of age. Five-eight. Roughly one hundred and fifty pounds. His last known contact was three days ago at approximately 10:23 a.m. The family reported him missing yesterday when they couldn't get in touch with him via cell."

"Cell service is low here," Javier noted. "How good was the quality of the livestream video?"

"Not great, but good enough to establish where he was

and what he was doing," Kaya replied. "If he fell during the hike and injured himself, he might have lost his cell phone or damaged it. That's the working theory. He left his car on the access road to the northeast. Deputy Root will fly the surveillance drone once we get to the top. I plan on combing every inch of this mountain and the surrounding area until we find Higgins. If we need to bring in more search and rescue people, we'll do so."

"Nobody knows Ol' Whalebones as well as me and Ellis," Everett explained. "He'll join us tomorrow, if need be. We'll find Higgins. I'd like Lucas to wait here with the horses since there've been signs of predators about."

She inclined her head. "Fine. Let's split into groups and hit the trail."

Chapter 2

"Ol' Whalebones wasn't always yours," Kaya told the cowboy. It was better than telling him to hold up and slow the eff down. Bastard was like a cat as they hiked toward the summit. She could hold her own athletically. But his legs were nearly the length of her body.

Everett took a glance back. He stopped, planting both feet in the rocky hillside. He extended a hand.

He wasn't even winded. She gritted her teeth as her bad leg shouted in protest and she took the offering. His touch was rough, taking her back to the day she'd been shot.

My hands are only good for cattle branding...

It was hard to reconcile the hard face of Everett Eaton with the pale shell he'd been in his cattle barn that day. He'd been using those hands to stop the bleeding in her leg—or trying. She liked his hands, and she was afraid she'd told him as much as she'd faded in and out of consciousness.

She had saved his life once, too. Hard to believe things had come full circle.

He pulled until she was even with him. She let go of his hand to take hold of the branch of the shrub tree to her left. "Thanks," she said.

"Take a minute," he ordered.

"No," she said. "We'll be losing the light before we know it."

"You can't climb if you can't breathe," he told her. "Here."

He unclipped the water bottle from his belt. She took it when he unscrewed the lid.

He watched her drink. She was aware of him enough to know it. She wondered if he counted the number of times her throat moved around her swallows. It made her hot.

Stop it, Kaya. She was sheriff now. There were those who thought she'd earned the position, and those who didn't. The latter had a strong sense she'd been voted in out of sympathy when she was shot by the former sheriff, Wendell Jones.

She might wear the badge, but she had a lot to prove. There was no time to lust after a long, tall cowboy with issues of his own. She handed the bottle back to him.

He took a sip, too. Then he lowered the bottle back to his belt and fastened it. "I know Whalebones didn't always belong to us. It was Apache."

"It didn't belong to anyone," she argued. "It was a sacred place. The Jicarilla called it Mountain That Breathes Water. Water is sacred to our people."

He grabbed the wrist of the hand she had wrapped around the branch. "Don't use trees for leverage. They've got shallow roots. A branch can snap. If you need to grab onto something, you grab onto me. I'm not going anywhere."

She pushed off the tree. Instead of grabbing him, she clambered her way up the mountain. It was best just to keep going—ignore the low simmer and smooth timbre of his words and what they did to her. "Do you get hikers out here often?"

"Sure. Ol' Whalebones was once the place to go for

camping in Fuego. Ellis and I led a few expeditions ourselves. That all changed when Tombstone established his territory."

"I looked into it," she admitted. She could hear Everett coming at the same easy pace behind her. She wanted the lead. His Wrangler-clad buns were too distracting. "There've never been reports of hikers at Eaton Edge. Not officially."

"When they do it the right way—knock on the door at headquarters and ask for permission—we normally give them the go-ahead. They can't leave any trash, must be out by a certain date and time and are responsible for any injuries or loss of gear that happens on the mountain."

"That's big of you."

"It was Ellis's idea. Dad went for it. I had to go along."

"Should've known it was your brother's idea." The brothers Eaton didn't have much in common other than height, horsemanship, ranching and the web of laugh lines they carried around their eyes even when they weren't amused. While Ellis was easygoing by nature, Everett had a well-earned reputation for being difficult to deal with. He was loyal as hell to anybody he thought of as his—family, hands and the few friends he counted as his own... Anybody else was practically the enemy.

Ellis was a frickin' marshmallow by comparison.

Kaya may have been an officer of the law for a decade, but she was also a single, red-blooded woman who liked the look of cowboys. She'd been wondering for a while why her glands had danced toward prickly over princely. She liked things that lined up. Puzzle pieces that fit neatly together. Her clear-cut certainty came from years of honed gut instinct.

Everett Eaton was a gray area.

She'd been toeing that gray area for a while.

There was nothing certain about him. She hadn't yet had the nerve to cross the line in the sand she'd drawn between herself and Fuego's most storied cattleman.

"Did Higgins contact anyone at Eaton Edge about climbing Ol' Whalebones?" she asked.

"I checked with Ellis and Paloma. Requests normally go through them. Nobody'd heard of him before yesterday."

She climbed to an embankment and stopped to look around. As he climbed to her position, she bent over double, planting both hands on her left thigh. It sang an ugly operetta that made her molars grind. She heard him closing and straightened. "No sign of a hiker."

He stopped, too, and scanned. "No tracks, either."

She took the radio off her hip. "Root."

"Yeah, Sheriff?"

"Status report," she requested, cutting into the hissing static. As she waited for a reply, she took the bottle Everett offered her again and sipped. The breeze was high, cooling the perspiration on her face and neck.

"Javy and I made it around to the east side. We're making our way up to the top."

"Any sign of Higgins?" she asked, passing the bottle back to Everett.

"Not even an empty Doritos bag."

"I want updates every ten minutes," she told him. "Higgins had to climb either the east or south side, and it hasn't rained. Signs should still be there."

"Ten-four. We'll check in soon."

"Thanks." She clipped the radio into its holding on her belt. "Damn."

"What about the live broadcast?" Everett asked. "Didn't the kid say which approach he took?"

She shook her head, shifting her weight to her right leg. "He kept going on about climate change, cultural landmarks… His profile took up much of the frame so there aren't any discernible background features. And the livestream was cut off just before the summit."

Everett assessed her. "You're hurting."

"I'm not," she lied through her teeth. "We need to keep moving."

"Does your leg bug you like this all the time?" he asked as she established the lead again.

She dismissed his worry. "It doesn't bug me anymore. Period."

"Should've left you with Lucas and the horses."

She rounded on him, happy when her feet didn't slide down the slope. "If I'd known you were going to nag this much, I'd have thought better before calling you out to help."

He tilted his head. "My land, my call."

She scowled. It would be so easy to dislike him, as most people did. Why had she never disliked him? She sniffed and caught a strong enough whiff of something foul to distract her. "Didn't you shower this morning?"

The blade of his nose sharpened, and his nostrils narrowed as he took in a long breath, scenting the air. "It's not me." His eyes narrowed, too, as recognition hit his cobalt blue eyes. The pupils grew larger. "That's something dead."

Her head snapped in the direction of the wind. "That way." There was a clutch of trees clinging to the cliffside. She picked her way in that direction, crossing from the trail into the shrubby undergrowth.

"Let me go first," he said, taking her arm.

"Hi, I'm the sheriff. Nice to meet ya," she drawled, refusing to give up the lead once more. "Stay behind me or I'll make you wait here."

Her stomach tightened as she made steady progress sideways across the mountain. Automatically, her hand went to her hip, fingertips brushing the sidearm on her belt. She squinted, trying to see into the shadows of the trees. She recognized the smell. Death, a scent ingrained in the walls of her memory. "Goddamn it," she said under her breath as she narrowed the distance to the grove. "Stay back," she told him firmly, holding up a hand.

"Like hell," came the response at her back. He was coming, too.

She cut the urge to roll her eyes, tilting her chin as she peered into the stand. She took a step into the stubble of thicket that grew at the base of the trees.

It would have taken her longer to find it if not for the flies. Near the center of the stand, a small pile of dead leaves and natural debris gathered. She crouched, narrowing her eyes. Holding her breath, she brushed away the detritus. She hissed at what she found, sitting back on her heels.

Over her head, Everett cursed. "That's a body," he said.

"What's left of one," she confirmed. She pressed her lips together, careful not to breathe too deeply.

"It ain't human."

"No," she agreed. She tried to recognize something of the small animal. "This is something's prey. And it's fresh, so that means—"

Everett cursed again, filthily. He yanked her to her feet. "Get up now!"

"What?" She saw the pallor of his face. It was achingly familiar. "Everett, what—?"

"Look at the trees," he said, bringing the rifle he'd strapped to his back around to his front.

She saw the markings on the trunks. Claw marks. She lifted her Glock from its sheath as her pulse clambered into high gear. "You think…"

"Hell yeah," he confirmed, all but herding her back the way they'd come. "He knows we're here."

"He who?" When Everett continued to push her out of the trees, she raised her voice. "Everett!"

"Move!" he ordered.

Underneath his pallor, she recognized fear. Her response was visceral. It urged her into a sprint. Everett followed close on her heels. Her heart beat in her ears when his hand clamped on her shoulder, keeping her within arm's length.

They made it back to the trail. Everett kept his rifle up. "Look for the ears in the underbrush," he said, pivoting. "You see them first."

Kaya scanned. With everything waving in the breeze, she couldn't detect anything. She shook her head. "Who do you think is out there?"

"Christ, woman. Don't you know this is Tombstone's territory?"

Tombstone. Stories of the one-eyed cat had seemed mythical. "Tombstone's…real?"

"*Hell yeah,* he's real!"

She saw the sweat on his neck and blinked. "You've seen him."

"Saw him hunting in the summer and heard his screams just three months back."

Kaya released a breath before she raised the barrel of the gun to the sky and squeezed off a round. She did it twice, then again. Birds scattered and the thunder of the shots echoed off everything.

Nothing sprang from the grass except a fluffle of rabbits.

She lowered the gun. "He's not here. They run at the slightest sign of humans."

Everett was still tense as a board. "You don't know Tombs. Not like I do."

She observed the tight line of his mouth, the successive lift of his shoulders as his lungs cycled through quick, quiet breaths. She opened her mouth, but the radio on her hip crackled. "Altaha. You read?" came the brisk sound of one of her deputies.

She took the radio out of its holding and raised it to her mouth. "All clear."

"You fired?"

"Three shots. Affirmative. We came across a cougar den. Had to make sure we weren't being stalked."

"Ten-four. You want us to keep going for the summit?"

"Yes," she agreed. "Be watchful and keep checking in. Over." She clipped the radio back in place. "Relax. We're not getting carried off like your calf."

"Yeah," Everett bit off, watching the boulders in the near distance as if one of them would pounce at them if he let his guard down.

Kaya laid her hand flat against the warm line of his back. "You're really spooked."

"I'm not spooked," he said with a deep frown as he lowered the weapon a fraction. He didn't stop scanning the hillside. "I'm ready."

She noted the half step he took toward her, until her front buffered his arm. "You'll have to tell me what that's about."

"You ever seen a cat that size take down an animal?"

"Haven't had the pleasure, no."

"You don't see it coming," he said. "Its prey doesn't see it coming. Hell, the devil doesn't see it coming. It'll wait an hour if it must for its prey to feel secure—for it to get close enough. And it moves like a wraith. It goes for the throat, mostly. Tears out the guts. It feeds. Then it buries the rest for later."

She fought a shudder. "It's an animal, cattle baron. Flesh and blood. Not the bogeyman."

"Let's keep moving. We'll have better visibility from the top."

She pursed her lips when he took the lead this time. Keeping her hand on her sidearm, she followed no less than a few feet behind, her eyes trained to the periphery.

Everett propped the rifle muzzle on his shoulder as he watched Kaya assess the day's findings.

No hiker. No body, either, other than Number 23's calf, or what was left of the spindly little thing. Everett didn't figure Tombs had gotten much of a meal off it. Calves weren't particularly meaty.

As Kaya's gloved hands handled the tennis shoe Deputy Root had found near the top of the east trail, Everett noted the line buried like a hatchet between her eyes. She turned the shoe, checking the bottom, then pulled back the tongue to peer inside. "Men's size nine," she reported to Root as the man took notes. "The tread's new. Very little wear. No tear. Make a note to question the family. See if any of them know if he recently bought a brown pair of Merrell Moabs. Have them check for receipts." She lifted the shoe's opening to her nose. Her studious frown deepened as she lowered it. "Definitely fresh." She placed the shoe gingerly in an evidence bag and sealed it. "This needs to be labeled."

"Yes, sir," her other deputy, Wyatt, said as he took the bag from her.

She pulled off her gloves as she scanned the other evidence bags. They'd found one half-full canteen, one selfie stick, two crinkled foil gum wrappers and one bullet casing. She lifted the bag with the casing and walked to Everett's position. Holding it up for him to see, she asked, "You do any shooting on the mountain?"

"Not in ten years," he replied. She allowed him to take the bag. He laid the plastic-wrapped casing across his palm. "This is newer. Maybe not from the last week, but recent."

She nodded, taking it back. "You know anybody else who shoots on the mountain?"

"No," he said. "We haven't had hikers since last spring, and we make it clear—no shooting unless it's necessary to defend against wildlife." When she continued to measure him, he sighed. "I can track down the waiver the last campers signed. It'll have contact information. I'll have Ellis pass it on to your department."

"I'd appreciate it," she whispered.

He wanted to smooth the line between her eyes away with the rough pad of his thumb. "You got that same funny feeling in the pit of your stomach that I do?"

She blinked, the thoughtful glimmer disappearing as she lowered her gaze to his chest. "I've got questions."

"Like why we found one shoe and no kid."

She nodded. Her lips disappeared as she pressed them inward.

"Sun's going down," he said when her attention turned again to the mountain. "There's no use searching after dark. Cougar's most active between last and first light. We'll hit it again in the morning."

"I know."

Everett shifted his feet when she didn't look any less

discomfited. He spoke in an undertone he knew she didn't want to hear. "You know if that kid's alive, he'd have said something, called for help, after you took those three shots."

"Maybe," she muttered. "Doesn't make leaving for the night easier." She looked back at the shoe Wyatt carefully labeled. "My gut tells me Miller Higgins never left Ol' Whalebones. I can't face his family until I have more."

It'd weigh on her. It'd weigh her down hard. It took everything in him to stand his ground and keep his hands to himself.

Lucas called to him from the horses gathered near the river. "Boss, we should head south for home. Don't you have that hot date?"

Kaya's eyes widened as she looked in the boy's direction. "Who with?" she called.

Lucas fumbled at the sheriff's attention. "Ah…he never said. I just know he was real jazzed about it."

Kaya turned a stunned look back at Everett. "What's that look like?"

Lucas filled in the blanks. "Oh, you know, he's not much a grinnin' man. But once he got word that the date was on, he's been slaphappy."

"I'd like to see that," she mused, scrutinizing every inch of Everett's face. She might've looked amused to anyone else, but he saw the gleam in her eye and his heartbeat skipped. That look was damn near predatory. He cleared his throat and looked long in Lucas's direction.

The boy's smile subsided. "Sorry, boss. Ready when you are," he said before turning away to busy himself with Crazy Alice's bridle.

"Hot date, huh?" Kaya said, refusing to take her attention elsewhere.

"I think so," Everett mused.

"Hmm."

"Sheriff," Deputy Root said. "I put the evidence in your saddlebags."

"Good work," she said. "Mount up. I'm coming."

Everett gave Lucas and Javier the signal to do the same but walked Kaya to her leopard Appaloosa. "Nice horse," he commented, touching its nose. The horse breathed on him, its nostrils filling his palm and warming it with a searching snuff.

"Name's Ghost," she said, adjusting the stirrups. "She likes sweets."

The deputies walked their horses at a safe distance. They were far enough away. Everett felt free to touch her finally, turning her to him. With Ghost's long form between them and the deputies and his own men, Everett filled the space between them. "Are you okay to ride?"

Her smile came slowly. It didn't stretch to fill the ridges of her cheekbones as he'd seen it do at its height, but it warmed. "I was born on the rez. I can ride with the best of them."

"You can find the access road okay?" he asked. "Dark's coming on quick."

"We'll find it," she assured him. She paused, her gaze tracking the line of his throat. Her voice lowered a fraction. "You better get along. Wouldn't want you to miss that date."

"You're not backing out?"

She lifted her eyes to the passing clouds. With the sun low to the west, they burned. "I'll let you know."

"Don't back out," he said.

A laugh sounded in her throat. "Careful. You sound a little slaphappy."

"Lucas doesn't know what he's talking about."

"No?" she said, and she ran a hand down the length

of his shirtfront, making the skin underneath the buttons judder. "Pity."

He caught her wrist before she could feel his muscles quiver under her fingertips. "Eight o'clock, right?"

"Better make it nine, at this rate."

He grinned. "Sure, Sheriff. Sweetheart."

She brought both hands to his lapels and pulled him down to her height. Dropping her voice to a whisper, she cautioned, "Easy on the endearments. I have a reputation to establish."

"I'm aware of your reputation." All he saw…all he wanted…was her mouth under his. "Just as I'm aware it took me three months, thirteen days and nine hours to talk you into going out with me. I'll be damned if I screw this up now." He bent his head to hers and took her mouth.

She made an involuntary "*Mmm*." He released her, stepping away just as fast as he'd swooped, lest he take more than he should with his men and hers within shouting distance. His blood had quickened at the taste, the promise of her. "Don't back out," he whispered.

She pressed a hand to her horse's saddle, touching her mouth. She dropped her hand when she saw him watching. "Ride on. Isn't that what cowboys are supposed to do?"

He tipped his hat to her. "Ladies first."

Chapter 3

Kaya was more tired than she would have liked. And she was worried. She'd expected to find more of Miller Higgins on Ol' Whalebones than his right shoe.

The shell casing bothered her long after she left the station house. She'd stayed long enough to stable Ghost and update the mayor on the hiker's whereabouts—or lack thereof. Then she fielded the phone call from Higgins's mother and arranged for the next search party to meet at the base of the mountain the following morning.

Her house was near downtown Fuego. It was small. She liked to think of it as cozy—cozy enough for one… and that was stretching it. Its one redeeming aspect was the little windowed alcove off the kitchen she used for her round bistro table and as many potted plants as she could squeeze in along the walls. She set her bag down there, taking out the file on Higgins.

She opened it. His smiling photograph stared back at her.

"What happened to you on the mountain?" She wanted to know. He was just a kid—one with strong convictions… But a kid just the same.

She closed the file and told herself to end the questions for the night. If she continued, questions would spring into more before she had a hydra-like situation on her hands. She wouldn't be able to concentrate on anything if she didn't let the inquiries lie.

She checked the time on the stove display and cursed. It was a quarter past eight. She unbuckled her weapons belt and slid it off as she veered toward the bedroom.

As she showered, the questions didn't stop coming.

If it was an accident, what happened? Did he fall down the mountain? Was that why there was only one shoe, the new selfie stick and his half-drunk canteen? Where was Higgins's pack? Every hiker carries a pack. Where was his camera and cell phone? What caused him to stumble? Was it the cougar?

No, Kaya thought. *No.* If it had been the cat, there would have been evidence of that...

Everett's visual came back to her, accompanied by his grim baritone.

...it goes for the throat, mostly. Tears out the guts. It feeds. Then it buries the rest...

There had been no tracks on the summit. No blood they'd been able to see. No remains of any kind...except for the shoe. There weren't drag marks through the brush.

Which brought Kaya's questions around to...

Foul play? Did someone else beat Higgins to the top of Whalebones? Had the perpetrator been waiting? Was their meeting coincidental? If so, why did the perpetrator attack? Was the shoe left behind when the perpetrator carried the body off?

She remembered the absence of blood or drag marks.

Was the perpetrator smart enough to cover his tracks?

Dogs, she thought. They needed search dogs on the summit tomorrow. She needed to call Root, set it up...

She pulled back the shower curtain and checked the watch she had left on the counter. *Eight-thirty.*

She quickly washed the shampoo out of her hair and shut off the tap. She towel dried her hair before she remembered to shave.

It had been so long since she'd dated, she was out of her routine. Placing one leg on the closed commode, she lathered one part of her leg after the other before dragging her razor over it, as carefully as she could manage in a hurry. She nicked herself only once on the knee before she finished. She bounced on the toes of her left leg a bit as she lowered the right back down to the ground. It ached in the center of her thigh. Telling herself to remember to take a pain pill before she left, she went into the bedroom to find something to wear.

The little black dress wasn't new. She shimmied into it, grunting a bit to fit it over the wide points of her chest and hips. She was more muscular than she'd been when she bought it. She tried not to think about her mannish shoulders as she turned to look in the full-length mirror she'd mounted to her closet door.

The dress hit her midthigh. She didn't remember it being that short.

"Hmm," she said as she turned to the side, examining. It was hardly appropriate for someone of her rank.

She thought about her former boss, Sheriff Jones, in something this short and snorted in reaction.

She trailed her fingertips over the gunshot wound he'd put in her. It was completely visible below the hem.

She sighed. That wouldn't do. Nothing halted revelry like a solid reminder that she'd almost lost her life in her date's hands.

She decided on a maxi dress that exposed her shoulder

line and one leg up to the knee in a slit. Seeing that another ten minutes had passed, she rummaged through shoes until she found a pair of wedge heels that matched, then went into the bathroom to find her makeup bag.

"You're sheriff now," she said out loud as she applied mascara, wary of messing it up and having to start over. "Men should take you seriously, Kaya, with or without mascara…whether you're cuffing them…dating them…" Still, the thought of going on this date without mascara… "Nuh-uh," she decided as she switched eyes.

She felt the minutes tick by as she pulled the towel down from her hair. The strands fell to her waist, wet as a drowned rat. "Be late, cattle baron."

The doorbell rang promptly at nine o'clock, causing her to groan at the state of things. Her hair still wasn't dry. There would be no fancying it. "Hold on a minute," she said with bobby pins between her teeth as she knotted her hair on top of her head and hastily pinned flyaways.

By the time she threw open the door, he'd taken to pounding on it with his fist. "Yes," she said, exasperated. "I can…" She trailed off, noting the sport coat over his clean-white button down. His hat was in his hand. His tousled black hair was thick and clean. His dark beard had a nice sheen. He'd trimmed it. "…hear you," she finished, lamely. "Wow. You look…decent."

She'd never seen Everett Eaton look so shiny. Not outside of a wedding or a funeral. And he always looked like his family dragged him to those kinds of things.

"I should hope so," he said. "Paloma threatened to hold me down and shave me." His smile came slowly as he lowered his gaze from her made-up face to her bare shoulders, over the pattern of the dress, down the long slit. "You look fine, Sheriff. Damn fine." And he made a noise in his throat that shot straight through her.

She gripped the door, feeling his eyes everywhere. *Here we go again.* What was it about this cowboy? She made the mistake of shifting onto her left leg in a casual stance. She ruined it by moving to the other leg quickly. Hissing at the pain, she closed her eyes for a moment and touched her brow to the cool wood underneath her hand.

"Hey," he said, stepping over the threshold. "You doing all right?"

"Mmm." She mashed her lips together and offered a nod. He wouldn't get the best of her tonight. If they were going to do this…if she was going to take this leap with him—ill-fated or otherwise—she wanted to be at her best. He'd saved her life, after all. The least she could do was wait for a night when she wasn't worn down. "Listen. I hate to do this. But it's late and there's a lot on my leg… I mean, *my mind.* Maybe we should do this another—"

"Nope."

She jerked her head back. "I'm sorry. 'Nope'?"

"That's right," he said with a decisive bob of his head. "Nope."

He made the *p* come to a point at the end. She narrowed her eyes. "You don't want me tonight, Everett."

He didn't miss a beat. "I beg to differ, sweetheart."

"I'm distracted," she said, ticking the excuses off on her fingers. "I'm tired. I'm a little cranky. I'm more than a little sore…"

"I'll take you any way I can get you. Distracted, tired, cranky… If you're hurting, I'll carry you," he revealed.

"Oh," she said, not at all swept off her feet. "That's nice."

"As for the sore part, I plan to buy a large bottle of wine

for our table when we get to the restaurant for our reservation in…" He checked his big, silver watch. "…a half hour. And I'm not waiting another three months for you to decide that this is right again, so get your bag because otherwise I'm hauling you over my shoulder and we're leaving without it."

She blew out a hard breath. "I'd like a word with whichever barnyard animal raised you."

"Can't," he said. "We sold it for beef a while ago."

When she only stood staring at him, he made a move toward her.

"All right!" she shrieked, dancing out of his reach. She muttered as she went back into her bedroom. "I am the sheriff," she reasoned as she shoved her Glock down into her beaded bag with her wallet and phone, then yanked a sweater off a hanger and stalked back to the door.

"Why wasn't there more?" Kaya questioned. "Why weren't there signs of a struggle? If he fell on the trail, we should have found his body near the trail. Unless something or someone dragged him off…"

Everett bobbed his head in a nod as she went on about the day's search and all the questions that had arisen from it. He poured her another tall glass of wine. At least she was drinking it. He wondered how many glasses it would take for her to forget about work. She was well into two.

He raised the label of the wine toward the light, squinting to read the alcohol ratio. He raised a brow and set it back down on the table.

Kaya Altaha was far from a cheap date.

She'd ordered a steak, like him, and wasn't that just a turn-on? She looked good in candlelight, so good he wondered why he'd taken her out in public and not back to the

Edge where he could kick everybody out of Eaton House and distract her with something other than red meat and wine…

Because clearly those two things weren't doing the job. Neither was the fancy restaurant with its crystal chandeliers, fine china, white tablecloths and overdressed servers. He picked his whiskey glass up off the table, tossed back the contents and savored the burn of top-shelf liquor. Setting the glass down, he leaned forward and asked, "You wanna dance?"

She fumbled in the middle of another question. Her mouth hung open, red as a poppy and glistening, like she'd coated it in gloss. She looked around, as if noting the chandeliers and other well-dressed patrons for the first time. "Yeah, there's no dancing here," she pointed out.

"There could be," he considered. He reached across the table and laid his hand next to hers on the tablecloth.

"No," she decided.

"You're a fine dancer, as I recall." And he smiled at the memory of spinning her around the kitchen at Eaton House.

A glimmer of that memory lit her eyes and shined.

He nudged his hand toward hers so that his first finger grazed hers.

The glimmer faded and her hand retreated. She looked away. "I haven't danced. Not since then. My leg…"

"It's hurting you," he knew. "It hurts a sight more than you let on."

"I get through it," she said, clutching the stem of her wineglass without lifting it.

"Do you take something for it?"

She thought about it. "Not tonight. Damn. I forgot."

He could see a web of pain floating translucent over the powerful line of her brow. He remembered the pain in his chest waking him up in the middle of the night for weeks after Whip Decker shot him and all the mixed-up nightmares that had made it impossible for him to sleep through the night during that time. "Here," he said.

Her eyes widened as he scooted his chair around the table, making enough noise with the legs screeching across the marble floor that the restaurant patrons swiveled toward the commotion. "What are you doing?"

"Gimme," he said, reaching underneath the tablecloth to wrap his hand around the smooth slope of her calf. He pulled it into his lap, edging closer still. Her perfume was heady, and he got lost, so lost he almost didn't see her grimace. "Easy," he murmured, keeping his eyes on hers as he followed the trail of satin skin up the slit of her dress to her thigh. Digging his fingers in, he urged himself to be gentle as he massaged.

He heard the quick, almost inaudible catch of her breath. "You know," she said, "this is more of a third date kind of thing."

He chuckled, then gentled the kneading when he saw the line of her mouth tense. "Are my hands too rough for you?"

"Your hands," she murmured. She closed her eyes. "No. Not for me."

He fought a curse. He was afraid she'd have him panting like a cartoon character by the night's end. "You see someone about the pain?" he asked, diverting his mind elsewhere as his fingers continued to work.

"I'm told it's normal," she said, tipping her head back slightly. Her eyes rolled once before she closed them. "I'm still going through physical therapy."

"Hmm," he said, biting the inside of his lip when she made an agreeable noise. "I'm not a fan of doctors on the whole, but PT helped me." Almost as much as talk therapy, but he didn't mention that. He still had his qualms about telling people he saw a psychiatrist.

"You need to stop," she said, placing her hands over his.

"Why?"

"Because people will think you're doing something else under the table."

"I am doing something."

"You *know* what I mean."

"I don't give a hot damn what people think," he reminded her. He grinned because he could see the touch of pink at the crests of her cheeks. "And as much I like where your head's at, sweetheart, that's not a first date kind of thing, either."

"No?" she asked as he pulled his hands away. She sat up straight, her leg easing off his lap. "Most cowboys expect that sort of thing."

"I'm a bit more refined than your average cowboy," he revealed, lifting a finger to a passing server. He raised his empty glass.

She snorted. "You? Refined?"

He slid her a long look, rattling the ice in the glass.

She licked her lips. Her gaze touched on his wrist. "Sorry."

He saw those dark eyes dart elsewhere and frowned down at his wrist with the expensive watch. Wondering why it made her uncomfortable, he fit his shoulders to the back of the dining chair and tried to read her. Hammond had bequeathed the watch to him...one of the few nice things his father had collected through the years for himself. Like Hammond, Everett was a simple man. He didn't like fuss. But the occasion had called for a bit of shine. He felt the sting of his father's loss as he watched the low light dance across the band.

"Tell me the truth," she asked, carefully. "When was the last time you took someone to bed?"

He tried not to be thrown by the question. "It's been a minute," he mused.

"Not since Decker shot you?" she asked.

"Hell no." He'd been in no place to think in terms of sex or what led to it.

"How long then?" she asked.

"Is this a first date conversation?" he teased as the server brought another glass of whiskey. "Thanks."

"I don't care," Kaya replied.

He raised his hand in an empty gesture. "I don't know. Two…maybe three years?"

Her brows hitched. "Why that long?"

He lifted a shoulder. "Haven't found anyone worth courting. 'Til now, that is."

"You need to court a woman to sleep with her?" she said in amusement.

"Well, yeah."

"Is that why you're here with me—because you're courting me?" she asked, picking through the words carefully.

He bobbed his head and kept her locked in his sights as he raised the glass to his mouth again. "I'd say that's a fair assessment."

She narrowed her eyes as he tossed the whiskey back. "At least he's honest, ladies and gentlemen," she murmured and took a long drink from her wineglass.

"What's wrong with me courting you, Sheriff?"

"It's not the courting I'm worried about," she said with a shake of her head. Dangling the glass with her thumb and two fingers on the rim, she studied him with her cop eyes. "Why me?"

"Why *not* you?"

"That's not really your answer, is it?"

He shifted in his chair. "Cards on the table?"

"I'd like that."

"Fine." He cleared his throat. "I want to find out what this is."

"What?"

He gestured from him to her and back quickly. "This. You know what I'm talking about." When she eyed him uncertainly, he groaned. She was going to make him spell it out in this fancy schmancy restaurant over candlelight and frickin' canapes. "I want to figure out whatever it is I feel—for you."

She stiffened. Her eyes bounced between his in quick succession, but she stayed quiet, waiting for him to elaborate.

He gripped the whiskey glass hard. "During my recovery—" he continued, carefully "—the one person I looked forward to seeing, or even really wanted to see, was you. The one person who never failed to make me grin like an idiot was you. And when the sheriff took a shot at you, I nearly lost that. It scared me more than I thought it could."

"Everett…"

"You wanted to hear," he reminded her.

She settled back, a line digging deep between her eyes as it had earlier that evening.

"I've done a lot over the last several months to eliminate my fear," he revealed. "I've lost people and I'm still dealing with it. It hasn't been easy. It helps, whatever this is. You help…just having you here…lookin' at you. I'm drawn to you, and I want to know why. I want to know you better. I need it."

Her throat clicked on a swallow. "What if…" She stopped, thought about it, then continued, perturbed. "What if I'm a disappointment? You've put me on a pedestal, from the sound of it. That's a tough way to begin a relationship. Expectation's already through the roof where you're concerned."

"The hell with expectation," he dismissed. "My question is, what took you so long to say yes?"

She measured the width of his shoulders. "You're a complicated man, Everett. Some would even say you're a hard man. I'm the sheriff, and you don't have much regard for the law when it comes to your own."

"Who does?" he asked, raising the glass for another drink.

"Me," she replied pointedly. "I do."

"So…you don't want me because you assume I'm not an easy person to live with," he weighed.

"I *know* you're not an easy person to live with," she retorted. "I have it on high authority you're a verifiable pain in the ass." She hesitated, looking down at her lap to fiddle with the cloth napkin she'd laid there. "And I never said I didn't want you," she added quietly.

Why did she have to look away? He wanted those dark eyes on him, always. "Damn, but I'd like to see you with your hair down. Just once."

She closed her eyes. "Don't change the subject. This is serious."

"How long?"

"How long what?"

"How long have you been living with the fact that you want me and keeping me at arm's length?" he asked.

She chose not to answer.

He went a step further, urgency driving him. "I nearly died last summer. I had to watch you bleed. I'm no longer in the business of waiting around to see what life's going to hit me with. I'm tired of getting hit. I see something I want…something I need… I chase it. It'd be nice if you'd let me know how much longer I'm going to be chasing you—because I'm too deep in this to stop."

She propped her elbow on the edge of the table and cradled her temple. After a minute of watching him watching her, she sighed. "All right."

"All right what?" His heart banged in anticipation.

"We do this," she considered. "We see where it goes. But on my terms."

"Name 'em," he said.

She leveled an accusing finger at his chest. "If you brush up against the wrong side of the law while we're together, I'm out."

He offered a crooked smile. "Okay."

"Let's keep this between us. I'm new as sheriff. I'm still trying to gain the respect of certain parts of the community. I don't need talk interfering with that."

"You know how hard it is to keep a secret in Fuego."

"I do," she told him. "Which is why I assume you made reservations out of town."

"I'm banned from Grady's Saloon," he reminded her. "Hickley's BBQ doesn't exactly scream 'date night.' And the steak at Mimi's isn't much to write home about. Third?" he prompted.

"I won't sleep with you," she decided.

He hissed. "That hurts a little."

She held up a hand. "No matter where the courting, as you say, leads… Until I know what we're about…until I'm sure, we keep it PG. Okay?"

He let his eyes rest on her exposed collarbone. Her skin was the color of wheat before harvest and the hollow at the base of her throat fluttered with her pulse. "Can I still think about you naked?" he asked, low.

It shocked a laugh out of her. Smiling widely, she gave an affirmative nod. "Yes," she granted. Then she groaned. "It won't be easy."

"I'm a hard man," he replied, "as you say. I don't do things easy."

"I'm aware of that," she mused. "I'll give it a month. If this doesn't burn out or fizzle and we don't disappoint one another, we'll see if it's worth staying the course."

He raised his glass. "You drive a hard bargain. But I'll take what I can get."

She raised her glass, too. They tipped them together, clinked. "You're worth it," he said as he lifted his glass and drank.

She sipped and muttered, "You'd better be."

As Everett pulled up in front of her house, Kaya unbuckled her seat belt. "Well, this was…something."

He cranked the gearshift into Park. "I'll walk you in."

She grabbed his arm to stop him from turning off the ignition. "No."

"But we're courtin'," he reminded her. "I should walk you to your door like a gentleman."

She leaned into his warmth. "You're not a gentleman and I'm not a lady. We've got something warm and yummy here. You walk me to my door, I'll be tempted to invite you in, despite what I agreed to in that classy restaurant. You'd best stay put."

He raised his hands from the steering wheel. "Hey, you're the sheriff."

"That's right." Grappling for his shoulders, she brought him closer and dropped her voice to a whisper. "Now, I order you to kiss me good night—like you did earlier—so I can go in and think about what I've done."

His quiet laugh blew across her mouth. "You might be a woman after my own heart. Isn't that something?" He gripped the back of her neck, long fingers splaying up into the taut nest of her bun as he tipped his head to the side and took the kiss further, his tongue sliding over her lips to part them.

She caught herself moaning. He made her feel soft, pliant, female. She was so stunned that her mouth parted, and she felt the quick, hot flick of his tongue against hers.

She was practically panting, she found, as his hand firmed against the dip of her waist. She pushed her arms through the parting of his sport coat, all but bowing her torso to his to gather his heat for her own. Her head dipped back on her neck as he took what he wanted, and her hands splayed across the long, firm line of his back.

The big, tough cattle baron had been pining for her— Kaya. Wasn't that a trip?

She was tripping, all right—high on his earthy scent and the sound of his breath clashing with hers in the quiet.

She felt his hand scale her ribs, cruising toward her breast.

She twined her fingers through his before sliding it away. She broke away from his mouth in a faint protest she'd have to chide herself for later. Pressing her lips together, she edged away, toward the passenger door where she'd have stayed to begin with if she'd known what was good for her.

She lived off her mind and her gut and the cool voice of reason. One drink of Everett Eaton and it all turned to ash.

He knocked his head back against his headrest and groaned. "And here I was thinking you didn't want to get all hot and bothered," he said between his teeth. "That'll linger."

"You just hold that thought," she suggested, making herself turn the handle and open the door. She hopped out of the cab.

"I'll see you tomorrow, Sheriff Sweetheart," he called in his distinctive baritone. "Bright and early, like I promised you."

Her legs weren't steady. She blamed it on the wine he'd bought her. "Good night, trouble," she volleyed back and closed the door between them.

Chapter 4

"We've covered most every inch of the east and south sides of the mountain, and we've swept most of the north side as well. It's been two days and we've found nothing else but an old hair scrunchie, two empty beer bottles and some rusty tent stakes," Kaya said. She was back on the summit of Ol' Whalebones for the third morning in a row with her deputies and a ragtag team of professionals and volunteers.

Word of Miller Higgins's disappearance had spread. They'd found a news van from Taos at the end of the access road where they unloaded their horses for the ride to the mountain at dawn. Kaya had forbidden them from coming farther than the eastern trailhead. "If we don't find anything today, we're going to have to bring in a chopper."

Deputy Root's attention was on the screen of his minilaptop. His reconnaissance drone was in the air, searching the rocky west side of the ridge. "You're comfortable having members of his family come out to help?" he asked.

Kaya shook her head. "Not in the least. If we find remains… And with cameras waiting at the base of the hill… It's hard for people to keep their heads when shock and grief are taking a sucker punch at them."

"The father's a decent tracker," Deputy Root reported.

"With him and Wolfe Coldero, the drone and dogs you had the handlers haul out here, chances are good we'll find something."

Kaya hoped she wouldn't regret involving the Higgins family in the search for Miller. "I put Wyatt and Ellis Eaton with the father and son team. If they find anything first, those two are the most calm and compassionate. I warned the handlers about the cougar den. That's probably going to occupy most of the dogs' attention."

"Is it true about Tombstone?"

Kaya narrowed her eyes at Root. "I never saw him. But I'm told this is his territory. If he's still alive. Seems a bit of a stretch. Stories of Tombstone are older than my niece, Nova, and she's driving now. Still, every team has protection and is on the lookout."

Root paused, handling the drone's joystick. "Is it possible Higgins isn't on the mountain?"

It had crossed her mind. Higgins's mother had searched his room at their home in San Gabriel and found an empty Merrell shoe box with a receipt dated a week prior to the boy's livestream. Size nine. Brown. Moabs. They had one shoe and no Miller. The information fed the deep pit in Kaya's stomach.

Everett had sent men out to the four quarters of Eaton Edge. If Higgins had run in that direction, she could only hope they'd find him alive. It had now been five days since Higgins's last contact. "We can't assume anything until we've searched every inch of the mountain. Is there a clear path to the western part of the ridge?"

He panned and zoomed on his screen. "It'll be a lot more challenging than other parts. You up for it?"

She hated the question but understood it. Three days of hiking had given her a noticeable limp. She'd had to skip this week's physical therapy session, too. "Call a handler and Wolfe Coldero's team. Tell them I want him and half the dogs with us."

Like Everett, Wolfe Coldero was a polarizing figure in Fuego. The tall, dark cowboy was mute, his origins a mystery. He had come to Eaton Edge as a boy, lost and broken, and he'd served time as an adult. It didn't matter that he'd been exonerated of the crime Wendell Jones had sent him up for. Some people still talked of him only in whispers.

Kaya knew him to be a man of exemplary character, if mysterious. He was also one of the best trackers she'd ever worked with. As the dogs yanked their handler onward over the tumble of rocks and boulders that pitted the northern portion of the mountain, Wolfe followed at his own pace, stopping to crouch on and off the path.

When he stopped again, Kaya let the others go ahead. She chugged water from her canteen. While no was looking, she choked down some Advil.

The sun was high so she could discern little of Wolfe's face under his worn, black felt hat other than a contemplative frown and sharp-bladed jaw. His finger had dug a circle in the dirt. He shoved aside a small rock, another, then he raised his head, finally, and whistled in her direction.

She moved to him, kneeling with a short wince. "What'd you find?" she asked.

He pointed to a small object in the soil.

Kaya lowered her head further. "It's metal." She reached into her pocket for her gloves. After pulling them on, she took further precaution by prying the metal object out of its dirt bed with a pair of tweezers. She lifted it to the light so they could both examine it. "An earring," she said.

"Gold. The real thing. It's not tarnished or corroded. I'd say it's been here awhile if you had to dig it up like that."

Wolfe nodded his agreement.

"I doubt it's to Miller's taste," she went on. "But I can't see a situation where a camper would wear something this nice out in the elements." Reaching into her back pocket, she pulled out a small evidence bag. "God, your eyes are good."

He rolled his shoulder in a shrug and stood. When she shifted from one foot to the other to do the same, he grabbed her under the shoulder to help. "Thanks," she said as she put the bag and the tweezers away and pulled off her gloves. "I should catch up."

He walked on with her, scanning the ground.

"How're wedding plans coming?" she asked. "It's only a month from now, isn't it?"

He nodded and sent her a small, sideways smile to show her that plans were going well.

"You and Everett getting along?" she wondered.

Wolfe made a so-so motion with his hand. Kaya made a noise in answer. Everett's long-running feud with Wolfe had only just cooled in the last year when Wolfe and Everett's sister, Eveline, fell in love. Kaya had never known what Everett and Wolfe had fallen out about when they were teens living on the Edge, but it had divided the house, with Wolfe going to live with the operation's foreman, Santiago Coldero. Not long after, Everett's mother, Josephine, had left her husband and three children to join Santiago and Wolfe at Coldero Ridge on the other side of town.

The resulting scandal had lit the touch paper for town gossips and was still the subject of their tongue wagging at times. It was exacerbated by the fact that the events over the last summer had stirred the mystery surrounding

Josephine's and her youngest child Angel's deaths seven years ago.

The sound of a dog's baying carried on the wind, followed by a second and a third. Kaya quickened her pace. She had to climb over a rocky ledge to get to the handler's position. "Did they find something?"

The dogs were straining against the handler's lead. "They won't get away from the edge," he informed her. "Something must be down there."

Kaya tested the ground, looking for cracks. The outcropping hung lengthways over a sharp drop. This side of the mountain more closely resembled the buttes that littered the high desert landscape. "Get them back," she advised, edging closer to the cliff. The wind came up to meet her, teasing the flyaway strands that had come loose from her bun. Holding on to her hat, she turned her gaze down below the outcropping.

"There's another ledge down there," she noted. "I can just see it. Other than that, there's nothing for thirty feet or more."

"There's no way for us to get down there safely," the handler said.

As Wolfe came forward, she asked, "Ever done any abseiling?" At his frown, she course-corrected. "Rappelling?" At the shake of his head, she pursed her lips.

"Could be the dogs smell that mountain lion again," the handler explained. "Though that's a long drop…even for a cat."

Her thoughts exactly. She unseated the radio from its holding on her belt and brought it to her mouth. "Root, do you copy?"

"Ten-four."

"We made it to the north ridge," she relayed. "And we

need your drone. Tell Wyatt to bring climbing equipment. Does anybody have experience with cliff descent?"

Static hissed momentarily, then the familiar timbre of Everett's voice called back. "Affirmative."

She frowned. Of course it would be him. "I need you, too."

A pause hovered before Everett's message came back. "On the way."

"Are you sure you know what you're doing?"

Everett glanced up from the climbing harness Ellis secured around his middle. Kaya's gaze was on Root's drone as it sailed over the cliff edge, scanning. But he knew she meant the question for him. "Ellis and I used to do this every weekend," he told her. "Didn't we?"

Ellis gave a jerky nod. "During the misspent years of our youth, yes."

"Did you do it here?" she asked.

Ellis shook his head. "There're some canyons and cliffs at the state park we liked to hit."

Kaya held her elbows and leaned back slightly—to keep the weight off her bad leg, Everett knew. She met Ellis's stare, probing. "Is he any good?"

Ellis's mouth moved in a small grin. "He's a risk-taker. But he knows what he's about."

"Why does the first part not surprise me?" she said, looking to Everett with an ounce of accusation.

He smiled broadly, feeding the rope through his hands. "You worried about me, Sheriff?"

Root yelped.

Kaya leaned over his laptop screen. "Do you see something?"

"Directly below," he said, making minute adjustments with the joystick. "Do you...see that?"

Kaya's hand came to the deputy's shoulder. "Can you zoom in?"

Everett watched the hand flex. He heard Kaya's breath stutter and moved forward. "What's wrong?"

She held up a hand. "Stay back."

"Why?" Everett asked. "What's down there?"

She raised herself to her full height. His lips parted when he saw that all the blood had drained from her face. "We may have found him."

Kaya had everyone pulled back from the north ridge and a perimeter established. She ordered Wyatt to get Higgins's father and brother to the base of the mountain with a reminder to keep them clear of reporters.

She called in crime scene technicians. It took most of the afternoon for Miller Higgins's body to be recovered from its unlikely resting place.

Along with others.

"Jesus God Almighty." Deputy Wyatt, normally a stickler for professional lingo, swallowed hard as the bag containing the final unidentified victim came into view via a complex system of ropes and pulleys. "That's *four*."

Kaya had seen the bones underneath Higgins's in the drone footage. But she hadn't counted on four, either... "Three unidentifieds."

Root had been reticent since seeing the images on his computer screen. He was several shades beyond pale underneath his freckles. "Where were the birds?"

Kaya narrowed her eyes. "What?"

"The birds," Root said again. His voice sounded dull and his eyes tracked the movement of the techs as they carried the body away. "They should've been here—for Miller, if not the others. He was…fresh."

Kaya lifted her chin, understanding.

It was the medical examiner, Damon Walther, who answered. "The birds have already been here, deputy. They'd finished their job before your search began."

Wyatt blew out a full-length curse, shifting his feet on the uneven ground.

"That'll make determining cause of death more difficult." Kaya knew. "I want this to be priority when you get these bodies back to the morgue. I don't have to tell you what kind of case we might have on our hands here."

Root's lips parted. They were the same color as his skin. "I…I think I'm going to…"

She gave him a light push. "Take a minute. Get yourself together. Miller Higgins's relatives are waiting below. We all need a handle on this before we meet them." She'd be lying if she said that grim feeling she'd had in the pit of her stomach throughout the day hadn't grown. On the back of her tongue, she could taste something bitter and acidic that didn't make it easier to negotiate what was happening in her stomach. She took her hat off as the techs passed by and felt more than saw her deputies do the same.

When the techs had carried the body some distance away, she settled her hat back on her head and scowled at the view from the top. "What the hell happened on this mountain?"

Chapter 5

Everett waited his turn. There was no getting to Kaya through the snarl of people at the trailhead. He waited with Crazy Alice, holding her reins and those for Ghost, who'd been busily munching sweets Everett had stashed in his saddle bag.

He wasn't sure exactly what condition Miller Higgins had been in when Kaya and the others had found him. He'd known by the grim set of her mouth and the appearance of crime scene technicians on the scene that it wasn't good. She'd sent Everett back behind the police perimeter, despite his insistence to stay.

I need you to do this, Everett, she'd told him. *Don't argue with me.*

The words hadn't wavered, but he'd seen what was in her eyes.

She'd seen death. They'd been too late to save the kid.

The choppers had come and gone—not one, but three, which had given everyone at the bottom of the mountain more to talk about. The Fuego police had thankfully separated the kid's father and brother from the small herd of journalists.

He saw Kaya come off the mountain, cutting a swath through the reporters and cameras. She'd gone straight to where police had ensconced Higgins's family and stayed there for half an hour.

By the time she came back to the horses for Ghost, the circles under her eyes were as dark as bruises.

"You okay?" he asked.

She didn't meet his gaze. "I need to return to the station. I'm meeting the rest of the family there. And I need to make a statement to the press. It won't wait until morning. Dispatch called. Apparently, there are more reporters gathered there outside."

"You're tired," he told her.

"I know what I am," she snapped. Then she paused, taking the reins from him. "Sorry. It was rough up there."

"He's dead," Everett said quietly.

She pressed her lips together, unable to confirm or deny. "Listen, if reporters show up at the Edge—"

"No comment," he said and nodded. "I know."

She searched his face, then lowered her voice. "This could be trouble for you. Your family."

"Whatever happened, happened on our land," he stated. "Yeah. I expect there'll be a fair few questions."

Her scanning eyes fell on the buttons on his front. "I can't discuss it any further—with you or anyone. Don't push me."

"No," he replied. "So long as you promise me you're going to eat something when you get back to the station house. You need energy."

She shook her head. "No, I…" For a moment, her lips trembled. She cast a look in the direction of Ellis and Wolfe who were close by. "No."

Everett felt the lines dig into his brow. "Christ. Must've been bad up there."

Silently, she motioned for him to step back so she could mount her horse.

He stood by for a few seconds before reaching out, just enough to brush his knuckles across the tense muscles of her jaw. "Get back safe. You hear me?"

She jerked a nod, placed her foot in the stirrup and boosted herself up, swinging her other leg over Ghost's back. She settled into the saddle, let the Appaloosa shift underneath her, then clicked her tongue. The horse walked on.

Everett watched as Root and Wyatt joined her on their mounts. They broke into a trot, then a gallop.

Ellis's mount, Shy, nickered close behind him as his brother crossed to Everett. "She thinks there's trouble in it for the family?"

"Mmm," Everett responded. He saw Wolfe come to stand on Ellis's far side. His hands moved to communicate in sign language. "What's he saying?" Everett demanded.

Ellis watched his friend's motions. He and Wolfe had bonded soon after the latter had found a home at the Edge. Their friendship had lasted through the twisted forays of their family histories. "He says whatever happened to the kid wasn't an accident."

Everett frowned at the man in the black hat. He didn't feel a lot of warmth for Eveline's fiancé. But Wolfe's instincts tended to be better than others'. "How do you figure?"

Wolfe signaled. Ellis translated, "She didn't talk to the press. Neither did either of the deputies. And why would there be three choppers for one body?" Ellis braced his hands on his hips. "She did tell us, didn't she, that this was going to bring trouble to the Edge?"

Everett picked through Kaya's words. "And here I

thought we'd put trouble to rest with Whip Decker's death and Sheriff Jones's arrest."

"We need to know what happened up there," Ellis countered. "Preferably before reporters come to call. We need to know how to respond."

"Simple," Everett said. "No comment."

"Everett—"

"You heard me." He intervened before his brother could voice any more cautions. "Whatever happened on Ol' Whalebones, I aim for us to pass well below the radar. We've been through enough trouble to last us a lifetime— and Eatons tend not to live as long as others."

"Don't remind me," Ellis muttered. "And you won't be saying that around my fiancée."

Wolfe gestured in agreement.

"It's a bad legacy," Everett acknowledged. "But we don't have a choice other than to live with it." He patted Crazy Alice's muzzle when she nosed his elbow. "If I don't get you home to your women, I'm going to be persona non grata. Let's ride."

Kaya could deal with the press. She could deal with the curious bystanders who'd come to her office, expecting a definitive word on the situation. She could even deal with the questions inside her head and the sick feeling that wouldn't leave her alone.

Sitting down with Miller Higgins's mother, father, brother and sister, however, was something else altogether. This part of the job wasn't easy for anyone in law enforcement. Her emotions played close to the surface. When handling family of the deceased, she struggled even under the best of circumstances.

This was far from the best situation. She had four bodies in the morgue.

When she saw the mayor stride past the press pack and into the station, she allowed herself a lengthy sigh.

True Claymore was all swagger, even on bad news days like today.

His smile didn't quite meet his eyes, as it normally did. He was classed up, as always, in his embroidered black Western coat that was open over a pressed, white shirt complete with all the sterling accoutrements he felt necessary to reinforce his white-collar status—bolo tie with its prominent, engraved *C*, and an enlarged belt buckle with its crossed pistols and the words "GOD, FAMILY, COUNTRY" displayed underneath—up to the buckle of his hat band.

Kaya steeled herself. For all his charm, the good mayor did nothing to whet her appetite for his regular visits. He liked his finger in every pie if they smelled well enough of power and influence, which he'd enjoyed in this town for too long.

Her becoming sheriff hadn't pleased him. He'd done what he could to sway the election a different way.

Chiefly because he knew, unlike her predecessor, that she could not and would not be bought.

He tipped his hat to her. "Hell of a day, Sheriff Altaha. Hell of a day."

"I didn't see you on the mountain, mayor," she stated, "though I'm assuming you know as much as those people outside, which is next to nothing at this point."

"Come now, Kaya, honey," he said, sinking his hands into his pockets. "You know I've got my sources. You didn't find just one person dead on Ol' Whalebones."

Kaya caught the gasp from her assistant, Sherry, at her

desk. Irritated, she jerked her head toward the door of her office.

"Sherry," Claymore said in greeting as he passed her by. "How's the baby?"

"He's doing great, Mr. Claymore, sir," Sherry stuttered.

"Ah, that's fine, real fine," he schmoozed.

Kaya spread the door open. "We're all on the clock here."

As an invitation, it was poor. But the thought of having to deal with this clown inside the enclosed space of her office made her already upset stomach clutch. Claymore's cologne all but strangled her as he moved into her office. She shut the door and went behind the desk to put space between them. "The details of this case are being kept under wraps until we know more. In fact, they're on a need-to-know basis."

He messed with his tie. "That's just the thing, honey." Spreading his hands, he raised his brows. "In order to handle the press and questions from my constituents, I need to know. The bodies were found on Eaton Edge. There's been quite a lot of trouble out that way over the past year. I'd say you should start your investigation there."

"I never said there was foul play involved," she noted. "I won't know that until I speak with the medical examiner."

He rolled his eyes. "Come on, Kaya—"

Her restraint snapped. "It's *Sheriff,* actually. When I held the position of deputy, you never addressed me as anything but that. I don't recall the two of us getting any more familiar with each other over the past three months nor do I anticipate that happening anytime in the future. So you will address me as Sheriff Altaha and when I tell you the details of this case or any other are need-to-know you will take that as my word. Do I make myself clear, Mr. Claymore?"

His good-natured smile slipped. He was too smooth a man to let aggravation take hold, as she had. She knew, though, as the playful light in his eyes dimmed and a muscle in his cheek flexed, that she'd hit the mark. "We'll see about that, Sheriff. Yes, we will see. Have you dealt with the family of the hiker?"

She curbed the urge to club him over the head. "Have I *spoken* with Miller Higgins's father, mother and siblings? Yes. At length. They should be left alone. Instead of focusing on the press and the curious gaggle of townspeople outside, why don't you utilize your mayoral powers to inform people that the Higginses should be left alone? I'm sure they'd appreciate it."

Claymore took in a long breath. "Very well. You will keep me apprised of the nature of this case. It'd be best— for all involved."

He strolled out. Sinking into her chair, she pressed her hands to her temples. She was distressed when they shook. Pressing them between her knees, she willed herself to get it together.

She hated how much True Claymore still rattled her.

Unable to dwell on the reasons why, she opened the top desk drawer and found the Advil she kept there. There was a half-drunk Pepsi can on her desk from the day before. Claymore had left the door open so she called through it. "Sherry?"

"Yes, ma'am… I mean, sir." The woman, who wasn't but a few years younger than Kaya, bustled in. "What can I do?"

"Could you get me a bottle of water?" she asked. "And

maybe something small to eat. Nothing heavy. I'd appreciate it."

"I can run down the street and see if the deli's still open," Sherry offered.

"Thanks," Kaya said. "And you know not a word to those outside…"

Sherry bobbed her head quickly. "Mum's the word."

Kaya tried to fix a smile in place. Sherry had been hired by Jones, so Kaya had inherited her as an assistant. Knowing she had a baby at home, Kaya hadn't contemplated firing her, though she'd been cautious with her, unsure whether she still felt allegiance to her former boss.

Sherry hesitated on the threshold, worrying the pad of sticky notes and pen she carried with her. "Did you really find more than one body?"

Kaya closed her eyes briefly. The images were still fresh in her mind. And after her visit to the morgue, there'd likely be more to contend with. "It's late," she countered. "Once you come back from the deli, you need to go home and see your family."

Sherry handled her disappointment well. "Thank you, ma'am. Sir. I'll be back shortly."

Kaya found herself alone in the station house. Root was dealing with reporters. Wyatt had escorted the Higgins family home to San Gabriel for the night.

She'd seen her share of the dead. She'd been a rookie cop on the streets of Taos where the crime rate was anything but low. Her two years in uniform there might have made her, but they'd also exposed her to victims of overdose, homicide, accidental death and suicide.

She'd learned early that she could either compartmentalize it all, funnel it away or get overwhelmed so she'd done the former—to survive. To keep going because being a cop was the only ambition she'd had that mattered. Failure was not an option.

It still wasn't. She hadn't come back to Fuego County and joined the sheriff's department so that she could take over Wendell Jones's position. She'd had no ambitions there whatsoever. Nor could she turn her back on the people who'd thought she was best suited to the position.

She'd wanted to find Miller Higgins alive. She had needed to find him and return him to his folks.

She flicked open the report on her desk and stared at his photograph, as she had so often over the last few days.

There hadn't been a homicide in Fuego County in well over a year. But she had little doubt that Higgins had been murdered...along with the other three people they'd found with his body on Ol' Whalebones.

Murder had come to Fuego four times, which meant her department wasn't just dealing with a dangerous perpetrator. They were dealing with a serial killer.

Kaya pushed through the doors of the morgue. There was no one at the reception desk. Dr. Walther had volunteered to stay in after hours to see that the bodies were well cared for. Half the fluorescent lights in the lobby had been switched off.

As she turned toward the swinging doors of the examination room, she came up short. Her hand nearly jumped to her sidearm before she stopped it. "Damn," she said as the man just before the doors turned and she was able to see his face in the small amount of light from the lobby. She swallowed the curse because the mystery man was Reverend Huck Claymore. "Sorry. My nerves are on a hair trigger."

"It's understandable," he said in his level voice. The

only place she'd ever heard him raise it was during passionate sermons from the pulpit of the local church.

Kaya had always felt conflicted about him. He was True Claymore's older brother. He'd grown up at The RC Resort, same as the mayor. Neither man had wanted for much. Huck's suit might not be as flashy as his brother's, but even she could see that it was tailored. His tie was silk, and his boots weren't the least bit scuffed. He rarely smiled. She'd never heard him crack so much as a meager joke. He was a sober, weary-eyed man whose presence was a comfort to the citizens of Fuego.

He studied her closely with his unchanging expression. "How are you, Sheriff Altaha?"

She wasn't looking for comfort any more than she'd ever sought any of his preaching. Still, it was a kind, even question she'd be rude to rebuff. "I'm all right," she lied. When he lowered his chin, she sighed. "I've been better. May I ask what you're doing here, reverend?"

He didn't so much as blink. "To pray for the poor souls you took off the mountain this afternoon."

"Right," she said, feeling like an idiot. "That's kind of you, reverend. But we can't allow you beyond this point."

"I understand," he said with a passive nod. "Will the Higginses be returning tomorrow morning to identify their son?"

Kaya nodded. "Ten o'clock."

"I'd like to be here," he requested. "They might need some comfort during this time."

"Of course," she granted.

His lips curved but his eyes didn't track. "Thank you, Sheriff. I hope my brother hasn't been giving you any trouble over your investigation so far. He tends to overstep in these matters."

"I can handle the mayor."

As he regarded her, his eyes followed the path of his smile for the first time in Kaya's memory. Something gleamed to life there that he quickly shuttered. "I have no doubt you can." He reached up and pinched the edge of his white Stetson. "God be with you, Sheriff Altaha."

"And with you." The words didn't come as easily to her as they did him. She waited until she heard the entry doors swing shut behind him before she pushed through the doors into the exam room. "Sorry. I'm behind schedule."

Dr. Walther peered at her through his protective eyewear. He used a scalpel to point to the wall. "Gown. Gloves. Hairnet."

She grabbed what he told her to and donned each, carefully. There was one body on the table. The other victims were likely locked up in the cooler already. The ME's office was small and understaffed. The complete results of each autopsy were weeks out. But she'd wanted to gather any early impressions Walther had as well as view what had been collected with the remains.

The drone had been far enough away to give her only a vague impression of the damage done to Higgins over the last three days. It had given her more than enough, however, to tell her that he was no longer part of the living world. And yet she still felt sucker punched when she leaned over the table and viewed him close-up.

"The wildlife did their work," Walther acknowledged.

"Will you still be able to determine cause of death?" she asked as her stomach flipped the deli sandwich Sherry had brought her.

"After a proper examination," Walther granted. "There are tears and lacerations to the face, arms and torso."

"His family's coming tomorrow," she cautioned. "They can't see him like this."

"His wallet was still in his pocket," Walther revealed.

"Identification and cash?"

"Both," he said, pointing to a tray. "He had upwards of two hundred dollars on his person. Technicians also found a pocketknife with his name carved into the handle."

"What about his phone?" she asked. "He was livestreaming with it or a camera at the time of his disappearance."

"No phone, no camera," Walther answered.

"His pack?" she asked. "Hikers always have packs."

"Yes. Its contents have been catalogued. Would you like to see the full list?"

"I would," she said. "Have you found any other wounds on the body other than tears and lacerations on the front?"

Silently, he instructed her to help him turn Higgins's body onto its right side so the back of his head was facing her. "There's a large wound on the back of his head—a result of the fall, but it also could be consistent with—"

"A killing blow or gunshot wound," she observed. "You'll have him tested for gunshot residue?"

"Samples have already been taken. They'll be sent to the lab first thing in the morning. We'll also be sending DNA from the other victims."

"Maybe we'll get one or more matches with Missing Persons," she hoped. "I hate that we couldn't bring him home to his family alive."

"He was the same age as my oldest, Libby," he mused, nursing his scalpel. He rocked back on his heels, viewing the dead with more compassion than clinical interest.

"Take all the time you need for results. I want the killer found as much as the next person, but you won't get any pressure from my department if it means a thorough report."

"The mayor's going to have something else to say about how fast things should be done."

"I'll take care of True Claymore and anybody else who tries to interfere so you can focus on the dead. I'd like to see the rest of what was found at the scene. Personal belongings of other victims…anything the killer might have left behind…"

"The first tray is what we found on the boy," Walther reported. "The second contains everything else taken from the scene."

"Thank you," she said, veering around the exam table. Miller Higgins's clothes had been bagged and tagged, as had his personal belongings. His library card lay alongside his driver's license. Something about that tugged at her heart. His pack had contained three calorie bars, a half-full hydration pack, a compass, waterproof matches, a minitorch, a machete and its sheath that looked unmarked as if he'd yet to have had a chance to use it, a stick of deodorant, dissolvable wipes and a first aid kit that had never been opened.

The name carved in the handle of the jackknife hadn't been engraved by a professional. It looked like something he might have done himself.

Kaya frowned deeply when she saw the lone shoe among the clothes removed from his person and moved to the second tray.

Her eyes skimmed over one belt buckle, several more boots—these dirty and weathered—a slender wristwatch that was feminine in appearance, one hoop earring that could have been a match to the one Wolfe Coldero had found and then landed on a bracelet. It was a C-shaped cuff that wouldn't have gone all the way around the wrist. It was lined with silver.

She reached for it, turning the face of the piece toward her.

Her heart stuttered.

The cuff was inlaid with turquoise. In its center was the letter *S*.

Her focus narrowed on the simple inscription. She went numb. Her ears filled with distracted buzzing.

She must've made a noise because Walther's gloved hand came to rest on hers.

She jerked. "I…" She was breathing through her teeth. Her pulse was high and the buzzing was incessant. "This piece," she stammered. "I know this. I know who this belongs to!"

Chapter 6

Everett hadn't heard from Kaya in two days—unless listening to her press conference on the local news counted.

...recovered the remains of a sixteen-year-old male. He has been identified as Miller Higgins of San Gabriel. While searching the area, three other unidentified bodies were found...

She'd sent her deputies to the Edge to interview everyone on the premises. They asked questions about the comings and goings in the northern quarter over the last week—casual, routine questions that shouldn't have put his dander up.

But they did. Everett couldn't believe the police thought anyone at the Edge was responsible for Higgins's death. Rumors were rampant in town. Ol' Whalebones had been cordoned off. He and his men had been asked to leave it alone, pending further investigation.

Kaya hadn't said it on the news or otherwise, but everyone from Fuego to San Gabriel had. There was a killer on the loose.

That wasn't the only thing putting Everett on edge. Because the four bodies had been found on his family's mountain, the name Eaton was firmly entrenched in rumor and suspicion. With Eveline's wedding coming around the bend, people were pointing fingers.

There was nothing he disliked more than gossip. Unfortunately, Fuego was the gossip capital of the civilized world.

Even the church on Sunday stank of tittle-tattle.

Paloma always insisted he, Ellis and Eveline attend church with her. She'd somehow won the trifecta this week, roping all three of them into the front pew alongside Luella, Wolfe and Ellis's girls, Isla and Ingrid. Everett passed much of the service ignoring the whispers exchanged behind hands at their backs, swapping folded notes back and forth with his youngest niece, Ingrid, instead. She had a head for mischief and an intolerance for sitting still for more than five minutes at a time—two traits she shared with her uncle.

They had to be sneakier than sneaky to not draw the attention of Paloma who wouldn't hesitate to put a stop to it. Eveline caught his eye once, then subsided when Ingrid placed her finger over her mouth. His sister had smiled and looked the other way.

Ellis was distracted with Luella. She was tense amongst the other townies and with good reason. As Whip Decker's daughter, she'd been branded as troublesome the moment she was born. Whether she deserved the moniker or not, she'd long been branded "Devil's Daughter" by the people of Fuego County.

Everett saw Ellis place his hand on her bouncing knee where he drew circles with his thumb. If anyone could ease Luella's troubles, it was Ellis. He had a way with the woman he'd claimed as his own in high school. She'd slipped through his fingers, and he'd gone on to marry Liberty Ferris. But after the divorce and a fateful winter, Ellis and Luella had come together once more and it didn't look like they would be parting again.

"Psst!"

Everett glanced at Ingrid on his left. He took the note she slid across the surface of the hard bench. Making sure Paloma was still listening to Reverend Claymore, he unfolded the small scrap of paper to find another sketch of a horse.

Ingrid was turning out to be quite the artist.

Everett played along, knowing she was looking for his insight as much as his praises. He picked up the pencil without an eraser he'd found next to the Bible underneath the seat and scribbled, *Nice one. Pass it to LuLu.* He folded the square, then held out his hand as if to shake. She squeezed his fingers, taking the little note as she did. She opened it and read it while he did his best to look uninvolved. Then she folded it again and reached over her father's lap to tap Luella on the wrist.

Both Ellis and Luella looked. Silently, Ingrid did the same faux-shake with Luella she had with Everett, leaving Luella with the folded scrap. She unfolded it with hands that shook only slightly…

A smile bloomed across her face. She swept red curls from her cheek and greeted Ingrid with a soft look. *Thank you*, she mouthed.

Ellis reached his arm around Ingrid's shoulders and drew her close against his side. The child went willingly, casting a grin back at Everett as she did so. He gave her a thumbs-up but stopped when Ellis caught his eye. Shrugging, Everett tried to tune back into the reverend's spiel about sin and damnation and stopping the devil's wicked work in their good community.

Everett glanced over his shoulder, restless. The sanctuary was packed. The question was which of these sinners had been on his mountain. The killer hadn't been on the back of Ol' Whalebones just once. They'd returned over and over and over again. Everett figured it was someone from the county, likely Fuego itself, though he'd thought they'd combed out a fair good many wrongdoers over recent months—Jace "Whip" Decker, Wendell Jones…hell, even lewd Rowdy Conway had been flushed out.

He aimed to do any amount of legwork possible to catch whoever had brought death to Eaton Edge and stop them from killing anyone else there.

His gaze roved over those assembled, searching each face. He knew them all by name. He'd gone to school with some of them. He'd been on the rodeo circuit with others. Hell, he'd raced cars with a few. There were friends and there were rivals.

When his eyes hit the back of the church and Kaya standing near the door, arms crossed over her sheriff's uniform, he felt his heart give a lurch.

She'd been avoiding him. He had no doubt about that. The question was why? Why had she sent Root and Wyatt to question him, his family, his men? Why hadn't she told him about the bodies herself?

Was it because—deep down—like the rest of them, she was distancing herself from everyone at Eaton Edge because she thought somebody there might be involved in the body count?

He turned back around, rolling his shoulders. She hadn't met his stare, but he could feel it like an itch between his shoulder blades. Restless from having sat too long and the strong ache in his chest that he would not name because he knew what was good for him, no matter what had passed between him and the good sheriff of Fuego County, he leaned over his knees, wishing Huck Claymore would just shut up already so he and his family could escape with their dignity intact.

A movement out of the corner of his eye caught his attention. It was a wave from the left of the pulpit where the organist Christa McMurtry sat, watching him.

She was always watching him. She beamed, curling her fingers his way.

"Hellfire." His mutter fell into one of Reverend Claymore's pauses. Heads turned, Paloma leaning clear out in the open to scowl at him. He looked away, up at the pulpit, and saw the elder Claymore eyeing him with strong disapproval.

Join the party, reverend, he thought bitterly.

Everett fought his way to the back of the church once the service was over. He fought so hard, he elbowed several people out of the way and nearly knocked down Turk Monday, the former manager of Fuego's bank. Once he found sunlight and fresh air again, he nearly stumbled down the length of the church steps...

...and found that Kaya had escaped already.

"Ah... Mr. Eaton?"

"What do you want?" He settled down when he saw that it was Nova, a waitress at Hickley's BBQ. She had long raven locks that were straight as an arrow, wide dark eyes narrowed against the angle of the midmorning sun and prominent cheekbones that marked her as Kaya's niece. Kaya's sister, Naleen Gaines, was Nova's mother. "Sorry," he said when he saw her take a half step back in retreat. He sank his hands into his pockets, hoping for a less menacing impression. "Church makes me mean as a woke bear."

The lines of her mouth wavered, and he wondered if

that wasn't amusement lurking beneath. "I've been meaning to speak to you, Mr. Eaton."

"Call me Everett, Nova. I've known you since you were in diapers. And nobody calls me Mr. Eaton," he told her.

"Everett," she said, treading lightly. "I was wondering if you'd consider taking on a new hand at Eaton Edge this summer."

He made a thoughtful noise. "Depends on if they're any good at the kind of work I need them for. I'm already apprenticing one man. Not that he's much of a man…"

"Are you talking about Lucas?" she asked. "Lucas Barnes?"

He groaned. "The pain in my ass." When he heard the last word slip out, he sighed. Now he was going to have to apologize.

She surprised him by laughing. Catching his stunned gaze, she lifted her hand, subsiding. "Sorry. It's just… I know him—from when he was still in school. He gave the teaching staff fits."

"I'll bet he did." He inclined his head. "You know somebody I can take on?"

"Yeah," she said, standing a little taller. "Me."

"You?"

She narrowed her eyes. "Just because I'm a girl doesn't mean I don't know how to herd. Don't you have a sister? Doesn't she ride out with the men?"

"Occasionally," he said. "And it's got less to do with you being a female and more to do with the work itself. We don't just herd. We feed, wrangle, fix fencing, pipes, brand, tag, sort, vaccinate… No matter the season or the weather—hot, cold, rain, high desert sun, snow—we ride. It's tough on a grown man. Much less a teenage girl."

"My stepfather, Terrence Gaines, has been showing me

the ropes at his ranch," she said. "It's a small operation, but we do all those things there, too. And my father...well, my biological father—Ryan MacKay?"

"I know him. He's my stable manager Griff's son."

"He's been teaching me to rope since I was a toddler," she revealed. "And my aunt, Kaya, she taught me to ride with the best of 'em."

"Did she now?" he asked.

"Yeah. She did a lot of trick riding back in the day."

"You don't say." He considered. The girl hadn't wavered when he'd spoken about the work or the elements. "Wouldn't you rather spend your summer raising hell?" When she shook her head, he had to think harder. "Or... at the mall?"

"You don't know much about teenage girls, do you?"

"No. Look... I'm not going to say no to more help. But I'll need to speak to your mother first. I'm not aiming to get on anyone's mother's list, if you know what I'm saying."

"Sure," she said.

"I can't pay you much of a wage," he said. "At least not at first, while you're still learning the ropes."

"I learn fast," she assured him.

"And there's no way in hell you're sleeping in the bunkhouse with the men," he warned.

"Fine by me," she said. "Spring break's coming up. If you'd like, I could use that time to show you my skills. That way, you'll know what you're getting in the summertime."

"Why not?"

The beginnings of a cautious smile touched her mouth. "You're really saying yes?"

He found himself nodding. "I'm really saying yes."

"Wow. My mom said I didn't have a shot in hell." She beamed. "I love proving her wrong. Thank you!"

He was so shocked when she threw both arms around him, the hug sent him back a step. "Whoa." He caught himself, laughing. "There'll be none of that around the men. And you said your aunt was a trick rider?"

She bounced anxiously on her toes. "Uh-huh."

"You'll need to tell me more about that," he advised.

"Why? Are you interested?"

"In your aunt?" He bobbed his head. "Guilty."

"I didn't know the two of you were—"

"We've been keeping it quiet," he said.

"Oh," she said, lowering her voice and darting a look around. "Right. Okay. Well, what do you want to know?"

"How she's doing, for one?" he asked, feeling lame.

Her expression morphed quickly from playful to troubled.

The mob was beginning to file out of the church en masse. He stepped closer. "What's wrong?"

"I shouldn't say. Mom told me it's a family matter."

Everett tensed. "Does it have anything to do with what they found on the mountain?"

"It has everything to do with that."

He nodded. "I don't want to get you in trouble. Just do me one favor."

Kaya put the phone back into its cradle. She called Root and Wyatt into her office. She closed her file drawer with a thud and folded her hands on the desk. "That was the FBI. They're sending a man here."

"They'll shut us out of the case," Wyatt complained.

"We'll have to turn over all the evidence," Root said. "All those bodies…"

She nudged the file on the desk with her hands. "I've been speaking with Walther, off and on. I've also been coordinating with the Fuego, San Gabriel and other county police departments and Missing Persons from each bureau."

"That's a heck of a thing," Wyatt muttered. People tended to go missing in the desert quite a bit.

"Together, we may have turned over some results," Kaya revealed, "but we'll have to wait for DNA to confirm." She picked up the folder and thrust it at them.

Wyatt took it. He flipped it open. "Mescal, Sawni. Missing since… Geez, boss. This woman's been missing for eighteen years."

Kaya nodded. She threaded her hands together to stop them from fidgeting. "She was seventeen when she disappeared. She wasn't native to Fuego. She grew up on the rez."

"Like you," Root said, innocently enough.

Kaya felt it like a blow. "Like me."

"Did you know her?"

Full disclosure. There had to be full disclosure if there was going to be trust. "There's a personal connection," she admitted. "I'm not willing to elaborate much further."

They both exchanged a glance, then let it lie. "Last known whereabouts were—"

"Here, in Fuego," she continued. "After three months, local police and sheriff's departments stopped looking for her. Though her family and others on the rez never have."

"Without DNA confirmation, why do you think it was her?" Wyatt asked.

"It's not wishful thinking, if that's what you're implying. A piece of jewelry was found at the site. It matches one I know she owned and wore often." *I had one to match— with a* K. Kaya had had her mother bring it over from their old house where she'd left it when she joined the police academy in Taos. Her piece and the one at the lab were a dead match. "Her grandfather made it for her and one other that I have in my possession."

"Maybe somebody duplicated it," Root noted.

"Maybe she pawned it before she went missing…or somebody could've stolen it," Wyatt said.

"All good thoughts," she acknowledged. "But the pieces line up…a little too neatly now that there are four bodies in the morgue…one of which could very well be hers."

"If one of the bodies does belong to Mescal and the FBI comes in here and says we're off the case, are you going to allow that?" Wyatt wondered.

She weighed the question and all the implications. "I'm not sure," she said truthfully. She flipped open the next file on her desk. "The other possible is Merchant, Bethany. You probably remember her name from the papers. She disappeared a year before Mescal while she was in her senior year at Fuego High School."

"I do remember this one," Root said. "I was a freshman when she was a senior. Head cheerleader, Miss Rodeo like three straight years in a row… She dated all the high-profile rodeo kids. Terrence Gaines. True Claymore. Sullivan Walker. Everett Eaton…"

Kaya pretended her breath didn't snag on the last. "Eaton."

Root nodded. "Oh, yeah. Real hot and heavy, that relationship. 'Course, then his mom up and left his dad for Santiago Coldero. Everett dropped out of school… Things cooled real fast between him and Bethany."

"Her last known whereabouts were at the Lone Star Motel," Kaya noted from the file. "They found an overnight bag, her wallet, keys, even her shoes in Room 10. The bed was still made, however, and it was between her check-in that evening, which she paid for in cash, and her check-out time the following morning that she disappeared."

"How do we know it's her in the morgue, too?" Wyatt asked, his brows low.

"Something that was not found among her possessions in the motel was a wristwatch, one her mother claimed she never left the house without. It was an heirloom that belonged to Bethany's grandmother and was given to her when the woman passed." Kaya sat back. The chair squeaked beneath her. She closed the file on Bethany's picture-perfect smile. "A watch of the same description was found at the crime scene. The family supplied samples as well as dental X-rays. If it's her, we'll know in due time."

"Which would leave one unidentified person," Root said.

"Did Walther say whether or not he's determined cause of death for any of them?" Wyatt asked.

"Just one for certain," she said, grim. "Our hiker, Miller Higgins. Gunshot wound. His skull was tested for gunpowder residue and the wound there is consistent with a gunshot to the back of the head fired at close range."

Root winced a little. "Sounds mercenary. The others must have contusions on the back of the skull as well. That's why the FBI's coming. If a pattern's been established, they must think we've got a serial killer on the loose."

"I don't have to tell you not to pass on any of this information," she reminded them. "The press is on us as it is, not to mention the public. I've had four separate families in my office over the last few days requesting to know whether or not one of the bodies belongs to their son or daughter. One of them was the Merchants. We must keep as many of the details under wraps as we can so that we can build a solid case."

"And then hand it all over to the FBI," Wyatt said dismally.

Kaya frowned. "We'll see."

It was raining cats and dogs before she left the sheriff's department and drove home. She thought about stopping by one of the takeout places in town and grabbing something, knowing she was going home to an empty fridge. She hadn't had it in her to face the supermarket or its patrons—not yet, anyway.

She wasn't avoiding people, she told herself. She just wasn't hungry.

Messages had been left on her voice mail at her personal number. There, she'd heard the voices of her mother, her sister, the Mescals…and that was hard to swallow.

And Everett. He'd called, twice—once to leave a message.

That was three days ago. Maybe he'd given up by now.

Just as well, she thought, escaping the rain for the comfort of her home. She'd likely be called back in before daybreak to deal with the arroyos that resulted from these spring cloudbursts. She took off her weapons belt and shrugged off her sheriff's button-down so that her shoulders were bare in her black tank top and she could breathe somewhat easier. She put her official phone on charge as well as her radio, ignored the pit in her stomach by avoiding the pantry and poured herself a cup of coffee.

She was watching the steam rise from the surface as it sat, untouched, on the counter when the doorbell rang.

Wary, she didn't move from the space over the brick cobbles of the kitchen. Fuego was small so it was only natural that some of its residents knew exactly where to find her during her off-duty hours. There had been a few who'd knocked on her door during the week, fishing for more on the case. She'd stopped answering.

She picked up her mug when the doorbell sounded again and then again in quick succession. Thoughtfully, she raised it to her mouth and blew across the surface, letting the coffee's scent curl up her nostrils. Maybe it would help settle her, as nothing else had since she'd recognized the turquoise and silver cuff.

Her mind wouldn't leave it alone. She set the coffee back down, tired and heartbroken all over again.

Had she really thought she'd find Sawni alive? After all this time?

She'd been a fool.

The doorbell was replaced by the sound of a hard knock. A voice followed, terse and familiar. "Hey! Sheriff Sweetheart! Open up!"

Kaya found her feet moving toward the door, abandoning her coffee. She crossed the living space. He was pounding on the door so hard, it was rattling on its hinges. She unlocked the dead bolt, undid the chain and turned the knob, then yanked the door open before he could break it down. "What are you doing?"

The porch light spilled over him. He was standing on her stoop under his hat in the rain. The drops hit the raised concrete platform beneath his boots and splatted noisily, breaking apart and coming in the house. He squinted at her. "What's the matter with you?"

Her jaw dropped. "What's the matter with *me*? You're the one about to break my door down!"

"How else was I supposed to get you to answer?" he asked. "Your family thinks you've done well to isolate yourself. You won't return their calls or mine—"

"How do you know what my family—"

He took a step closer to the threshold, crowding it and her out of the doorway. "What'd you find on the mountain that's made you shut down?"

Her teeth were gnashed and anger ground between them. It felt good, feeling something other than the bone-chilling fear she'd been walking around with. "Get off my porch before my neighbors see you lurking."

"You're going to have to arrest me," he challenged. He scanned her. "Christ. Have you slept since I saw you last?"

Had she expected him to be charming? Women who counted on Everett Eaton turning on the charm would be severely disappointed. She convinced herself she wasn't one of them. "Of course I've—"

"Don't lie to me," he said, grim around the mouth. He planted his hands on either side of the jamb. "I'll bet you're not eating much, either. You look like you're about to drop."

"Why are you here?" she asked him, exasperated.

"You're trying to back out," he decided. "You don't want any part of our agreement anymore."

"I've got more important things to worry about."

"At least call your sister and your niece. They're worried sick."

"Why do think I'm going to take orders from you?" she countered.

"Because you're alone and you're trying to keep it that way—however much you might need somebody right now," Everett stated. "Maybe that person isn't me. I can live with that. But the least you can do is tell me—not dodge my calls."

"You're right."

He opened his mouth to argue further, stopped midword and screwed up his face. "I am?"

Kaya closed her eyes. They wanted to stay closed. "I haven't slept. I'll cop to that. The situation on the mountain...it's far more complex than I thought it could be. There's more I can't tell you. It's personal and it's eating at me. I won't even have the authority to finish it or bring closure to the families. The Feds are on their way. They'll be taking over the investigation as early as Wednesday."

"Why the Feds?" he asked. "Your department's small, but you're capable. You won't stop until you've caught this son of a bitch."

He was going to have so many questions, none of which she could answer. "I want that," she said. "More than you know."

He straightened. "Are you hungry, sweetheart?"

She blinked. "I should eat. I haven't been hungry."

He picked up something off the stoop. A to-go container. "This is from Rocko's."

"Rocko's... Pizza?" she asked, bemused. "That's two towns over. Why—"

"Don't ask me to give away my sources," he said, holding the box out to her, "but I was told it was your favorite restaurant."

She felt the warmth of the cardboard box. "You brought me pizza from Rocko's."

"I want you to be okay. I aim to see to it that you are. You take care of the community, everybody in it. But if you need someone to take care of you, you know where to find me. Are we clear?"

She only stared at him, the scent of Rocko's thick crust supreme curling up her nostrils. Suddenly, she was awake, and she was ravenous. "I don't know what to say."

"Say yes."

There was no refusing him. She pressed her lips to-gether.

He didn't waver. "Is there anything else you need?"

You. In my house. In this space. With me. Her face burned as the thoughts hit home. She settled for shaking her head in response.

"Let me know if that changes," he demanded. "And answer the phone."

"Anything else?" she asked, wryly.

"I'd be inside the house if I didn't think you'd tase me for muddying your floors," he said. "The next time I leave the Edge and track you down, I'm coming in."

She didn't think it'd be wise to tell him she didn't care about her floors. She liked the idea of stripping him down layer by layer just so she'd know warmth again.

This man burned hotter than anyone she'd ever known. It was wiser to keep him out—keep him at arm's length, like she'd planned. But his eyes glinted and the longer she looked at him, the more she wondered just how hot his core was.

"Eat," he said in no uncertain terms. "And get some sleep. I'll say good night."

"Good night," she said. He turned away, walked off the stoop. She shut the door. It took her several seconds to move her feet. She walked back to the kitchen, set the box on the stovetop. She opened the lid. Saliva filled her mouth.

Before she could reach for a slice, one of her phones rang on the counter. She glanced over to see the screen of her personal device lit up. Everett's name was splashed across her caller ID.

This time, she didn't hesitate. She picked it up, swiped, then raised it to her ear. "Hello?"

"Just checking," came the sound of his baritone.

A small smile tugged at her mouth. It kept tugging and she gave in to it. "I thought we said good night."

"We're going to say a lot more good nights before this is all over. You know that, right?"

"Yes," she whispered.

"I'm looking forward to the night I don't have to say good night. I'm livin' for that night, baby."

"I can't handle you when you talk like that," she informed him.

"Good. Maybe it'll make you impatient."

"Good night, Everett."

He cursed but said it anyway. "Think of me, sweetheart." Then he hung up, leaving her with an appetite and need that were suddenly and magnificently awake.

Chapter 7

Everett stalked into the hacienda-style ranch house ahead of his dogs after a long day of tagging calves and counting cattle. He wanted to drink a beer, put up his feet and leave the paperwork he knew was sitting at his desk for later. The house smelled damn fine, and his stomach rumbled, needing whatever Paloma had thrown together in the kitchen.

No sooner had he taken off his hat than the dark-eyed housekeeper his father had hired over thirty years ago rounded the corner and snapped her apron at him. "Take off those boots. You're tracking in dirt. Don't you have any sense, or has it all vanished with the altitude?"

Everett hung his hat on the nearest peg and stretched his arms from one side of the mudroom to the other. "I was awake with the cock this morning. I don't need you pestering me when we both know I wiped my feet a dozen times before entering."

"You got witnesses to that?" she asked, eyeing him beadily.

Everett growled low in his throat before he turned, opened the door and stepped out onto the welcome mat. He scraped the bottom of his boots on the coarse fibers in exaggerated motions like a mama cow stamping the ground while he tagged her calf. When he was done, he came back in and slapped the door shut with a resounding thud after letting the dogs in, too. "Satisfied?"

"Turn them up for me, one after the other."

"No," he drawled and stomped around her in the direction of the kitchen. The clickity-clack of the dogs' nails followed him across the hardwood.

Paloma pulled him up short with an urgent hand on his arm. "Don't go in there looking like that!"

"Why not?" He loved her. She was more mother to him than the woman who had made him and run away. But he was hot and drained and all he'd thought about for the last hour was settling down with a beer and his dogs.

"There's a man," she hissed, down to a whisper.

Everett raised a brow. "You got a man in here?" He shook her loose. "Does he know he'll never be good enough for you? Never mind. I'll tell him."

She grabbed him again before he could turn the corner. "Not that kind of man, you lout. And haven't I got enough problems keeping you decent without some good-for-nothing boyfriend hanging around?"

"That's the spirit," he muttered, still trying to get a look around the corner. "Who's the guy?"

"He says he's from the FBI."

Everett stopped straining away. "Say again."

"You heard me," she said, lowering her brow. "Everett Templeton Eaton, don't you go all Clint Eastwood on this one. He's no Sheriff Altaha, or Jones for that matter."

"I'll thank you never to mention the good sheriff and her predecessor in the same breath again," he warned.

"You misunderstand," she snapped, pinning him with an expression he'd come to know well over the misspent days of his youth. "An outside agent of the law isn't likely to give you the sort of understanding or leniency that local law enforcement has. Keep that tongue of yours civil. I don't have the wherewithal to bail you out of federal prison."

It wasn't exasperation that gripped her. Not entirely. She was worried about him—more than usual. He felt himself soften. So few people filed away his rough edges, but she could do it in a look. Without answering, he bent to her level and pecked a kiss on her round cheek. Then he ducked into the kitchen to face the man sitting across the room at the table.

Built like a boxer in a flat gray suit that strained around the points of his shoulders, the fella didn't fool Everett into thinking he was as refined as either his clothing or rigid posture suggested. When he stood to greet Everett, opening his mouth to do so, Everett pivoted for the fridge and opened it. He took out his beer, twisted the top off the bottle and tipped it for a long pull as his dogs Bones, Boomer and Boaz drank from their water bowl under the picture window.

The FBI man cleared his throat. "Mr. Eaton, I presume."

Everett drank until the contents of the bottle were half-gone before coming up for air. He checked what was on the stove. Enchiladas. *This better be quick, secret agent man*, he mused before shutting the fridge and turning to face his latest opponent. "If she invited you to dinner, she's overruled. I'm not in the mood for strangers at my table."

The FBI man looked amused. "The sheriff said you're a real mean cattle king. I was half expecting John Wayne to walk through the door."

"Altaha sent you?" Everett asked.

"She asked me to wait until she could smooth the introduction," the stranger said, talking fast with hints of Boston around his consonants, particularly the *R*s. "But I was keen to form my own impression of Fuego's newly minted cattle baron. This is quite a spread," he added. "I understand you're second-generation. Quite an inheritance for a man still shy of forty."

FBI man would have done better to bring the sheriff with him. Everett lifted the beer for another drink. "Just."

The FBI man took that as his cue to introduce himself, stepping forward. He pulled aside his coat to show the badge strapped to his belt. "I'm Agent Watt Rutland."

"The hell kind of name is Watt?" Everett asked.

"Birth name's Walter," Rutland explained. "Father raised six boys on his own, had monosyllabic names for all of us."

"Now, that's fascinating," Everett muttered, kicking out a chair for himself. He turned it and sat down backward, leaning on the ladder-back rail. After another drink, he hung his arms over it to pet Boaz who came looking for a scratch. "What can I do for you, Watt?"

"I think I prefer Agent Rutland for now," he said thoughtfully, pulling a small pad of paper from the lining of his sport coat.

Everett heard someone clearing their throat from the direction of the door. He turned his head only slightly, knowing Paloma was just out of view. He remembered her warning, the plea in her eyes, and rolled his. Gripping the bottle in both hands, he asked, "Will you be taking some of the caseload off the sheriff?"

"What do you know about the case, Mr. Eaton?" Rutland asked, shifting on his chair. He clicked the button on the top of his pen, ready to scribble on the pad he'd spread open on the tabletop. "Or can I call you Everett?"

"Eaton's fine," Everett admitted. "Just leave out the mister. I'm not my father."

"He passed recently, didn't he?"

"Nine months ago," Everett said. Long time to go without the leathery sound of the old man's voice or the sight of his time- and work-worn boots crossed on top of the office desk. Covering up his grief the way his therapist had told him to stop doing a long time ago, Everett sipped his beer again, then swallowed hard. "I know there were several bodies pulled off our mountain. Three unidentified females and one boy. The kid, Higgins, that went missing recently from San Gabriel. Foul play's involved though nobody's saying how, specifically." He frowned at the stranger across from him. "If the FBI's here, I'd say foul play's been chalked up to murder and it's serious business."

"Is murder ever not serious business?" Rutland asked conversationally.

The casual tone wasn't fooling Everett one bit. Rutland had come to Eaton Edge to study Everett and study him hard. *I'm not going to squirm for you, secret agent man*, he determined. "You've got to look in my direction because you see it as my land."

"Well, isn't it?" Rutland asked.

"It belongs to the family," Everett told him. "So does the business. And there's not a thing going on here that we don't know about."

"If that tracks," Rutland considered, "then one of you knows what happened on Ol' Whalebones. Don't you?"

Everett didn't answer, nor did he lower his stare from the FBI man's. He finished off the beer.

Rutland unclicked the pen and placed it and the notebook back in the lining of his coat. "How's about this? You clean up. Get your story straight. Then you come by the sheriff's department tomorrow morning where my team and I can interview you formally."

As Rutland rose from his seat, Everett raised a brow. "Do I need to bring a lawyer with me?"

Rutland paused. "Representation isn't necessary. But if you've got reason to believe you need counsel, you're well within your rights."

"As a suspect," Everett assumed.

"As a person of interest," Rutland said evenly. Then he stuck out his hand.

Everett didn't bother to stand or shake it.

Rutland dropped it. "I'll note that in my report."

Everett waited until the sound of his high-priced brogues faded before he gave in to a long exhale, trying to release the tension from his shoulders.

Another bottle of beer dropped to the table in front of him. Paloma's hand touched his shoulder. "We got trouble?" she asked, taking the empty bottle from his hand.

"Why would we when I didn't kill Higgins or any of the others?" he asked.

Paloma dropped to the seat Rutland had abandoned. Everett was shocked to see a full beer in her fist, too. To his knowledge, he rarely saw Paloma drink more than champagne at New Year's or wine at Christmas dinner. He recalled the time he'd had to pick her, Eveline and Luella up at the police station where they'd been detained on a trumped-up drunk and disorderly charge after Margarita Night. It nearly teased a smile out of him. She choked the bottle top, twisted off the cap and tipped it to her mouth for a delicate sip.

When he and Ellis were troublemaking youngsters, she'd known how and when to put the fear of God into the two of them. A ranching woman to the core, she could boast as many callouses and scars as either of them.

But Everett had never had any doubt that Paloma was

a lady. She'd tried her best to breed him, Ellis and Eveline to be polite and well mannered.

He'd given her hell. There were times he felt sorry for it. She was the only woman who'd ever loved him for who he was without condition.

"If he's got nothing on you," Paloma considered, "why'd he come all this way to make introductions?"

"To his mind, it's my mountain. He and his team are going to be crawling over this place like ants." It was going to annoy him. Everett opened the new beer. It hissed and the cap clinked when he tossed it onto the table. He crossed his arms over the top of the chair and peered at the view of the barn and corrals from the window over Paloma's shoulder. "They better not do anything to stall operations."

"You don't think he's already looked into you and everybody else here?" Paloma asked. "You don't think he may not like something about your past and was trying to shake something loose?"

The concerned light in her eyes hadn't ceased. Rutland was causing Paloma to worry, and that angered Everett. "He won't find anything, will he?"

"What's this formal interview about tomorrow at the sheriff's then?" Paloma asked.

Everett thought about that. "Hell if I know."

Paloma watched him drink. "You need to call Ellis, Eveline and the others."

The others being Luella and Wolfe, as they were family all but in name as far as Paloma was concerned. "No use getting them worked up, too, over assumptions."

"My assumptions come straight from my intuition," Paloma informed him, "which is rarely wrong where the lot of you is concerned. I'd have thought by now you'd have learned to pay attention."

As she picked her bottle up off the table and got up to leave, Everett waited until she brushed by his chair to reach up and take her by the wrist. He waited until her dark eyes swung down to meet his. "I wouldn't lie to you. You know that."

He saw her lips firm but not before he saw the heavy lower one tremble. "Everett, I know you would kill to protect your own. I've never doubted that. But what happened on that mountain was nothing less than evil. That isn't you. I know it wasn't you. I will not abandon you to this scrutiny. I just wish the sheriff's boys and the FBI would leave us well enough alone. Hasn't this family been through enough?"

He held her for another moment, long after he dropped his eyes. The sight of her unshed tears gutted him. "They won't be looking our way for long," he pledged. "I'll make sure of it."

"Don't do anything stupid, *mijo*," she muttered. She *tsk*ed as she passed a rough hand through his hair. "Get a haircut while you're in town tomorrow or I'll take the scissors to you myself."

"You'll have to catch me first," he warned her.

"Hmph."

As she passed into the kitchen to put plates together for the both of them, the tension jammed taut between his shoulder blades and his thoughts didn't stray far from the meeting with Rutland tomorrow morning.

Kaya tried to gauge Everett's face from the corner of the room. She'd been invited to observe Rutland's interview with him—but not to participate.

He'd had his hair trimmed. The tips had been cut far enough back that she could see the pale stripe the sun hadn't touched at the peak of his brow. There were fine notes of gray there, mixed with black. His hat was hooked over one knee of his Wranglers and his plaid shirt was open over a gray T-shirt that fit him well enough she could see hints of definition underneath.

She steadied herself. She'd known the FBI agent would investigate Everett, his family and his employees. She'd had her deputies do the same. She'd wanted him clear. She hadn't wanted his name anywhere near the list of possible suspects. When Root confirmed that his alibi for the window of Higgins's disappearance had checked out, she'd shut herself in her office to breathe a long, hard sigh.

If she was going to go to bed with the man—and after that pizza business at her house, it felt inevitable—he couldn't be involved in this.

Kaya knew Rutland had to go through the same motions and come to the same conclusion about Everett's involvement. It didn't make her any less wary of what Rutland had hidden in the bland file folder on the desk in front of him.

He'd been working Everett for over half an hour with all the routine questions that Root and Wyatt had already asked. But with the latest news from the forensics lab and Walther's office, there were more questions to be asked.

Rutland reached into the folder and pulled out a photograph of a blonde girl. It was over a decade old. "Do you recognize this woman?"

Everett raised one thick eyebrow. "Her name's Bethany Merchant. She went missing after I left school."

Rutland nodded. "What was your relationship with Miss Merchant?"

"We were involved," Everett informed him.

"Intimately?"

Everett peered at Rutland. "Are you asking if we had sex?"

"I'm just trying to get a more detailed understanding of what happened between you and Miss Merchant before her disappearance."

Everett stared Rutland down. Finally, his shoulders lifted. "We were together. We drank, kissed, partied and yeah, we had sex. Multiple times. You want a list of the places or are you more interested in the positions?"

"There's no need to get testy, *Mr.* Eaton," Rutland said evenly.

Everett tilted his head just slightly and Kaya came to attention when she saw the ready light in his eyes. It meant there was a fight ahead and not a pretty one. "You're the one prying into my personal business. *Watt.*"

She sucked in a breath.

Why was he using Rutland's first name when she hadn't heard him say hers since he'd started asking her to consider him more than a friend?

The hitch of pain came as a surprise. She didn't want it. She wanted nothing but to focus on the remainder of the interview and get back to the county's and the town's needs.

The hurt persisted, nonetheless. And that set her as ill at ease as the realization in the restaurant that he had put her on some kind of pedestal.

It made no sense. Why would he have all these expectations of her and who they could be together…if he couldn't say her name?

Rutland placed another photograph on the table. "Do you recognize this individual?"

Everett frowned. After a moment, he leaned forward.

Kaya's heart was in her throat as he studied Sawni's

picture. *Why?* she thought helplessly as she watched her past and present collide.

Everett shook her head. "No," he answered. "Though she does look familiar. Who is she?"

"Sawni Mescal," Rutland revealed. "She worked in Fuego, not long after Bethany disappeared."

Everett watched Rutland as he shuffled the photos back into the folder. "She went missing, too, I assume." He glanced at the wall. His eyes locked with Kaya's. She felt the impact in her knees. "That's who you found on the mountain?" he asked her.

Rutland cleared his throat. "We can neither confirm nor deny at this time—"

"That's where Bethany's been?" Everett asked, undeterred. "All this time? Her body's been at the Edge…"

The awareness came. Kaya saw it dawn on him. As he trailed off, his chin lifted in understanding. To Rutland, he said, "That's why you think I'm involved. Beyond the fact that Ol' Whalebones is part of the Edge, you think I…what—killed Bethany weeks after I ended things with her and dumped her on the mountain?"

"Mr. Eaton—"

"No," Everett said. He climbed to his feet. "They looked into me. There are files, records that'll show I was cleared after her disappearance." Again, he looked to Kaya. "You still got those files, sheriff?"

"We do," she answered. "Missing Persons cleared you…"

Everett sensed more. "But?"

Kaya stepped forward. "There were rumors that you and her fought at the rodeo the day before she went missing…"

His gaze circled her face. "So?"

"You may not have killed her," Rutland said. "But you

were a man of means, even then. You had enough money and privilege to hire someone to—"

"That's bull," Everett dismissed. "You're talking about my trust fund. If you'd followed through, you'd know that money didn't come into my possession until I was twenty-one. I was barely eighteen when Bethany disappeared. And that wasn't a fight at the rodeo. She came after me, hankering for a dispute for ending things with her after I quit school. I walked away from it. I'd already made my position clear."

"Which was…" Rutland prompted.

"She always talked about going east after graduation," Everett explained. "She wanted to go to college and live there, get out of New Mexico. She had the grades to do it, too. She could've gone to any school, Ivy League or otherwise, and her daddy had the money to pay for anything her scholarships didn't. She wanted me to tag along and start a life with her, wherever she went. But I knew I'd never leave Fuego. I never wanted to. She resented that just like she resented me leaving school because my father needed me at the Edge. I ended things between us because she got her acceptance letter from Princeton, and she needed to know there wasn't anything holding her back."

"If there wasn't anything holding her back, why did she argue with you the day before she went missing?" Rutland asked.

"She was mad because I didn't want to go," Everett explained, "and because I'd told her I didn't love her."

"Did you love her?"

Everett set his jaw. "I don't see how that's relevant."

"Everything's relevant," Rutland explained. "Her parents deserve an answer as to why she was murdered and left on that mountain—a mountain that belongs to your family, Mr. Eaton. Answer the question."

"No," Everett snapped.

"No, you won't answer the question? Or no, you didn't love her?"

"I didn't love her," Everett shot back. "Not enough to follow her across the continental US. Is that the answer her parents want? That I didn't love their daughter the way she wanted me to love her? Is that going to comfort them in their grief?"

Rutland chose not to answer these questions. He'd opened the file again, splaying it wide. Turning it, he revealed the discovery photos and the photos Walther's technicians had taken of the dead in the lab. They scattered under Everett's nose.

Kaya stepped forward, wanting to shuffle them back into the folder where they belonged.

Everett saw them before she could round the table. His hands lifted. The skin of his face seemed too thin. He released a rough breath and stepped back.

He wavered and she dove.

Before he could stagger or fall, she grabbed him by the shoulders. "Sit down," she murmured. Looking around for his chair, she hooked her toe around its leg and slid it closer. "Just sit, okay?"

"Why would you…?" he groaned as she pushed him into the seat. "You think…"

"Quiet." Kneeling, she framed his face with her hands. The skin around his mouth was white. His lips themselves had turned a shade paler than his skin. She cursed, hooking her hand around the back of his neck. "Put your head between your knees and breathe."

"You think I…" he said again even as he did what he was told.

She didn't like how small he sounded. "Put those away," she snapped at Rutland. "He's had enough."

It took Everett longer than he would have liked to pull himself together. It was bad enough that he'd nearly passed out in the interrogation room.

When he closed his eyes, he could still see the photographs of Higgins, Bethany, the Mescal girl…and whoever the fourth person was.

Higgins's brain cavity had been exposed. Bethany's blond hair had still been visible but her skin had faded away from bone—same with the Mescal girl, only her hair had been dark. Nothing remained of the fourth person except skeletal remains…

The images would live rent free in his mind for the rest of his life.

Everett splashed water across his face again in the men's room. The back of his throat was raw. He'd lost the fine breakfast Paloma had made for the two of them that morning before seeing him off with a reminder about getting his hair trimmed…

He felt older, more burdened. He was far angrier than he had been after Rutland's visit the night before and the reasons weren't settling well.

He'd grown up on a ranch. He knew what became of animals left out to die.

But those bodies in the photographs were human.

The image of Higgins's skull floated back to him. Everett ducked his head to the sink and drank water from the faucet. He swished it around his mouth, trying to rid himself of the bitter taste, then spat it out and shut off the water, finally. He ripped brown paper towels from the dispenser to the right of the mirror, wadded them up and dried his face.

His reflection was clear now, but his eyes weren't. They were bloodshot. Pulling the aviator sunglasses from the neckline of his T-shirt, he took his time cleaning the lenses with the open corner of his plaid button-down before he covered his eyes. He tossed the wad of paper towels in the overfull trash can and opened the door.

Kaya was waiting.

He lowered his head and beelined for the door.

"We'll speak again, Mr. Eaton," Rutland called from the open door of the interrogation room.

Everett ignored him. He could see the outdoors through the glass. He pushed through the door, letting the sun hit him in the face.

Before the door could swing shut at his back, Kaya exited, too. "Everett," she said when it closed behind her.

"Nope," he said, shaking his head as he pivoted in the direction of the parking lot. His voice was raspy and weaker than he needed it to be.

Her hands closed around the bend of his elbow.

"You don't want to do this right now," he warned.

She scanned him. "You shouldn't drive."

"I'm fine," he bit off. He felt naked under the glide of her black, knowing gaze and he didn't need her to know it. "I'm walking, aren't I? Now let me go. I'm not feeling peaceable, and I know you don't want to do this dance in town, seeing as you're determined to keep our relationship a secret from everyone."

She didn't loosen her grip. "I'm sorry about what Rutland did in there. It was dirty."

He made a noise in his throat. He extricated himself and took long, retreating strides to the door of his truck.

"I didn't know what he was going to do," she told him. "I wouldn't have agreed to it if I had."

"That's nice," he drawled, opening the driver's door. "I'll see you around, sweetheart."

Before he could boost himself into the seat, she grabbed him again. "Everett."

"I can't do this right now," he growled. "Step away."

She pushed herself farther into his space, taking a handful of his shirt. "I can't let you leave 'til I know you're okay."

"I'm okay."

"You're not."

"Just tell me one thing," he said. "I need to know if any part of you believes any of it."

"Believes what?"

He pointed at the building and what had happened inside. "That I did *that*. That I'm *capable* of that."

"Would I be here if I did?" she asked.

"I don't know anything right now," he replied. "You want me to be okay? Turn me loose."

She hesitated, her eyes doing circles around his face. Finally, her hand released his shirt and she shifted onto her heels.

Everett placed one foot on the running board and settled into the driver's seat. He shut the door. He cranked the truck and gripped the wheel.

He saw Kaya walking back to the door. He thought about rolling the window down and saying something but stopped himself. She'd been in that room. Even if she didn't think he was capable of killing Higgins, Bethany and those other people, she'd stood back while others who did questioned him.

He put the truck in gear and pulled out of the parking lot, unable to deal with what was under the surface.

What had he expected? He was someone who notoriously surrendered to nothing in life. So why had he begun to surrender his heart, of all things, to the goddamn sheriff of Fuego County?

Chapter 8

Kaya didn't want much to do with Agent Rutland, despite their departments working together on the case. She'd spent the majority of time over the last week out of office seeing to her sheriff duties. At some point, she had even stopped checking her personal cell phone. Everett hadn't called or texted once since the debacle at the station.

She patrolled with Root and Wyatt, answering a trespassing call outside of Fuego, which turned out to be a landlord and tenant dispute. That led to a destruction of property charge for the tenant.

A drifter was spotted outside Fuego. When his location was called in to dispatch, Kaya took it. The man turned out to be dehydrated. His shoes were falling apart. When she led him into the sheriff's station to see to his care, she ran headlong into Annette Claymore, the mayor's wife, who had plenty to say about his kind being invited into town. Kaya enjoyed putting her in her place, much like she had put True Claymore in his the day the bodies were found.

"You better be careful," Annette warned her. "If the citizens of this town don't like the way you do your job, they can remove you just as quickly as they appointed you."

"Have a nice day," Kaya said as she led the man into the air conditioning.

There was a medical emergency down the street at the barber shop. When Kaya arrived, Root was performing CPR on one of the cosmetologists, sixty-year-old Mattie Finedale. Paramedics arrived and Kaya helped keep people back so that they could do their job.

Even as Mattie was being loaded into the van, Turk Monday tugged on Kaya's elbow. "When are you going to release the names and cause of death of those poor people on the mountain?" he asked.

It brought attention from others. Soon more questions were hurled at her.

"The Merchants say it was their daughter. Is that true, Sheriff?"

"Was it a serial killer?"

"How close are you to nabbing the killer?"

"Settle down!" Kaya shouted over the ruckus. She heard the doors of the ambulance close at her back as she held up her hands. The siren started up and tires rolled. As its screech wailed into the distance, she shook her head. "People, Ms. Finedale just had a stroke. How would she feel if she knew that before she could be driven off to the hospital, you were causing a scene about a closed investigation that has nothing to do with her? I know you want answers. But there's a reason the investigative team is keeping the details under wraps."

"Do those FBI people think it was aliens?" When others turned to stare openly at Turk, he lifted his shoulders. "What? We're not that far from the rez and Dulce. Y'all know what happened there."

Kaya rolled her eyes as the shouts started back up again. "Quiet!" she yelled.

It worked but for a level voice from the back of the crowd.

Annette Claymore spoke up, asking, "Sheriff, is it true you knew one of the people who died on the mountain?"

Kaya frowned at her. If she wasn't mistaken, there was something smug hidden beneath Annette's careful expression.

"The rumors say one set of remains belongs to a girl named Sawni Mescal," she went on. "Wasn't she a friend of yours? You know, back when you were little rez girls."

...little rez girls...

The words struck Kaya. Her head snapped back as if she'd been lashed. The sharp, cold shock washed over her.

The boss wants you to remember what happens to little rez girls when they don't learn to leave well enough alone!

The shouting that echoed from long ago was loud in her ears, as was the sound of her own screaming.

She'd screamed. She'd thought she'd been so tough, so formidable in her own right. But that day she'd screamed loud into the quiet desert void, and no one had heard— except the man who had hurt her and the other who had held her in place.

She drifted back to the present and realized she was facing almost the entire town in the middle of the street, breathing unsteadily. Sobs...or memories of sobs...she couldn't tell...were packed against her throat. She was drenched in cold sweat and all she could see was the satisfied glimmer in Annette Claymore's eyes.

Does she know? Did Annette know what those men had done to Kaya that day on the road to Fuego?

How could she? That was before she married into the Claymore family.

Back when Kaya was a little rez girl, running after something far bigger and more sinister than herself.

"Well, Sheriff?" Annette piped up again.

Kaya's hands were wrapped around the front of her belt too tight. She loosened them and moved to speak.

"Nobody asked you!"

As heads swiveled to the sidewalk, Kaya spotted her teenaged niece standing tall and defiant there. "I've seen cows with more manners than all of you," Nova added. She looked to Kaya, her stubborn chin high, before fitting a pair of trendy sunglasses to her eyes and cutting through the swath of people between her and the door to the ice cream parlor. The kid, Lucas Barnes, who Everett had hired months before, followed her.

That had once been her, Kaya thought. She saw so much of herself in Nova, or who she had been before that day on the side of the road…before she'd had to work to reclaim her power.

The radio on her hip squawked and she took the opportunity to turn away from the crowd. She walked until their restless murmur was no longer a hindrance and unclipped it, raising it to her mouth. "Say again, dispatch?"

"Two-eleven in progress at Highway 8 and Miflin Road. Officer needs assistance."

"Show sheriff responding, code three," Kaya instructed as she stalked to her vehicle. She engaged lights and sirens, dispersing what was left of the rubbernecking hecklers downtown.

"Do you think people respect you, Sheriff?"

Kaya ground her teeth. Rutland rode shotgun in her truck. She'd left her service vehicle behind at the station. Her business on the Jicarilla-Apache reservation was personal.

Why had she agreed to let him tag along?

Stupidity, she thought. *Complete and utter stupidity.* "Is this really the conversation you want to have right now?" she asked him.

"The mayor stopped me outside the steakhouse yesterday evening," Rutland revealed, running a hand down his tie. The sun was low, and his brows came to a *V* as he squinted against its rays. "He has some doubt as to your ability to handle this job."

The mayor can bite me. Kaya wanted to say it. She was raw. Sawni's memorial was to take place in half an hour and Kaya was going to have to face her friend's parents. "I never heard him complain about the last sheriff, and he was corrupt."

"Might Claymore and Jones have been involved in corruption together?" Rutland asked curiously.

"It's never been proven," Kaya replied. "But Jones was swayed by Claymore. Jones wouldn't admit to anything under interrogation."

"Do you think Jones meant to kill you when he shot you in December?" Rutland asked. "From what I gather, he wasn't very supportive of his female deputy. It's why you never advanced within the department."

"He argued before the jury that he didn't want me dead," Kaya said evenly.

"He shot you when your back was turned."

She steered the truck over a rise. Jicarilla-Apache land spread out before her. The view was enough to back the breath up in her lungs. But that notion of *home* was as hurtful as it was sweet. Gripping the wheel a bit harder, she noticed the clouds throwing shadows to the west. "He did."

"It's clear to me, whether he stated it for the record or not, that he had something against you. The question is whether the mayor still does."

"It's not my job to find out whether the man likes me,"

Kaya told him. "The people in Fuego County wanted me to take this job. So I did. If True Claymore has a problem with that, or me, he's welcome to vote for someone else when my term ends."

"Small-town politics," Agent Rutland muttered. He shook his head. "They're just as messy as they are in DC."

"I won't argue that," she stated. "The way you handled the interview with Everett Eaton." She shook her head. "It wasn't right."

"I got what we needed," Rutland said, unfazed.

"Which was?"

"The truth about whether he murdered his ex-girlfriend," Rutland said. "The victims all had close-range gunshot wounds to the back of the head. My guess is their killer forced them to kneel at the edge of the cliff. He shot them and gravity took them over the edge to the ledge below. He knew their bodies would be hidden there. Any animal other than the birds would have a hard time getting to them, even the mountain lion. As long as no one knew the ledge was there, those bodies would never be discovered."

Kaya pushed the air from her lungs. She didn't want to picture Sawni kneeling on the edge of the cliff, but Rutland had painted too clear a picture. "This is what your profiler says?"

"Some of it," Rutland admitted. "They all died execution-style. It was cold. Mercenary. Nobody who could do that over and over again over time would have fainted or tossed their cookies the way Mr. Eaton did when he saw those photographs." He eyed Kaya's clenched hands over the wheel. "I'm sorry," he said. For the first time, he softened from the dogged, hard-edged investigator she'd come to know. "I asked you to bring me with you to your friend's memorial and I'm walking you through the details of her murder. My ex-wife complains I'm insensitive. Apparently, she's right."

"Why did you ask to come with me?" Kaya wanted to know.

"I haven't been formally introduced to her family and friends, other than you and your sister."

Kaya slowed for the speed limit signs. "You think this is the time and place for that?"

"Grief can be revealing," Rutland explained.

"Or maybe you're just being insensitive," she suggested, turning off the main road as he chuckled. The memorial was being held well out of town. Sawni had loved the outdoors, particularly the small cabin near the river. Her parents had chosen that spot to formally say good-bye. Kaya knew they'd chosen it to curtail any media attention, too. Nothing made saying good-bye harder than a nosy press pack.

"You seem nervous."

Kaya swallowed. "I'm fine."

"I spoke to your sister, Naleen. She said you and Sawni were very close. Like sisters in your own right. After she'd been gone for three months, investigators seemed to give up on finding her. You took up the mantle. She thinks that's why you became a cop—to find Sawni or those who made her disappear. Is that true?"

Kaya didn't want to answer. "It was a long time ago."

"Did you ever find anything?" he asked.

Nothing she'd been able to prove. She'd had to live with that, hadn't she? All these years, she'd lived with it. And facing Sawni's family again was so difficult because of it. She'd sworn to them she would find out what happened. They were still waiting for her to deliver.

Finding Sawni's body on Ol' Whalebones wasn't an answer. It'd only brought forth a whole new set of questions.

Yet Kaya wouldn't stop until she had an explanation. Knowing Sawni had been murdered made her more determined than ever to bring closure to the Mescals…and herself.

At the memorial, the Mescals looked at Kaya like they had for over a decade—with warmth, yes. But with those not-quite-hidden hints of regret. Their mouths said *thank you for coming* and *we hope you are well.*

But the eyes. The eyes said, *Why was it our daughter… and not you?*

No amount of time or reflection could make Kaya believe it meant something different. She was here, and Sawni wasn't. *Why?* Sawni's mother's soft, lined face had seemed to question her as she smiled without meaning.

Kaya was only too glad to drop Rutland off at the bed-and-breakfast on Sixth Avenue when they got back to Fuego in the late afternoon. At least he hadn't felt the need for probing questions or small talk on the way home. She couldn't stomach either. She was drained. She'd been holding her thoughts and emotions together with rubber bands.

Those rubber bands had stretched too far. They'd grown wear lines and fissures and were ready to rupture.

Kaya frowned when she pulled up in front of her house behind an Eaton Edge truck. Putting hers in Park, she spotted no one at the wheel.

Glancing at the house, she groaned.

Everett raised his hand in greeting from his position on the front stoop.

After a week of noncommunication, his timing couldn't be worse.

She didn't see another pizza box. Just a cowboy with a long face and even longer legs taking up space where she'd wanted him, thought about him, practically moped over him since he'd skirted tires pulling away from the sheriff's department days ago.

Bracing herself, she got out of the vehicle and stepped down to the ground. She reached across the seat to the console where the flowers the Mescals had given her, leftover from the service, were tied with a silver ribbon—Sawni's favorite color. She shut the door and crossed the small yard to the house where he was sitting on the stoop. It was so low to the ground that his knees were nearly drawn to his shoulders.

She stopped before him, shaking her keys so they jangled. "You look ridiculous."

"Fine, thanks," he replied. "How're you?"

She found the right key and held it in her hand. "Shouldn't you be castrating something right now?"

"Not until summer," he informed her. He knuckled his hat farther up his brow, gauging her expression. "It'd be rude to castrate a calf just after it's born."

"Kind of rude anyway, don't you think?" she asked.

"You come to the Edge when it's time for business," he advised. "Your perspective might change."

"Maybe." She shook her head. "You want me to ask you in?"

"I've been sitting here for half an hour," he said.

"Why?"

"You drive slow. Nova said the memorial was supposed to end at one o'clock. It's near sundown."

She looked at her front door. He was between it and her. "Are you going to get up so I can pass?"

He made a doubtful noise. "Pretty sure I'm stuck."

She cleared her throat because the urge to laugh filled her—great bursts of it. The grief pushed it, making it more forceful. She didn't give in because she was very much afraid there were tears close behind it.

Her feelings needed to stay in the bottle. There was no collecting them once they broke loose. "I'd make you my new lawn ornament, but people would have too many questions."

"Questions make you uncomfortable," he muttered, reaching out to grab her hand when she extended it.

She went back on her heels to pull him to his feet. He unfolded like an accordion. Ignoring what he said, she unlocked the door, then left it open as she pushed into the house. Laying the flowers on the kitchen counter, she dropped her keys next to them and heard his boots approaching. Trying not to feel insecure about the used sofa or the uneven brick kitchen floor, she watched him come.

The little house felt smaller with him in it.

"Coffee?" she asked, desperate to fill the void as he looked around, trying to get a read on what she surrounded herself with.

"Coffee's fine," he replied.

She snatched the pot from its holding in the coffee-maker and turned to the sink to fill it. "You like it black?"

"As your eyes."

The fine drawl drew the space between her shoulder blades up tight. "Don't do that," she urged quietly.

"Why shouldn't I?" he asked from the other side of the counter.

"I've already told you I won't sleep with you." But she knew exactly how many steps there were between them and the bedroom to the left.

"I'm not always trying to get into your pants, Sheriff."

The pot was full. She shut off the water. It was still dripping but she turned with it to face him anyway. "Why do you do that?"

"Do what?" he asked.

"Why do you call me Sheriff?" she asked. "Or sweetheart? Or Sheriff Sweetheart? But never my own name?"

He paused, frowning deeply. "I've called you by your name before."

"Before it was Sheriff or Sheriff Sweetheart, it was deputy or deputy sweetheart. You *don't* call me by my name, Everett. Why?"

He stared at her and the vehemence on her face. She was breathing hard between them. His gaze skimmed her shoulders, her chest, then lifted up to circle her face again. Dropping his head altogether so his hat hid whatever he was thinking or feeling, he shifted his feet.

She took the opportunity to reel it in—the ready urge to yell at him. The hurt behind the accusations. She did well, normally, to hide these things. She'd had to learn to separate her feelings on the job. She'd done it early and often.

But Sawni's memorial had scattered all that to the wind. And for the past several weeks, Everett had made her feel... well, just *feel*. There was no hiding things. She'd known that from the beginning with him and yet she'd reached...

Stupid, she thought again. *You're so stupid, Kaya.* What a surefire way to get hurt.

Everett lifted his head, finally. His jaw was tight, but he met her gaze and held it. "I never call you by name because..."

She waited. "Because...?"

He licked his lips quickly, then spoke carefully. "...because the people who I love tend to get away from me. They leave. Or they die. So…the ones that matter… I tend to push them away somehow or other."

She made a frustrated noise. "Everett, you wanted this. You told me you'd be damned if you'd mess it up—"

"I know what I said," he acknowledged. "Doesn't mean some part of me isn't terrified you're not going to want this in the long run or something's going to put you so far out of my reach, there's nothing I can do to bring you back. Whatever it is that I want or need, it's hard to move past all that when the people who matter to me don't stay."

Love. In the long run. People who matter. The words dropped into the gulf between them and caused her heart to hammer. She didn't know what to say in response.

She placed the dripping pot back in its holding and turned on the coffeemaker. She should invite him to sit. She thought about going into the conservatory, but he'd look just as ridiculous folded into one of those tiny chairs as he had on her stoop. The used shaggy couch was not an option. So she simply waited for the water to boil and the machine to start glugging.

What felt like an eternity passed before the coffee was ready. She poured it, steaming, into two mugs and passed one over the counter to him.

He lifted it in acknowledgement.

"Don't drink," she warned quickly before he could bring it to his lips. "You'll scald your mouth. Nova told you about the memorial."

"She did," he said with a nod. "She's working at the Edge."

"She told me," Kaya said. "Thank you for giving her a chance. She's wanted this for a long time."

The corner of his mouth lifted. "Girl could be anything. Firefighter. Engineer. Rocket scientist. And she wants to be a cowboy. Your niece wants to ride cattle from sunup to sundown, and she may do it better than half the hands I have on payroll."

Kaya smiled. There was some pride there. Buckets of it. "Naleen wishes she'd move past it, but she's too much like me."

"Then why aren't you a cowboy?" he asked.

"I was," she revealed. "But this isn't about me."

"You're going to have to tell me more, anyway," he told her. "Starting with why finding this Mescal girl's body hurt you so badly you started pushing people away, same as I do."

Kaya nearly denied it. Then she saw the understanding beneath everything. He understood.

"I get what it is to grieve," he explained. "I get shutting everyone else out to do it. Everyone."

"That's not why I didn't tell you about Sawni." Lifting the coffee for a testing sip, she weighed whether she was ready to do this. The liquid was hot, but it didn't burn. She swallowed carefully and leaned over so her elbows rested on the countertop. "This is more than grief."

"Yeah?"

She tilted her head. "Look, if you're not great at listening, then this isn't a conversation you want to sit through."

"I'll sit through anything you've got."

Why did the man who regularly put his foot in his mouth know just what to say to bring her back to him? "Even if it means starting from the beginning?"

"Hey, if I start falling asleep, just kick me."

She snorted a laugh. The bastard. Backing up to the sink, she set the coffee aside and braced both hands on the counter. "Sawni and I grew up together on the rez. We weren't friends—not at first. She was quiet. She let herself pass under the radar in a lot of ways. I think she was afraid of confrontation, even if it was positive."

"And you?" he asked.

"Mmm." Kaya lifted her coffee and found her lips curving over the edge of the rim. She sipped again. "I wasn't quiet, and I definitely wasn't afraid of confrontation. I wasn't an easy child."

"You were a hellion," he guessed.

"That's one way to put it, yes."

Everett stepped around the counter to the other side, raising his mug in toast—one hellion to another. "That's my girl."

Her smile grew to the point she could no longer suppress it. She'd known the telling would be hard. She hadn't known he could make her smile through it. "You and I would have gotten along famously, I think. Sawni was treated as something of a doormat by the other kids. I started standing up for her. She needed someone big and loud and assertive to stand beside. Once she started talking to me, we decided we would be friends, always. It didn't make sense to others that we became so close. I was kind of mean. I could be a bully. She carried around a doll forever. She did everything she was told. I didn't understand why she wanted to be my friend until later. Sometimes the quiet ones will seek out someone stronger than themselves…for protection or…"

"Did you protect her?"

The smile tapered off, slowly. *Not well enough*, she thought. Not when it had really mattered, in the end. "In small ways, I guess," she replied. "Everything was great until we got to high school. Her parents blamed any trouble she got into on me, naturally. And they were right. But then we both started looking outside the rez. We set our sights there. We started going to the rodeo here in Fuego."

"You were half-pint buckle bunnies?" he asked, amused.

"We were spectators," she contradicted.

"I was on the junior circuit for a time," he revealed. "I don't remember you."

"Eaton, your head was so far up your ass you couldn't see past your own nose."

He laughed. Lifting his chin, he scrubbed the line of his neck with a rough, wide-palmed hand. "God, you're right. How'd you know that?"

"Lucky guess."

His grin turned sly. "You knew me. Or you knew who I was."

She raised a shoulder. "Never mind that. It became my single greatest desire in life to ride."

"Did you?" he asked.

"I worked with a trainer on the rez," she said. "Worked my butt off to raise enough money for lessons. Eventually, I joined the junior circuit, too, as a trick rider."

"Apache Annie," he suddenly blurted out, snapping his fingers. He pointed at her. "You were Apache Annie—with war paint and feathers in your hair."

"Yes," she said reluctantly.

"You were the real deal," he breathed. "The other boys and I… We used to watch you. *Everyone* used to watch you. You were mesmerizing."

She blinked at the praise. "I thought the whole lifestyle was mesmerizing. The circuitous nature of things. We traveled around, never stayed in one place. I wanted that—badly enough that I started lying to my mother. She found out and threatened to send me to Santa Fe if I didn't straighten out. She tried getting me several good jobs in

Dulce so I'd settle down or stay busy enough to keep me out of trouble. I quit every one of them, or never showed up to begin with. The trail riding job at RC Resort was my mother's last stand. It was either that or move in with my dad in the city, which felt like a fate worse than death. She threatened to sell my horse, too. So I started working for the Claymores…"

Everett's mouth worked itself into a scowl. "It didn't work, I take it."

"It worked okay," she said. "But I couldn't stop thinking about riding. So I asked Sawni to take over for me so that I could go train more and compete. As long as the position was filled, the Claymores had no reason to call my house looking for me. The crazy part was that the Claymores are so blind and idiotic that they thought Sawni was me, just because we have the same color skin. They called her Kaya and instead of asserting herself she went along with it."

Kaya lifted the coffee for a long drink. The next part was going to be most difficult. She hadn't talked about any of it for so long. It had lived inside her head. She'd picked through it over the years, combing through every minute detail, trying to find the point where things had changed, where Sawni's disappearance became inevitable. Was it the rodeo? Was it Fuego itself? Was it the resort? Where had it gone wrong? Who was responsible, other than Kaya herself? "She stopped communicating with me."

"Why would she do that?"

"I've never been sure," Kaya said. "For the longest time, I thought it might be resentment or anger. I was at the rodeo. She wasn't. Or the job sucked, and I was responsible for her being there. But over the years, I started to wonder if it might have been something else. She was seeing some-one at the time. She never would tell me who. She didn't want to be teased. She stopped sharing little things at first and then…the communication became less and less frequent. No more phone calls. No more meeting after work or school. She just kind of started to slip away. Then her parents reported her missing. At first, the authorities dismissed it. You know how it is. 'She's out partying.' 'She's at a friend's house.' It was three days after that they began to take it seriously. The first forty-eight hours after someone goes missing are the most crucial. By the time they started searching, she was gone."

"You say you were responsible for her being at the RC," Everett recalled. "Sounds like survivor's guilt."

Kaya nodded. "I am responsible. I'm the reason she's gone. Her parents know it. My mother knows it. My sister. Most people on the rez do, too. Her disappearance was a huge story. The entire community came to Fuego to search for her because that was the last place she was seen. There's security cam footage of her walking into the corner store downtown shortly after her shift. The Claymores said she worked the whole day, even though it was a school day. From the store, there's nothing. She didn't have a car. She took the bus, but there's no record of her getting on the bus that afternoon. The bus driver was subbing for the regular one and he couldn't say whether she got on or not. She never made it to the bus stop in Dulce. Somewhere between the corner store in Fuego and Dulce, she was abducted."

"You never bought that she ran away," Everett assumed. "They would have said she did. They said the same thing when Bethany went missing."

"She wouldn't have done something like that. She wouldn't have put her parents through it. She loved them, respected them. She stopped going to the rodeo because they asked her to. Even when I kept going, she stopped. She was the good one."

"Stop," he said firmly.

"Every time her parents look at me, they think 'It should've been you,'" she said.

"Do they say that?" he asked.

"No. But I know that's what they're thinking."

"No, you don't," he argued. "You've been punishing yourself for this way too long, Kaya."

She sucked in a breath. *Kaya.*

When she stared at him, thunderstruck, he closed the small space between them. His hands closed over the counter on either side of her waist. He leaned in, smelling of leather and horses. She could smell his soap, just a hint of it, and wanted to spread kisses up the chords of his neck.

Everything about Everett was long and rough and certain. She wanted every piece, she realized—every little piece of him. Even if it ruined her.

"Tell me I'm wrong," he drawled. "Tell me you haven't been destroying yourself over this for years because you think you put her in the hands of her kidnapper."

"Her killer," she said unevenly. "He killed her. I have to live with that now."

"I don't want you to," he said. "That's not a life. She would've wanted you to do better for yourself. That's why she took the job to begin with—so that you could follow the rodeo and your dream. But you didn't. And it's about time you stopped torturing yourself."

"I haven't told you the rest of it," she said. She hadn't planned to. Oh God, could she? She'd never told anyone… Not her mother, not Naleen, not the police or the men she'd shared a bed with through the years… No one. When he dropped his hand from her face and stepped away so she could gather her thoughts, she realized she could at least make the first steps. "I became obsessed with her case. I led search parties. I knocked on doors. I annoyed the police and sheriff's departments to the point where they'd lock their door when they saw me coming. I hung posters, rallied the community to spread the word. I made websites. It went on for a year or more, long after everyone else had given up on her."

"Did you ever find anything else?" he asked. "Any trace?"

"Nothing solid," she said. "I practically stalked the Claymores. I was convinced they had something to do with it. But I could never shake anything loose, exactly."

"Exactly." He latched onto the word. "What does that mean?"

She felt panic tearing at her insides. It trapped the rest of the story in. She closed her eyes. *Not yet*, she thought. She'd come so far already with him. She couldn't go on.

She inhaled, trying to control the fear. The terror. It was ridiculous. She'd been on the job for so long. But she was still scared, and that was the hardest thing of all to live with.

It made her angry. So angry she could scream. "I became a police officer because I wanted to find her. When the police gave up on her and let the case go cold, I felt like the only one who cared about her or any other rez girl who went missing, for that matter. So I joined the academy in Taos and became a beat cop there. Eventually, I got the job as deputy in Fuego County. I gained access to the case files. I fell back down the rabbit hole again and couldn't stop. I nearly lost myself to it."

Everett ran his hand over her braid, soothing. He did it over and over in a silent caress that salved something inside her.

He spoke low and soft. "You didn't give yourself over to it. You wouldn't be who you are today if you had."

"It was my mother, mostly," she admitted. "She deals well in hard truths. She said even if I was any closer to finding Sawni, I was far too close to losing myself in the process. I had to stop, or Sawni and I both would have been gone."

"I'm glad you're not," he murmured. "I've told you, haven't I—that I'd have been lost without you last summer?"

It didn't hurt to hear it again. "Where would your family be if you had been? They need you, Everett. Everyone at the Edge needs you."

He made a thoughtful noise. "I like your hair this way. Even if it's not loose like I want."

"Thank you," she muttered.

"If you never let it loose, why don't you cut it?" He wrapped his hand around the width of the braid, measuring. "There's so much of it."

"It's part of me," she explained. "It's a part of my story. I don't expect you to get it—"

"I get it."

He did get her, she thought. It was stunning.

"Kaya."

She shivered. It was involuntary and thorough, skating the length of her spine and spreading tingles at the base of her head where his hand came to rest. "Yes?"

"Will you let me take your hair down? I want to feel it in my hands. I want to see it shine."

She placed her hand in the bend of his elbow and followed it up, circling his wrist. "I don't think I can handle that. Not after today."

"Eventually?"

She sighed. "If I've learned anything about the two of us together, it's that it's inevitable."

"What?"

For a second, she couldn't say it. Then she thought about all the other things she couldn't say and pushed it out on a whisper. "Everything."

He sucked in a breath and straightened. "Damn."

She smiled softly. "You were the one who spoke about the long-term."

"I did," he acknowledged.

"You know, I told myself I wouldn't go out with you until I heard you say my name."

"So why did you?"

"You've got nice eyes," she told him. "And a tight butt. And you make me laugh. You're sexy and annoying and you know how to wear a woman down with your big mouth. I may be a cop, but I'm a woman, too. I have needs and feelings and for some inexplicable reason they've both been pointed in your direction for a while."

He removed his hat and tossed it on the counter. His lips moved to hers. He kissed her firmly, cupping the back of her neck as her head fell back and his toes came to rest between hers, the hard line of his body flush against her. She spread her palms against his back and pressed, bringing him closer. She wasn't sure what close enough was anymore. He was beyond that point, wasn't he? But she wanted him closer.

A whoosh of air escaped her when his hands ran down her shoulders and back, over her rear before splaying over the backs of her thighs. He lifted and set her on the sink's edge so they were closer to eye-to-eye.

She wrapped her hands around the counter for balance as his head tilted and his mouth came back to hers for more. She groaned because he was good at this part. His last kisses had lingered for so long. How long would these stay with her?

When he broke away, she started to protest. "I'm sorry," he said on a wash of breath.

"Sorry?" she asked, off balance.

"The other day at the station house," he reminded her. "I was bruised. When I'm hurt or raw, I lash out. It's been that way as long as I can remember, and I'm getting help for it—same as I was getting help for the PTSD last fall. Some habits die hard, and when you stayed silent during Rutland's questioning, some part of me thought it was because your thoughts were in-line with his." When she began to shake her head, he nodded. "I know they're not. You were trying to stay objective. That's your job, whether or not my name's called into question. But I'm sorry."

"It's okay," she said, holding him. "We're okay."

"Yeah?" he asked, tipping his brow to hers.

"Yeah," she answered. She smiled. "Am I still worth the wait, cowboy?"

"Hell yes," he asserted. "I'm not a quitter."

So many men had quit on relationships with her, unwilling to wait for her to give all of herself. Everett was in this, and she couldn't decide if she was terrified or thrilled. "I think I like the idea of being Everett Eaton's woman."

"My woman." He scooped her off the counter and held her so her toes dangled off the floor. His hum of satisfaction vibrated across her lips as his mouth dappled lightly across hers. "You're going to have to come to the Edge. I want to see you ride."

She raised a brow. "Is that so?"

"A horse, sweetheart," he said, but his wicked grin said something else entirely. When her fingers tangled around a hunk of his hair, he hissed and dropped his head back to belt a laugh at the ceiling. "I swear. I meant a horse."

She made a doubtful noise but loosened her hold regardless.

"Your niece hinted at your past life as a trick rider before you did, and I can't get it out of my head—you bareback on that Appaloosa, your hair streaming like a black flag behind you…"

"What is this obsession you have with my hair?" she wondered.

"I'll let you know when I figure it out." He kissed her again, thoroughly.

"Hmm." Her brows came together, and her arms tightened around him. If a swarm of butterflies really was called a kaleidoscope, that was the only way she knew how to describe what happened to her insides when Everett kissed her. "I'll come to the Edge," she agreed. "But only if Paloma cooks us something."

"I might talk her into that," he weighed. "Groveling might be involved."

"Tell her we'll do the dishes."

"She's going to like you so much better than she likes me," he murmured.

She had never understood Paloma Coldero's unconditional love for the eldest Eaton brother…until now. Everett might prove to be as hard to love as others had found in the past, but Kaya liked a challenge. She'd once reveled in them.

She was going to find out what this man was made of. And if those butterflies in her stomach were any indication, she was already too far gone in this particular game of risk.

Chapter 9

The Spring Festival was a chance for Fuego County residents to mix and mingle. It was a boost to small businesses, and it was considered good medicine for all.

Everett thought it was more headache-inducing than watching Lucas and Nova stack hay bales. He'd rather haul manure or square off with a randy bull than talk to Mrs. Whiting from the bank.

He'd rather pay bills, spray weeds or grind feed than talk to Huck Claymore about Our Lord and Savior, Jesus Christ.

He'd clear brush or even sit across from the family's longtime accountant, J.P. Dearing, discussing taxes before chatting up Christa McMurtry, the organist, who for some reason had moon eyes only for him.

"Poor girl," Eveline muttered, seeing Christa's gaze shining in Everett's direction, too. "If she's looking your way, she's a glutton for punishment."

Everett couldn't fight a sneer. "Her father's going to kill me because she looks my way."

"Can I watch?" Eveline asked in a low drawl that nearly made his lips twitch in approval. She took a loud, crunchy bite of her ice cream cone.

He had to admit, Eveline had come back into her own,

comanaging the stable at the Edge with Griff MacKay and recently opening an equine rescue with Luella at Ollero Creek across town.

His sister had come home. She and Wolfe Coldero had found each other, for better or worse. Everett may want to argue with what she was fast building with the man who had once been Everett's biggest rival, but he couldn't argue with Eveline finding herself again—any more than he could quibble over her happiness. "I can't wait until you're Coldero's problem. Not mine."

She wiped a drop of sticky vanilla from her chin. "I'm only leaving long enough to drink daiquiries on the beach and swim naked in the surf with my new husband."

"Washing cats."

"What's that?" she asked.

"I'd rather be bathing Luella's cat than having this conversation," he said.

She hit him in the arm. "You're not getting rid of me. After a week, we'll be back. Then you're going to hire Wolfe for that salary job you've been trying to fill since after Dad died."

He laughed. "I may have agreed to the bastard being my brother-in-law…" He winced, just for form's sake, and had the pleasure of watching Eveline cross her arms and spread her feet in a ready stance. "But that doesn't mean I have to coexist with him any more than necessary."

"Dad gave him a percentage of Edge shares," she reminded him, polishing off the cone and wiping her hands on a thin paper napkin.

"Coldero gave them up. Traded them all for a half-dead horse, as I recall."

"What's mine is his," she added. "And before that trouble with Whip Decker seven years ago, Dad talked about making him foreman."

"Don't remind me," Everett groaned.

"He loved Wolfe," Eveline murmured, "every bit as much as he loved each of us. You know that. You have to know that. He would have wanted you to give Wolfe that job."

"I'm done with this conversation," he replied.

"Fine," she said and rolled her eyes. "Shouldn't we be talking to people like Ellis is?"

"Why?" he asked.

"Public relations," she pointed out. At the sound of his growl, she gestured. "Look. Even Luella's speaking to people."

"She shouldn't have to," he stated. "None of us should have to. Every one of these people whisper about us in church every Sunday. They're the same people who shunned Luella after what happened with her father last summer. They're the same ones who haven't stopped calling our mother a whore though she's been dead for seven years. They made Ellis and Luella's lives hell, circulating rumors about an affair they never had when he was still married. They're the ones who sided with Liberty in the divorce. They wouldn't stop their gabbing after you and Coldero were caught together at Naleen and Terrence's wedding…"

"Of course they gabbed," she said. "We were both in an indecent state."

"That's putting it mildly." He studiously turned his thoughts away from finding Eveline and Wolfe together in the tack room at The RC Resort with their unmentionables down around their ankles. *Changing the tractor's oil. Digging ditches in an ice storm. Falling in a cow patty...*

All things he'd rather do than have this talk. "The point is, we don't owe the people of this town anything, least of all small talk. As far as I'm concerned, Fuego's one big dumpster fire."

"Now you've gone and hurt my feelings."

Everett whirled, bracing himself for what was at his back. Next to him, he felt Eveline tense in tandem with him.

True Claymore beamed from the shadow of his large black hat. His belt buckle caught the sheen of the light and shot sunbeams. The thing was nearly as big around as a tricycle tire. He threaded his thumbs through his belt loops, keeping his wife, Annette's, arm looped through his. "Ms. Eaton," True said, bowing his head to Eveline. "Annette here was just telling me we aren't invited to your wedding next week."

"It's a small ceremony," Eveline informed him. "Family only."

"Word is Javier Rivera and his family warranted invitations," True said thoughtfully.

"He's foreman at the Edge and has been for years," Everett put in. "If that's not family, it's as good as."

"And Rosalie Quetzal is invited," Annette rattled off, counting the names on her fingers. "*And* the Gaines family *and* Ms. Breslin from the real estate office...even a sprinkling of people from your modeling days in New York, Eveline. But not us. You didn't even ask our sweet Huck to officiate."

"Griff MacKay is ordained," Eveline explained.

"You would rather have a grizzly old stable boy conduct your ceremony than a man of the cloth?" Annette asked, round-eyed.

"He's family," Everett said. "It doesn't hurt that his name isn't Claymore."

Annette's mouth puckered, making her look waspish. True's fingers closed over hers, soothing. "Now, Eaton," the man said, shifting his weight. "You've gone and hurt my wife's feelings."

"Didn't know she had those," Everett said philosophically. He didn't back down from Annette's glare. He knew who had started the rumors about his mother, Ellis and Luella, and Eveline and Wolfe and who stoked them tirelessly. He knew what lawyer had put her weight behind the lawsuits and legal claims the Claymores had aimed at Everett and his father through the years, even after he died.

Everett knew who had tried to lure Paloma into leaving Eaton Edge and joining the staff at The RC Resort at his father's wake.

The Claymores had been poaching ranch hands and staff from the Edge since True and Annette had laid claim to it, throwing untold piles of money to transition it from working cattle ranch to luxurious resort and spa. They'd tried to take a piece of the Edge for themselves, crying foul at the informal way their fathers had drawn the narrow margins that existed between Claymore acreage and Edge lands...

Something niggled at the edge of Everett's train of thought. He tried to dismiss it.

The land claim... It had verged on the mountains and the trails. Everett had thought when studying the map that the Claymore's grab for the territory hadn't been about heritage. It had been about hiking. Their spread was flat like Ollero Creek. They wanted to make money off what the Eatons gave hikers free claim to as long as the rules on the mountain were obeyed.

Mountain.

Everett's chin firmed as he looked at True once more. "You son of a bitch."

"Excuse me?" Annette blustered.

True's good ol' boy smile had gone bye-bye. "Better to be the product of a straight bitch than a flaming whore."

Eveline made a disconcerted noise in her throat and stepped forward. Everett grabbed her. "Hold up," he said.

She whirled on him, fury writhing over her fair features. "You cut your knuckles on his real teeth last July for a lot less. You'll let me knock the rest of them out so he has to replace them, too. He won't be able to look in the mirror again without thinking of our family. I call that justice."

"The sheriff'd be a better judge of that," True estimated. Everett saw his nerves in his shifting stance and Annette's readiness in her hard face. "You'll wind up behind bars. There won't be a wedding."

"And won't that be a shame?" Annette chimed.

"Sure would," Everett considered, watching Eveline closely. Goading had always done its job where she was concerned.

Eveline shrugged, bristling his hand off her shoulder. She backed down.

That's right, Manhattan, he thought. *Eyes on the prize.* Whether she married Wolfe or Wile E. Coyote, there would be a wedding at Eaton Edge next week, if only to spite Buffalo Bill and Calamity Jane here. He tipped his hat and said, "Have a nice day, folks."

As he pulled her away, Eveline muttered, "Have you lost the rest of your mind?"

"Everyone's always on me about my mouth and my manners," he said. "I act right, and you still take me to task."

"Do what you want with those two," she invited. "Or better yet, let me."

"You're too skinny to take either one of them," he informed her. He milled through the crowd, dodging plates of BBQ and funnel cakes and pointy metal sculptures from one of the arts and crafts booths. He scanned the crowd, moving on until he neared the sheriff's department. Outside it, under a blue booth, he spotted the two-toned uniform. Picking up his pace, he ignored Eveline's cursing and all but charged.

Kaya crouched in front of a young boy in cowboy boots, smiling as she pinned a plastic sheriff's star to his shirtfront. "You're the real deal now, Officer Lawson," she said as she settled back on her heels and straightened his hat. "Now the first order of business as junior sheriff is to hunt up all the best grub on Food Truck Row. Think you can do that?"

The bespectacled youngster nodded eagerly.

"Report back to me with any signs of doughnuts," she advised. "And make sure to treat yourself to a snow cone. Morale is very important."

"Yes, ma'am," he said, grinning at her toothily before wandering off, parents in tow.

Kaya's smile didn't waver when she found Everett and Eveline. "Well, if it isn't my favorite brother and sister team. I've got some stars leftover. Let me pin one on you."

"Take a break," Everett advised, letting go of Eveline to take Kaya's hand.

She picked up on his urgency. Her smile fled. "Is something happening?"

"Come inside and I'll explain," he said.

She looked to Eveline who shrugged and said, "Don't look at me. He dragged me here."

"I'm on duty," Kaya replied to Everett.

"Handing out buttons?" he asked pointedly.

She let go of his hand to cross her arms over her chest. "It's called public relations, cattle baron. You should try it sometime."

He dismissed her. "I've got no time for that and neither do you. Do you have maps of the mountains north of the Edge inside?"

She nodded. "We have one pinned on the board in the conference room. But you can't—"

"Good," he cut in, starting for the door. "Bring your ass."

"Rude," she said at his back.

He opened the door. Cool air spilled out of the building. "Bring your fine ass," he amended and held the door open for her and Eveline who slapped him in the stomach as she passed.

He merely grunted and moved on. He saw Rutland through the glass in a large room toward the back of the department and rushed the door.

"Everett!" Kaya called. "Don't!"

He ignored her, flying into the conference room. Rutland jumped to his feet. "What are you doing here?"

Everett came to a halt. There were two boards, one nailed to the wall and another that had been rolled in for the FBI agent's use. The grisly images from the crime scene met his eyes. Before Eveline could step inside, he yanked the sport coat Rutland had hung on the back of his empty chair and draped it over the worst of them. He made certain it would stay, then pushed the rolling board with a clatter against the wall behind it so he could get to the map mounted to the other wall. There was a red pin on the side of Ol' Whalebones and another stuck in the location of the state park's parking lot where Higgins's car had been found.

"He can't be in here, Sheriff," Rutland said as Kaya entered.

"I know he can't," she replied. "Everett, I need you to leave. Now."

"Hang on, sweetheart," Everett muttered. "Everybody just hang on." He looked around for a writing utensil and found a Sharpie on the conference table amidst folders and photographs of the victims they had confirmed identification of—Miller Higgins, Sawni Mescal and Bethany Merchant.

He uncapped the marker and followed the lines of the mountain with his finger. He drew an additional one.

Rutland and Kaya made noises of protest. Eveline noted, "You *have* lost your mind."

Everett kept spanning the aerial distance with his hand, using the map scale. He made three more marks before stepping back. Using the marker, he pointed at what he had done. "Claymore."

When the others only stared, he groaned, capped the marker and tossed it on the table. "True and Annette. They wanted the mountain. Last year, they refiled a claim for this section." He stabbed the map over the west side of Ol' Whalebones. "And everything from that point west to their spread."

Kaya closed the door to the conference room. "Are you sure?"

Rutland gripped the back of his chair. "I thought everything north and west of the crime scene belongs to the state of New Mexico."

Everett frowned. "Fine investigative work you're doing here, Watt. How much is the government paying you?"

Eveline joined Everett, scanning the marks on the map. "Everett's right."

"Say it again, Manhattan," Everett requested. "Louder this time."

"Shush!" she hissed at him, then pointed at the map. "From here to here, everything that runs north is state territory."

"Including the river," Everett put in.

"That's how people get to Ol' Whalebones without having to trek across private property. The parking lot belongs to the state park. However, this narrow spit of land between the foot of Mount Elder and Big River Valley, right up to the edge of Ol' Whalebones is Claymore territory."

"My father, Hammond, laid claim to Ol' Whalebones and it was a bone of contention for Old Man Claymore when he was alive," Everett reported. "There's been talk of the Claymores taking it back for years. But nothing formal until my father's first heart attack."

"Which was?" Kaya asked.

"The year I left high school," Everett said. "The year my mother left for Coldero Ridge."

"The same year Bethany Merchant disappeared," Kaya said slowly.

"What if," Everett said, "the Claymores didn't want the mountain because their old man lost it? What if they didn't want it for right of access? What if they wanted it because they needed to cover up evidence?"

"You're accusing the mayor of quadruple homicide," Rutland pointed out.

"Or someone he knows," Everett said.

A shaky indrawn breath filled the quiet. He looked to Kaya who had gone pale. He reached out.

She backed off quickly. "Just... Just let me think it through."

"This could be a break in Sawni's case," he told her. "The one you've been looking for."

Rutland cleared his throat. "We're following other leads, Mr. Eaton. But we will take your information into consideration."

"That's a line of crap."

"Everett," Kaya said.

"Wait a second, sweetheart," he said slowly. He faced the agent. "You don't like me. Hell, you wanted me for these murders. Are you dismissing my information because you're on someone else's case or because it was me who gave it specifically?"

"Specifically," Rutland replied, "the investigative team is pursuing other leads." When Everett swore, he went on. "As you know, details of this case are being kept under wraps for investigative purposes. Which is why, again, you can't be in here."

"Everett," Kaya said again, "let's go."

"You want me to go?" he asked, offended.

"I'm asking you to come with me," she insisted.

There was trouble in her eyes. Scowling at Rutland, he jerked his thumb at the map. "I'll be following up on this, Watt."

"I look forward to it, Mr. Eaton."

Eveline followed them out. "Did he really try to pin four murders on you?" she demanded.

Everett stopped. "I'm clear, okay? He tried to make a connection between me and Bethany's, but it didn't stick. I'm all right," he said again. She shook her head in disbelief. "Don't tell Paloma or Ellis. It's over."

"You should have told us," she said. "How many times

have I bailed you out of jail? Just once, let it be for something I *know* you didn't do."

"Next time," he promised. Then he reached for her, skimming a hand over her shoulder.

"I need to speak to him," Kaya said to her.

Eveline nodded. "Sure." She smiled and lowered her voice. "How long have you two been—"

"None of your business, *hermana*," he told her, firm on that point. "Go find Ellis. Tell him I need to speak with him."

"And Wolfe, too?"

He rolled his shoulders with an impatient rumble. "Fine. Bring the bridegroom. Tell them to meet me at the house and that Bozeman should be there, too."

Chapter 10

"Shut the door," Kaya said.

Everett did as he was told, watching her close the blinds over the window to the bull pen. "What's going on?"

She planted her hand against the wall and leaned. He saw sweat lining her brow when she removed her hat.

"Kaya."

"I need to tell you something."

"Okay," he said bracingly.

"First," she said, "and this is really important, Everett— I need you not to go looking for blood."

He stilled. "This is about the Claymores."

"I need your word."

"Tell me first."

"Everett!" she shouted. "You said you wouldn't wind up on the wrong side of the law if we were together. Your word, please!"

He exerted a long rush of air through his nose, trying to deflate the foreboding built up inside him—the ready tension and anger. "I give you my word," he ground from between his teeth.

"I will hold you to it."

"Just tell me!"

She looked away. "I wanted to tell you before. But I've

kept it to myself for years and it's hard to let go. Even with you." She wet her lips when he fell quiet, anticipating. "I told you after Sawni disappeared that I became obsessed with finding her. I knew one of the last places she was seen was The RC Resort. I wouldn't leave the Claymores alone. I didn't trust that they gave so little information about her and weren't looked into further by the authorities. The police went light on them, likely because they were The Claymores, even then. So I snuck on site and I had a look around. I retraced her actions through what I knew of her day. Then I tried sneaking into the office. True caught me."

"What did he do?" Everett asked. His hands had curled into fists in his pockets.

"He told me he had a way of dealing with 'little rez girls who liked to stick their noses where they didn't belong.'"

Every muscle in Everett's body stilled.

"He took me outside. If True had handled me himself, I would have put him behind bars when I became deputy. Before the statute of limitations was up. But he never touched me beyond hauling me out of there and putting me in one of the resort shuttles. I never even saw him talk to the two security goons who drove me back to the highway. There's no evidence he told them to do what they did."

Words raked across his throat, hot as coals. "What did they do?"

Her hands shook once. Just once. It was enough to make him vibrate with rage. She culled the explanation out in a flat tone, as if reciting the Pledge of Allegiance. "They forced me out of the shuttle onto the roadside. One of the men hit me in the stomach while the other held my arms back. They told me to say I wasn't coming back. When I refused…"

Her voice hitched. Everett wanted to move to her, hold

her, but the vibrations had gone into the bone. He knew, all too well, that he didn't have a handle on himself.

"They grabbed me by the hair," she said. "I wore it loose. It was down to my waist. They made me get on my knees. The first one said, 'The boss wants you to remember what happens to little rez girls when they don't learn to leave well enough alone…' The other one held me while he…"

Everett filled in the blanks. His head nearly split. The images maxed out the capacity of his brain. Every single one of them was gunpowder. They torched his restraint.

Grabbing the first thing at hand, he flipped the visitor's chair on its head. He paced on the spot then faced the wall. It was cinderblock. It would splinter the bones of his fist if he hit it like he needed to.

With his back to her, he zeroed in on a fold of worn tape that had been left behind when a poster was removed. The anger didn't ebb. It was a restless wave pool that beat against one shore, then the opposite one until the swells met in the middle and clashed.

"I'm going to kill him," he said between his teeth.

"No, you're not," she returned.

"You're going to have to let me kill him, sweetheart," he said, revolving back to her.

She shook her head. She was steady, still and utterly calm. He was stunned by her bravery. He was awed by it. She'd had to live with this, on top of everything else. It wasn't long before she'd joined the police force, he knew. She'd come back to Fuego—to chase down her demons. Anybody else would have run from them.

"What about the goons?" he asked. "The men who did this to you. You didn't talk to the police?"

She looked away, her countenance flagging. "I was tres-

passing. I broke into the resort. And it stuck with me—
little rez girls. It followed me everywhere for a time. It was
my word against theirs."

"You came back," he said. "You came back to face
them."

She nodded. "I wanted them to feel threatened. I thought
my mere presence in Fuego in uniform would make them
quiver. I learned soon after I returned that True had replaced the two security goons with others. Worse, there
was no record of their employment with him. Their names
weren't even in the system. They were ghosts in the wind.
The first time I came face-to-face with True, he didn't recognize me. He's never put it together—the little rez girl
and the Fuego County deputy."

"Sheriff," he said, moving to her. "You're sheriff now.
And he should know exactly who he's dealing with. He
should damn well be quivering."

"I've been waiting," she said on a whisper. "I could
never build a solid case against him or Annette or the resort. Every time I got close, Sheriff Jones would shut it
down. After what you said in the conference room about
someone True knows potentially murdering the people on
the mountain... I knew."

"The security guys." He nodded. "True isn't the type to
get his hands dirty. If he'd wanted to put Sawni, Bethany
and the other woman in the ground, he would have used
someone else."

"They were killed execution-style," Kaya said. "One
shot to the back of the head. Mercenary." He heard the audible click of her swallow. "They were all likely on their
knees when it happened...like me on the side of the highway."

He cursed and pulled her to him. He folded around her.

She didn't tremor. She didn't relax, either. She was holding it all in. She'd held it in…all this time. "I want to kill him."

"No," she said, pulling away enough to look at him. "This is my fight. He's going to be my collar. I will gather enough evidence to bring him in. That's why I became a police officer, Everett. To find Sawni and to build evidence and a case around Claymore that he and his wife can never pull him out of. He deserves to rot in prison."

"He deserves to be throttled first," Everett inserted.

"I need you to listen," she said, eyes on fire. "I've waited my entire career to nail True Claymore. He might be looking at kidnap and murder charges if your theory pans out. And I will not let anybody stand in the way of putting that good-for-nothing behind bars once and for all. Not even you."

"God Jesus, you're incredible," he breathed. "But you're *not* alone in this. Not anymore."

"I'm telling you what I need and you're not hearing me," she said. "*Stay away from him.*"

"You mean don't fight for your honor," he amended, frustration stretching against the bounds of his skin.

"I'm asking you to trust me to fight for my own," she pleaded, "and the life and honor of every woman he's taken. I don't know how Miller Higgins is tied up in this. But women were his pattern. We can tie Sawni to him. I'll look for his connection to Bethany Merchant. He dated her, just as you did. We need to know the timing…"

"Rutland doesn't like my theory," he muttered.

"I'll work around him," she said.

"You're going down the rabbit hole again," he cautioned.

"I'm not alone this time," she recalled.

"No," he agreed.

"Promise me," she demanded. "Promise me you won't—"

"Beat Claymore to within an inch of his life?"

"Promise me," she whispered, holding both his arms, "you will not harm a hair on his head."

He scanned her face. Then he nodded, grimly, lips seamed tight.

"I need you to say it."

"Fine," he said. "I will not harm a hair on True's head."

She nodded. "Thank you. Now kiss me, cattle baron. I'm feeling queasy and raw and I need you, goddamn it."

He did as he was told, dipping his lips to hers in a slow motion. He kept it soft. He kept it tender. He felt the give in her muscles. He felt the release. He heard the longing report from the line of her throat and groaned in response, every bit as lost as she was.

"You're shaking," she said, running her hands up and down his arms. "I shouldn't have told you."

"Don't," he bit off. "There are no secrets between us anymore."

She searched his face. "No," she said, understanding. "No more secrets."

He made himself step back. "I'm meeting Ellis and the others back at the house. I'll have Bozeman get you copies of the Claymores' land disputes and any other legal documents they sent our way through the years."

"Everett?"

He stopped with his hand on the door. When he looked back, he didn't read vulnerability. He saw strength. She was strong—stronger than him. Stronger than anyone he'd ever met.

And he loved her.

The realization came like a thunderclap.

He'd known it would never come to this—loving someone uncompromisingly. Men like him didn't fall, not after watching his father's heartbreak over his mother kill him slow…excruciatingly slow.

Yet here he was and so was Kaya, and he loved her beyond doubt or reason.

"I'll see you," she told him.

He felt a quaver as deep as his marrow. Dipping his head to her, he yanked the door open and left.

Chapter 11

Kaya cornered Rutland in the conference room after seeing Everett out. She closed the door, hemming them in. "Why are you dismissing Everett Eaton? Last I checked, this case had run into a wall. We need every possible lead or it's going to go cold again."

Rutland considered the question. He'd taken his sport coat down off the board and was wearing it. Leaning back in his chair at the head of the table, he laced his fingers over his middle. "You're seeing him."

She thought of denying it. But Rutland wasn't going to trust her or her judgement if she lied. "I'm seeing him."

He lifted his brows but otherwise didn't move. "You're trying to earn the respect and authority your office deserves, and you think fooling around with a man who dances in and out of that Mayberry jail cell you've got in the back of your wheelhouse is the way to do that? You're smarter than that, Altaha."

She was still a little bit queasy and more than a little bit raw. She didn't feel stable. She curled her hands around the back of a chair, trying to rein it all in. She would not lose her composure in front of the agent. "My personal life doesn't interfere with my ability to do my job. But you're going to tell me why exactly you're willing to throw away evidence against the Claymores."

He tilted his head. "Are you insinuating something?"

"The Claymores have bought ranking officers for well on a decade," she informed him.

"You claim your personal life has no bearing on your police work," he said. "But it's starting to sound like you have a vendetta against this family. I've read the files from your previous sheriff. I know the Eatons most certainly have one."

"That's why you dismissed Everett?" she asked. "Because he's gone after True in the past?"

"Ask yourself this," he said, leaning forward so that the chair squeaked slightly. He dropped a file on the table. "If you were thinking objectively, wouldn't you have drawn the same conclusion?"

"That's not good enough," she replied. "You said we're pursuing other leads. You lied and tossed his theory out the window."

"I didn't lie."

She lifted her hands. "Is there another lead you haven't told me about? You haven't briefed me on one."

She saw him hesitate. Moving around the table, she said, "You're the one who wanted cooperation between our teams."

"I did say that, didn't I?" He turned his chair to face her. "I was going to brief you this morning. Then the business with the festival. And I saw what Mr. Eaton is to you."

"I'm dating a man you've cleared of all charges in this case and that gives you a right to squirrel evidence away?" she asked.

He let out a breath, then reached for two Baggies on the

table. "These arrived last night in the safe haven baby box at the volunteer fire department on Highway 7."

She took the bags. One contained a standard, unmarked bubble mailer, the kind that could be bought at any office supply store. The flap was open but it had been torn. There was no address or return address written on it.

The second bag contained a small book. Kaya thought it might be a datebook until she turned it over and saw the name written in the bottom corner. "What is this?" she asked in a quiet voice.

"I need to confirm the handwriting with her mother and father," Rutland stated. "But it appears Sawni Mescal kept a diary."

The letters blurred together. "No need," she said, setting the bags on the table. "I recognize it."

"It's her handwriting?"

"It is," she confirmed. "We passed enough notes... I've reread them through the years. Have you opened this?"

"It's bagged and will need to go to the lab for prints," he said, picking up the folder he'd dropped on the desk. "But my team made copies of the pages."

Kaya opened the file when he handed it to her. She had to take a measured breath when she saw the looping strokes of Sawni's handwriting that filled the first page.

"Did you know she kept a diary?" he asked. "Did she ever tell you?"

"She did," Kaya answered. "She let me read others she wrote. This was dropped last night in the fire department's box?"

"It was."

"Someone's had this this whole time... The killer?"

"Possibly."

"Why would they do that?" she asked, flipping through the pages. "When was the last entry?"

"The night before her death," he said. "There's reason to believe some pages were torn out."

She lifted her gaze to his, then went back to studying the final page. "She talks about working at The RC Resort... Nothing seemed to be troubling her."

"No," Rutland said, standing. He riffled back through the diary. "Look at this page."

She scanned the words. Sawni's quiet voice played through her head, as real as it had once been. Her eyes seized on a name. She read through the entry again, coming to the name once more. She shook her head. "I don't understand..."

"You told investigators at the time she was dating someone," he said. "Here she mentions him a week before she disappeared."

Kaya rejected it, offering the file back to him. "That's not right. It can't be."

"Sheriff, you said your personal feelings have no bearing on your work. You're not going to let them get in the way now when the answer may be staring you in the face."

"She's not naming her killer," she said, pointing to the file. "She's naming her lover."

"Wolfe Coldero. He's mentioned no less than thirty-three times throughout her journal. I checked back through her missing person case. No one ever checked his alibi for the day of her disappearance. No one checked him out in the Miller Higgins case, either."

"Wolfe Coldero didn't kidnap or kill Sawni," she stated.

"Why not? He lived in Fuego at the time. He worked at Eaton Edge and lived at Coldero Ridge. He's connected to Sawni through the rodeo. He was a bull rider. That's where and how they met. Why wouldn't either of them have told you?"

Her lips felt numb. She dropped to a chair. "Wolfe's mute. He's never spoken to anyone."

"Did he help with the search effort?" Rutland asked.

Kaya thought back. She combed through memories she'd gone over again and again, looking for clues or clarity or closure... "Yes," she answered. "I remember him being there. His father, Santiago, came. And Everett's mother, Josephine. She and Santiago were having an affair. They brought horses and were part of the mounted search party in the state park areas."

"I'd like to bring him in," Rutland said.

"He won't talk," she reminded him. "Not to you or anyone else."

"He can answer questions in writing," Rutland asserted. "If he doesn't, I can charge him with obstruction."

"He's getting married in a few days."

Rutland closed the file. "With a foreign honeymoon to follow, I hear. He's not getting on a plane until he's cleared."

"Wolfe Coldero isn't a killer," Kaya told him.

"Didn't he do time for shooting a man in the back seven years ago?" Rutland asked.

"Jace Decker," Kaya replied. "Wolfe shot him to stop him from throwing fuel on the cabin fire at Coldero Ridge. Josephine and her and Santiago's daughter, Angel, were inside. Wolfe tried to get them out, but he was too late."

"His record is against him," he said. "He'll be brought in at nine o'clock tomorrow morning. You can sit in."

The door to the conference room opened. Sherry peered around the jamb. "I'm sorry, Sheriff. Agent Rutland. But there's a situation."

"What kind of situation?" Kaya asked, coming to attention.

"It's the mayor," Sherry said. "The luxury vehicle he drives... It's been vandalized. He's agitated. Deputy Root is having trouble getting him to calm down."

"We'll discuss this later," Kaya told Rutland. "Where is the mayor now?" she asked Sherry.

"On Second Street where the car was parked," she said, trailing Kaya through the station. "He discovered the damage after leaving the festival."

"Thank you, Sherry."

The scene on Second Street was nothing short of chaotic. A crowd had formed. Kaya worked through it to the center. She could hear True Claymore hollering before she reached the center of the mass where he and his vehicle were located.

She stopped to assess. The mayor was without his hat. His hair was sticking straight up in places, finger-combed by frustrated hands. His hands flailed and he was on his toes, his red face in Root's. He threw invectives at the deputy, his voice no longer smooth. Nothing about him appeared to be collected.

Kaya walked around the parallel-parked vehicle to the driver's side. Damage had been done to more than the paint job. There was fender and other body damage. The destruction was so thorough, she doubted the vehicle was drivable.

Kaya didn't have to ask what instrument had been used. The offending sledgehammer lay nearby. It was the kind used commonly by farmers and ranchers to drive stakes into the ground. The paint on the front edge matched the color of the car.

"Did the perpetrator flee the scene?" she asked Wyatt, who was standing by.

True whirled at the sound of her voice. "Sheriff! He's done it now! Lock him up! Lock all of them up!"

She raised a hand. "You saw who did this?"

"I didn't have to see it!" True shouted. "He was standing right there with the sledgehammer when I got back!"

"Who was?" Kaya asked, though her gut stirred, and she was afraid she knew the name already. She looked around, searching.

Leaning against one of the closest building's support posts in a neutral stance, Everett stood. His aviator sunglasses reflected the scene. The bend of his mouth showcased nothing—not even amusement.

She knew when his eyes shifted to her. His stance didn't change or his expression, but she felt it.

"Did anybody see who did this?" Kaya asked the crowd at large.

Turk Monday stepped forward. "I saw that Eaton fella there going to town on it."

"He was heaving at it like a raging bull," another man piped up from the crowd.

Other witnesses' voices followed. Kaya rounded on Everett with a glare she hoped singed the fur off his hide.

"White trash, burnout, son of a bitch!" True Claymore yelled, stepping forward.

Root caught him by the arms. "Now, mayor. You're going to need to cool down if you want to press charges…"

Kaya walked to Everett. "Do you deny this?"

"Which part?" he asked. "The white trash, burnout bit?"

"Did you vandalize his vehicle?" she asked.

"That part I'll claim."

She stepped a hair closer. "You promised," she hissed.

He pointed at the mayor. "I promised not to harm a hair on his head. His hair's fine. So's every other part of him. You said nothing about his property."

"Turn around," she ordered. "Put your hands behind your back."

He straightened. "Sure, Sheriff Sweetheart. I know how it goes."

She reached around her belt for her cuffs. "Everett Eaton, you're under arrest…"

Chapter 12

Kaya stayed late at the sheriff's office, long after Rutland had left for the night, her deputies had gone home, and Lionel Bozeman had shown up with Ellis Eaton to bail Everett out of jail. She stayed behind her desk with the pages photocopied from Sawni's diary.

Annette and True Claymore had been there most of the afternoon. They'd railed at her deputies and her in turn. They'd even shouted at Rutland. There was no question Everett would be charged with criminal damage to a vehicle. They'd threatened her job if she let him out on bail.

Making threats to a sheriff in her own department was a ballsy move. She'd made a note of those who overheard and filed it away, as she'd filed so many other tidbits about the Claymores over the years.

The diary was revealing in ways Kaya hadn't expected. Sawni had dated Wolfe Coldero for much of the last year of her life. They met at the rodeo. When Sawni was forced to stop returning to the rodeo by her parents, there had been meetings with the two—on the reservation and off. Kaya read details about multiple rendezvous at the state park.

It made sense, Sawni and Wolfe, Kaya thought. It made perfect sense, actually. Wolfe was mute and Sawni was quiet. Their similar natures would have drawn them together. Sawni had been curious about boys and men but had never found one she could trust to experiment with...

Until Wolfe, apparently. Their relationship had turned intimate. Kaya had a hard time facing the fact that Sawni hadn't confided her first time to her. They'd sworn they would confide in each other, if no one else.

There was nothing violent about their relationship mentioned in the diary. There was no evidence that Wolfe treated Sawni with anything but care.

Kaya studied the photographs of the diary itself, taken before it was bagged for prints. At several junctures, the binding was ragged. Pages had been torn out. Quite a few of them. That called to question whether Sawni had ripped them or the person who had delivered the diary after all these years.

If it was the killer, why would they hand over the diary? To throw suspicion on someone else?

Someone like Wolfe?

Some of the answers would come in the morning when he arrived for his interview with Rutland. Kaya glanced at the clock. She frowned when she saw it was close to eleven. She closed the file and locked it in her filing cabinet before switching the lamp off on her desk. She changed from her sheriff's uniform to a more relaxed set of jeans and a button-down.

She locked the station door behind her since she was the last to leave. Walking to her vehicle, she got in the driver's seat and cranked the ignition. She pulled out onto the deserted street and started to turn the wheel for home.

She paused. As the traffic light at Main Street and Second changed, she looked down the intersecting road that reached into the black of night.

She thought about the diary. She thought about her bed and the complications she certainly wouldn't find there.

She turned the wheel to the left and followed the road well out of town.

Slowing, she made the turnoff for Eaton Edge and drove up the long, dirt drive to Eaton House. The motion lights flared to life as she parked. She noted the absence of cars in the drive.

She didn't know what she was doing exactly, but she took the path to the front door of the house and pounded on the door.

She expected Paloma to answer. When the door parted from the jamb, she found him instead.

Everett blinked at her in surprise. "Sheriff Sweetheart," he greeted.

When she stayed silent, he released a breath. "Look. I can take a lot. Scream at me. Hit me. You can bust my nuts or gouge me in the eyes. But don't give me the silent treatment. I can't take it."

She walked around him before she could tell herself not to. Beyond the foyer, she found a spartan living room he hadn't changed since his father died. There was a couch with space behind it. There, against the wall off the stairwell, she found the sideboard.

He didn't stop her from lifting the lid off its decanter. She turned an upside-down glass over and filled it with whiskey. She lifted it to her mouth and knocked it back straight.

"I'll take one of those."

She threw a look over her shoulder, quashing his attempt at camaraderie.

"Never mind," he decided.

She poured herself another, then, as an afterthought, a

second. She grabbed it by the rim and pivoted to extend it to him.

He took it, tipping his head to her. "Thank you, Sheriff—"

"Don't you dare," she warned.

He took a drink, instead.

She turned her back to the sideboard and leaned. Sipping, she pointed at him, lifting one finger from her glass. "You know…call me a sucker or whatever you like…"

"I wouldn't call you—"

"But I trusted you," she added, raising her voice over his. "I understand a lot of people have died on that hill, but I thought… I actually *thought* I could trust you."

"I didn't hurt him," he claimed. "Not a hair."

"His hair's gone! It's fallen out! He's so hoarse from shouting at me and Root and Wyatt for letting you out on bail he won't have anything left when he comes at you tomorrow, which he undoubtedly will."

"I'm not afraid of him and his froggy voice," Everett noted. "Though I'm mad as hell he came down on you hard."

"You don't get to be mad as hell," she informed him. "It's my turn now."

"All right," he conceded. He set his glass down. "How do you want to do this?"

"If I was smart, I'd leave," she claimed. "I'd go on with my life and wash my hands of this."

His eyes darkened in understanding. "But you're here."

"Because there's another part of me. The stupid, impulsive part that I never could kill. It seems to think you destroying another man's property on my behalf was sweet and maybe a little romantic, by Western standards."

He chose his words carefully. "You, uh… You like Western?"

"The sheriff in me doesn't."

"What about you?" he asked. "The trick rider. Apache Annie. The real you that ran away to the rodeo and never wanted to go back home."

"I'm here," she said.

His eyes shone, making her stomach flutter as only he could. "Yeah, you are."

She set the glass down with an empty clack. With both hands, she reached for her bun.

"What're you doing?"

"Be quiet, Everett."

"Shutting up," he replied as the pins came down and her braid unraveled, falling to her waist.

She didn't meet his gaze. Not until every last coil had been undone and she'd spread her fingers through her hair to make it spill loose over her shoulders.

Everett backed up until his hips met the back of the couch. He sat and gripped the edge with both hands on either side. "What're you doing to me, woman?"

"I'm not touching you," she said.

"Aren't you?" he asked. There was a bar between his eyes that spoke of danger and longing and her heart began to quake.

She crossed to him. With him sitting, they were nearly eye level. "Put your hands in it," she instructed. "Isn't that what you wanted?"

He made a noise. His fingers lifted to the ends of her hair. He fanned them out, letting the ends pass over the back of his knuckles in whispering strokes. Testing the weight with his palm, he wet his lips before twining one strand around his finger.

Kaya started unbuttoning his shirt. He hadn't changed out of what he'd worn earlier. She parted the chambray shirt over his front, pleased to see nothing underneath it but skin. Pushing the shirt over the hard, round points of his shoulders, she shed it.

In the center of his chest, she found the place where he'd been shot and the incisions where surgeons had opened him up to save his life. She traced the bullet wound, feathering her touch over the damage done.

His voice roughened. "I ain't touched anything as fine as you. Ever."

She smiled, in spite of herself. "Is that your way of telling me you love me?"

He cursed a stream.

"Steady there," she advised, planting her hand over the marks of his chest. His heart beat underneath them, big and forceful. "Steady on, cattle baron. It was a joke."

He shook his head slightly. "I did that earlier."

"You committing a third degree felony was your way of expressing your feelings?" she asked.

His hand came up to cradle the sharp line of her jaw. His mouth said nothing but his eyes, again, talked.

Her lips parted when she took their meaning, too. "Your love language may need a little work."

"I don't know," he considered, giving his attention to the buttons on the top of her blouse. "It's working just fine from where I'm standing."

When he removed her shirt, she stepped in the space between his parted knees. She grabbed him under the shoulders and confronted his smart mouth with her own.

He gathered her against his chest, his hands lost in the thick sheet of her hair. When he unclipped her bra, he tugged it away. Without lifting his lips from hers, he pushed to his feet.

Kaya dropped her head back, closing her eyes. Skin-to-skin, she let him feast on her mouth, absorbing the rough texture of his hands as they cruised over her in sure strokes.

When he unclasped her belt, she shimmied as he pushed the waistband over her hips.

He kneeled, tugging away one of her boots, then the other. The pants pooled at her ankles and his lips found the place on her thigh, the wound that still ached. He traced kisses around her thigh, then up, tickling the place behind her knee that was oddly sensitive.

She didn't stop him when he reached the juncture of her thighs. His mouth opened and pressed against her sex through the thin panties she'd chosen to wear that morning. It was her turn to groan, sinking her hands into his dark, cropped hair. His beard was rough, too. She felt it through the material as she had on her thigh and she shivered, bristled and shivered again as her arousal increased. If he removed the garment, he'd find how wet she was for him.

"Stand up," she directed. When he did, she yanked off his belt, whipping it free from the loops of his jeans. She undid the snap and pulled down the fly and would have reached in for him but met resistance when he took her wrist and held it. He took the other and she hissed at him.

"This isn't going to be fast, Kaya. I don't want you in fast gulps. I want to take my time. I want it drawn out. I want us both thirsty and begging. I want you in my bed."

"Long way to go," she noted absently as he guided her backward to the stairs. The promise of it all was enough to bring her up to her toes. She dragged his mouth back to hers.

Stumbling, they made it halfway up the flight before he turned her to the wall.

She found her cheek against the striped wallpaper and, as he nipped her shoulder, she sighed. "This wasn't on the list…"

"Shh…" His face was in her hair and his touch low on her navel. It cruised down, reaching the parting of her legs.

She planted her hands against the wall as his fingertips sank underneath the edge of the panties. When he traced the seam of her sex with his middle finger, she bit her lip to keep from crying out.

He made a noise when he parted her and found the cluster of nerves at the peak of her labia and the pool of arousal he'd caused. When he stroked, she drew herself up tight, arching her back.

She could feel him through his jeans. He was ready—just as ready as she was. But his touch glided slow, taking her up incrementally, stretching her pleasure to the point of affliction. "Never figured you for a sadist, Eaton," she said brokenly as she dropped her head back to his shoulder.

"You can take it," he whispered hot against her temple. "You can take all of me."

She pressed her hand to the back of his, forcing him deeper. "Don't. Don't make me beg. Not yet."

His laugh fell brokenly across her cheek. He inserted one finger, stroking. Then another.

Her mouth dropped open though she didn't make a sound. It was too divine, this point he was driving her toward. Too bright. She burned, moving against his hand, driving herself right up to the breaking point.

He held her there in splendor. The heel of his other hand pressed against her womb, as if he knew exactly where the heat was building.

She came apart. In diamond-edged rifts and shouts, she came apart in his arms.

He turned her. When she saw his wide grin and the triumph riding high on his face, she raised her open hand.

It cracked across his face. He hissed, but the grin didn't break. Instead, he laughed. "Why you gotta be so mean?"

She placed her hands on the back of his head, urging him down. She kissed his cheek. Then the other. She kissed them better.

He hummed, boosting her up by the hips so her legs wrapped around his waist and he continued up the stairs.

The last step tripped him. The landing came up to meet them. It knocked the wind out of her.

"Sorry, sweetheart," he murmured, sitting up.

"Stay down," she ordered, switching their positions so that he was down and she was up. She yanked at one of his boots, gritting her teeth when it didn't comply. It nearly sent her down the stairs when it loosened. She tossed it behind her so that it bounced all the way to the bottom before doing the same to the other. Then she pulled at the cuffs of his jeans.

He lifted his hips so he could remove them from his waist. Once she had them off, she balled them up and threw them over the railing.

He was fine-boned, long and just dark enough to be tan instead of white. She liked the way the muscles bunched across his flat stomach, the way his shoulders flared outward, defiant, from his collarbone.

She liked the cut of hair down the center of his chest and abdomen that grew thick underneath his exposed waistline. There were other things. So many other things she liked—his long thighs, the definition of his chest and the way he looked back at her with hooded, bedroom eyes, hungry and watchful.

He wanted it slow, drawn out? He wanted them both thirsty, begging? *Fine*. That was just fine…

She scaled the length of him slowly, from ankles to shoulders, dragging the ends of her hair across his front. His knees rose and his skin tightened, and she got to watch him bite his own lip for once. When his hand came to the back of her neck to urge her mouth down to his, she held back, raining kisses over every other part of him she admired. Shoulders, collarbone, neck, pecs and sternum. She traced ribs and abs and waist, letting the dark curtain of her hair cover him as she followed him down, down…

She wanted him as sensitive as he'd made her. She wanted him wild—enough to take a sledgehammer to her enemy's car again. More.

She wanted him wild for her. There was a part of her that reveled in the fact that he'd reached that point. She'd arrested him for it. But that didn't stop the flash of pride or sparkly satisfaction that knowing brought.

She wrapped her fingers around his girth. Passing her thumb over the tip, she grinned when he jerked. "People say you're heartless."

His lungs moved up and down in excited repetitions. He dropped his head back, rising at the bidding of her hand when she stroked. He cursed.

"They're wrong," she considered and caressed. She worked him as he'd worked her. She did it until he was breathless. Then she seated herself over his hips. She took his face in her hands. "They're wrong about you."

He took her hand and placed it over the healed wound on the center of his chest. Underneath, his pulse rocked and clamored and she dropped her lips to that point.

He sat up and grunted as he picked her up and carried her the rest of the way to his door, which was at the end of the hallway.

They made it to the jamb. He propped her against it so he could open the door. He stopped, nibbling on her lower lip before tracing a line down her throat as he discarded her panties and lifted her.

"Now," she said. "Right now."

He obeyed. She took him, all of him. Just as he'd wanted. "Oh," she cried. "Oh, hell yes!"

"I told you," he groaned. "I told you, sweetheart…"

She nodded in quick repetitions. "Don't stop."

"Bed," he grunted and carried her across the threshold, along the floor, then tipped her to the bed. "Just a second…"

She heard him fumbling in the drawer next to the bed. She blinked at the condom he found.

She'd forgotten protection. *How* had she forgotten?

He opened the packet, then fed the rubber to the base of his arousal. When his body covered her again, he uttered an oath, brushing the hair from her cheeks in sweet strokes. "I let you get cold."

"You'll fix it, baby."

His hair messy from her hands, he grinned in a quick, delighted burst. "Baby? I like that."

She smiled, too. It filled her cheeks to capacity. "Make me say it again," she whispered.

"Ten-four."

He was like a furnace. When he joined with her again, she felt like one, too.

Their bodies were already dewy with perspiration. Together, they slid, plunged, tossed. Her ankles crossed at the small of his back and he carried her up to the same point he had before, diamond-bright and stunning. When she moaned, he answered.

The flat of his hands came to the backs of her thighs and he pressed, fitful as he chased his own climax.

When he broke, she pulled his mouth to hers so that when he groaned again, it vibrated across her lips. And when he shuddered, she felt it from the toes up, just like him.

"You won't move," she told him long after he stilled.

"No. I won't."

"Wake up, cattle baron."

"Nah," he said even as Kaya shifted restlessly. His face was in her hair, his arms wrapped around her. At some point in the night, he'd tossed the sheet over both of them, unwilling to let her get cold again. "I'm good."

"The sun's going to be coming up fast," she explained. "Paloma will be here. We both have work. Don't cowboys rise early?"

He smirked. "Which part, Sheriff?" He grunted when she drove her elbow into his stomach. He wheezed a laugh but didn't relinquish her. "Hold still."

He growled his displeasure, turning to his back. He cupped his hands under the back of his head. Why'd he have to fall for a sensible woman? "Don't leave this bed."

She sat up, scooping her hair over one shoulder. She combed her fingers through it. He'd like to do the same once he roused himself enough, he thought.

"We need to talk."

He traced the absence of her easy smile and felt it. "You're wearing your serious eyes."

"Because I am serious," she said. "Are you up enough to talk?"

He propped himself on one elbow with some effort. "Yeah, yeah. I'm up."

"I stopped by last night for two reasons."

"Not to jump my bones?"

"That was a bonus. I stopped here so that I could pick a fight with you."

"I like the way you fight," he said, unable to hide a smile even in the face of her serious eyes.

"I'm not sure you fight fair," she considered. "The other reason I wanted to stop by was because I know who Rutland's going to target next."

He scrubbed his hands over his face and sat up all the way. "Why do I get the feeling I'm not going to like his new direction?"

"It's Wolfe," she told him.

"Coldero?"

"Two nights ago, someone dropped Sawni's old diary in the safe haven drop box at the fire station on Highway 7. It's hers. I recognized the handwriting."

"Who dropped it?" he asked, coming awake in full measure now. "And why did they have it?"

"I don't know," she said. "There were no security cameras. Nobody saw anyone outside. It's at the lab now being checked for prints."

"What does this have to do with Coldero?" he asked.

"There are pages missing from the diary," Kaya told him. "However, the ones that remain primarily talk about Wolfe and their relationship."

"You didn't tell me she was seeing him."

"I didn't know until I read the diary," she explained.

He saw the sadness and trouble on her face. "Come 'ere."

She didn't resist much when he caught her hand. She pressed her cheek to the wall of his chest as he leaned back in the pillows at the head of the bed. "What's all this mean, Kaya?" he asked.

"Wolfe's going to be called in for questioning this morning," she said. "If he doesn't give Rutland the right answers, there's a good chance his and Eveline's wedding will be delayed."

"They're going to lock him up," Everett said.

"I thought you should know. It's your sister who loves him. And you don't mind that as much as you let on."

"I'll warn them," he replied.

"You don't think that he killed Sawni and the others."

Everett frowned and found himself shaking his head. "For the longest time, people thought Coldero killed Whip Decker. He served time for it. But he's no killer."

"He'll need to hear you say it before this is all over," she said.

He made another noise and was relieved when she let him hold her awhile longer before the break of day.

Chapter 13

Wolfe arrived promptly at the sheriff's department at nine o'clock with Lionel Bozeman, Ellis and Eveline in tow. Since Bozeman was to serve as his attorney and Ellis would speak for him, Eveline was forced to remain outside the crowded interrogation room.

Kaya observed the proceedings. Wolfe confirmed his involvement with Sawni but had no memory of exactly where he was the day she vanished or where he had been during the time of Bethany Merchant's disappearance, either. Worse, he couldn't provide a witness to his whereabouts the day of Miller Higgins's death. Through sign language, he claimed he had been working at home. The only witness to that was his father, Santiago, who had moved in with him and Eveline after they built their house on a parcel of land outside Fuego town limits.

Santiago wasn't of sound enough mind to provide a statement. He'd been institutionalized shortly after the death of his wife and daughter seven years ago. Eveline had been working at Ollero Creek with Luella Decker on the day in question. She hadn't returned home until after dark.

"Can't you do something?" Ellis asked Kaya after Rutland requested Deputy Wyatt handcuff Wolfe Coldero and take him into holding.

"I wish I could," Kaya told him. "But if he can't provide an alibi for at least one of the murders, my hands are tied."

Facing Eveline was even more troubling. "How could you let this happen?" she asked, trailing Kaya through the department. "He trusts you. We all trusted you. You think he did this?"

"No," Kaya told her. "I don't think he's guilty, but Rutland believes he is and there's no physical or circumstantial evidence to fight that."

"He and I are getting married in five days," Eveline said. Her eyes were wet. "Kaya, *help him*. Please."

Kaya waited until the Eatons left and the reporters came and went. True Claymore showed up, demanding to know who they had in custody. He was only too delighted to hear it was Wolfe.

Kaya waited until Rutland left for the day before trailing Root back to the holding cells at the back of the building. "Unlock it," she requested when they arrived at Wolfe's.

Root opened the door for her and held it wide. She passed through. "You can close it," she told him. When he hesitated, she raised a brow.

Root gave a short nod. "Yes, sir."

She waited until he'd closed and locked the door before telling him, "Give us some room, please."

Root backed away at a respectful distance. Kaya crossed to the bench where Wolfe sat with his elbows on his knees and his hands together, his shoulders low.

She lowered next to him and stretched her legs. She leaned against the wall behind them, rubbing the spot on her thigh that hurt a little. Studying the strong line of Wolfe's back, she released a breath. "I knew she was seeing a bull rider. She never did say which one."

After a moment's pause, he eased back, too, until his shoulders touched the wall.

"I'm glad it was you," Kaya assured him. "I know you treated her right. She was in love with you." She swallowed because her voice grew thick. "She loved you, and you're being locked up for it."

He took her hand. The hold banked the grief and guilt, somewhat. She felt his anguish, too, in the quiet. "Did you know she was working at the resort?" she asked him.

He shook his head slightly.

"She stopped talking to me, once that started," she said. "Something happened out there. Something happened in the pages of her diary that were torn out. What happened, Wolfe?"

He lifted his shoulders. He had no more answers than she did and just as many questions, it seemed.

Kaya squeezed his hand before letting go. She raised herself to her feet. Passing a hand over her eyes, she made sure they were dry before turning back to him. "I'm sorry about the wedding." When he nodded, she turned away. Root beat her to the door and let her out. As it locked it back in place, Kaya met Wolfe's stare through the bars. "I'm not going to stop until the real killer is where you are."

Wolfe offered her a small smile before he lowered his head again, looking more than a little defeated.

Eveline rode out the next dawn to help tag the night's newborns. Everett was surprised to see her on the mid-morning drive as well. She was quieter than usual, but she and her mare, Sienna Shade, did their job well.

It wasn't until they stopped near the mountains that she came for his knees. "Did you and Kaya have a pleasin' time the other night?" she asked.

He heard the bitterness behind the question and raised a brow at Ellis. Ellis shook his head and moved away to a safe distance, leaving Everett to confront his sister's anguish. "Cut the crap, Manhattan, and say what you're needing to say."

"The man I love is in jail," she stated. "Facing charges *again* for killing someone he didn't."

"He's got a bad habit of being in the wrong place at the wrong time," Everett observed.

She stuck her finger in his face. "*Don't.* Don't accuse him of this. You know he didn't do this."

"I do," he said and watched her fumble into stunned silence. "You tell me what I'm supposed to do about it."

"There needs to be a wedding," she told him. "I *need* there to be a wedding."

"You want me to bring Griff down to the sheriff's department so you can marry Coldero through the bars of his holding cell? I don't see it working out any other way by Saturday."

"Do you love me?" Eveline asked and her eyes filled with tears.

He made a face. "Ah, hell."

"I can't do this alone, Everett. We need to get him an alibi. It was his connection to Sawni Mescal that made them look in his direction to begin with. If we can provide him with an alibi for the date of her disappearance, the case against him won't hold."

"How do you expect us to do that?" he asked.

"By going through Dad's old records," she insisted. "He wrote everything down. He kept everything. You didn't get rid of any of his old file boxes, did you?"

"No." The basement was packed with them, floor to ceiling. "It'll be like finding a needle in a haystack. And that's assuming anything's there to begin with. Wolfe wasn't a member of the family then. Who's to say Dad kept anything on him?"

"Because he wanted to adopt Wolfe when he was found wandering the Edge as a boy," Eveline explained. "He let Santiago care for him only because…"

Everett looked away when her eyes turned implicating. "Because of me."

"I don't know why you rejected the idea of Wolfe coming to the Edge to live," Eveline said, "and it doesn't matter now. What matters is that if there's something in Dad's papers that can help, I need your help to find it."

"Fine," he agreed. "Come to the house for dinner. Bring Ellis and Luella. I'm not promising we'll find anything to clear him…"

"I know," she said quickly. "Thank you, Everett."

"Boss!"

Everett looked around to find Matteo riding from the north. He and Javier walked out to meet him.

Matteo slowed his mount. "Tombstone's been spotted."

"Where?" Everett asked.

"Near the mountain. Seems folks are still hanging around, trying to get a look at the place those bodies were found."

"They need to be headed off," Everett said.

"I'll do it," Javier offered.

"Take your gun," Everett advised. "And Spencer, for backup. Both of you be back to headquarters by dusk."

"Tombstone's back?" Eveline asked as she stood at his shoulder and watched the two men ride off. Fear wavered across the words.

"He never left," Everett said before turning his attention back to their herd.

* * *

Everett was sleep-starved when he entered the sheriff's department the following morning. He'd missed Paloma's fine-smelling breakfast spread with Eveline nipping at his heels to get a move on.

The two of them and Ellis, Luella and Paloma had gone through their father's boxes in the basement. Everett had stared at papers until they were blurry. Not everything had been filed or labeled but most boxes had had the year etched on them.

It had been difficult confronting his father's words, photographs, hand-drawn maps and keepsakes. Because of what had happened over the summer shortly after his death, Everett hadn't truly processed his grief. It had come in fits and starts, dragging itself out over months, not weeks.

It was one of the reasons he'd continued to sit in the therapist's office once a week in San Gabriel after he'd learned to manage the bulk of his PTSD symptoms.

He'd heard Hammond's voice again when he'd confronted his handwriting, his little notes about the day-to-day events that he'd scrawled on calendars... He'd drawn plans on paper napkins and ideas on notepads with conference labels. The low, slow sound of the man's words had filled Everett's head.

Ellis had found wedding photos of their parents hidden in one box. Eveline had uncovered newspaper clippings in another, most of them yellow and soft with age. There were ribbons and trophies that belonged to all three siblings. Hammond had kept the boutonniere he'd worn while escorting Eveline to homecoming court.

Kaya came out of her office when she heard her secretary greet him. "Everett," she greeted. "What are you doing here?"

He felt bleary and not a little clumsy. His better judgement had disappeared along with the possibility of sleep, so he leaned over and kissed her. "Sheriff."

She jumped a bit, then settled. "Good news?" she asked, gesturing to the folder he carried.

"Where's Watt?" he asked.

"Mr. Eaton."

Everett found the agent standing in the open door of the conference room. He raised what he had brought for him. "I'm here to spring my brother-in-law."

Rutland eyed the folder. "I'm afraid it's not going to be that simple."

"Why not?" Everett asked. "I can prove Coldero wasn't with Sawni Mescal or Bethany Merchant on the days of their disappearances."

"Is that right?" Rutland asked.

Everett opened the folder and pulled out a newspaper clipping. "This is from the day Sawni was taken. He was at the rodeo. He won, which is how he wound up in the *Fuego Daily News*. There's the date for you at the top. It says right here that it was an all-day event. I resented him for it, too. The events were lined up one after the other, which tied Coldero up from the early morning until well after dark when he took the final cup. There's his picture with it right there."

Rutland took the glasses from the front pocket of his jacket and placed them on the end of his nose. He assessed the clipping thoroughly.

Everett took out the second piece of paper. "This is my father's desk calendar from the month and year Bethany

Merchant was taken. You can see his notation on the day she disappeared. What's it say right there?"

Rutland bent his head over the page. He tilted it to read the slanted, left-handed scrawl. "'Took Wolfe to auction. New bull bought and paid for. Stayed overnight in Santa Fe. Dinner and overnight at Renaissance Hotel.'"

"I recall that, too," Everett said, "as I wanted to be the one my father took to the auction. But he took Coldero. The man he wanted to be his foreman one day. He saw something in him. When he was gone, my father wanted me at the helm of Eaton Edge and Coldero as foreman. He trusted him. That's why I didn't need proof he didn't do what you're accusing him of. My father saw people for what they were. He saw Wolfe Coldero long before I could bring myself to do so."

Rutland took off the glasses. "That doesn't mean he didn't kill Higgins or this other woman."

"Wasn't that other woman killed close to forty years ago?" Everett asked. "I thought I heard that in the news. That's long before Coldero came to the Edge. As for Higgins, Coldero sent several text messages to my sister and Ellis. Ping his phone. He lives outside town limits. I guarantee there's no record of him being near the tower closest to Ol' Whalebones or the Edge. It'll be the one closer to his and Eveline's house."

Rutland cleared his throat. "I'll need to verify this."

"Before the end of the day," Everett demanded. "There's going to be a wedding at the Edge the day after tomorrow. I don't know if you've met my little sister, but she'll have my ass and yours if her groom is a no-show. You can thank me later for doing your job for you." Leaving Rutland with the folder, he passed Kaya on the way out. "You got a date for this thing?"

A spark of amusement entered her eyes. "I thought I was looking at him. I'll be the one in the black dress."

He winked and saw himself out.

Everett swung the double doors to Grady's Saloon open. The focus on the dance floor and jukebox shifted around to him and his companions. Activity slowed as the patrons came to a standstill.

"This way," he indicated, leading the way to the long line of the bar.

"You sure about this?" Ellis asked, close behind him.

"As a heart attack," Everett replied, locking eyes with the bartender.

Grady Morrison slapped his rag onto the counter. "You're not welcome here," he told Everett. "I told you that years ago. The brawl you started then resulted in over a grand in damages."

"Your memory's long, Grady." Everett had already reached into his pocket. He tossed a hundred dollar bill on the bar top. "How much for a chair?"

When Grady only stared at Franklin's face on the bill, Everett pulled another from his wallet. He flicked it onto the bar with the first. "How 'bout this, huh?"

Grady frowned at the money. Then he peeled it from the water rings it had landed in and stuffed it in his back pocket. He set three glasses on the bar. "What's your pleasure, gentlemen?"

Everett took a seat, motioning for the others to do the same. "Whiskey, straight." He turned to look at the person who settled on the stool to his right. "That all right with you, Coldero?"

Wolfe jerked his chin in affirmation. He took the glass Grady passed across the bar. He lifted it to Everett.

Everett lifted his briefly, then drank.

Ellis tossed his whiskey back in one fell swoop. He released a breath at the burn and set his empty glass down, touching two fingers to the rim for a refill.

Grady hesitated, wary. "Who's driving tonight?"

"I know someone," Everett asserted. "Keep it coming, old-timer."

Grady grunted and fixed Ellis another drink.

Everett watched him walk away. "You think he missed me?"

Wolfe shook his head automatically.

Ellis chuckled.

Everett raised a brow and sipped. He ran his tongue over his teeth and looked around. "I fought you here that night," he remembered.

Wolfe nodded.

"What for?" Everett asked.

Wolfe thought about it. Then he lifted one large shoulder in answer.

"I don't remember, either." Everett screwed up his face. "I don't remember most of the reasons we fought as often as we did."

Wolfe tipped his glass up, swallowing the rest of his whiskey. He eyed the bottom of the glass and shook his head.

Everett shifted on his chair, uncomfortable. "I'm in a pickle. My sister is over the moon for you. And let's face it, if you were going kill anyone over the last twenty years, it would've been me. I've given you nothing but cause."

Wolfe and Ellis remained still and silent.

Everett finished his whiskey, too. "You better make her happy or I'll wipe you off the face of the earth."

Wolfe's mouth slid into a small smile. He signed.

"He says, 'It's done,'" Ellis translated. When Wolfe's hands moved again, he added, "'Thank you.'"

Everett ignored that. "I don't like surprises. Is there anything else I need to know before I let you become an official member of this family?"

Wolfe shook his head.

Everett tapped the counter, signaling to Grady that he was done. He paused when Wolfe started to sign again.

Ellis coughed in reaction. Then he began to laugh again.

"What'd he say?" Everett asked, suspicious.

Ellis cleared his throat. "He says that, come fall, we're both going to be uncles."

Everett stared at Ellis, then Wolfe and the wide grin on the latter's face. His large hand fit to Everett's shoulder and squeezed before he got up and moved to the door.

Ellis grabbed Everett's arm and shook him. "You did good, brother."

"Jesus," Everett muttered, shrugging him off. He straightened. "Actin' like I cured cancer or something."

When Ellis left with Wolfe, Everett stayed at the bar. Grady returned to take their glasses. Everett held on to his. "Another," he demanded.

Chapter 14

The bride wore satin couture and carried a bouquet of desert flowers. Her elder brothers walked her down the aisle to the tune of Fleetwood Mac's "Songbird." Paloma Coldero served as Eveline's maid of honor, looking lovely in full-length chiffon and lace. The groom had been fitted for the occasion in head-to-toe black, including a new felt cowboy hat and snakeskin dress boots.

Eveline and Wolfe exchanged vows under a rustic awning that framed a stunning picture of Eaton Edge. The sun took its last gasp over the distant peak as he dipped her back for a long, satisfactory kiss to a raucous round of applause. They beamed at each other as they came up for air and the wedding party kicked into high gear.

Kaya spotted the security the Eatons had hired to block reporters and photographers—or anyone nefarious—from intruding on the pleasantries. *Smart move*, she thought, sipping champagne on the outskirts of the reception. The happy couple had chosen the wide flagstone patio of Eaton House for the party. Guests spilled down the steps into the yard, milling as far as the white barn with enchanting fairy lights trimming the eaves. She counted four guards, each wearing a spiffy black tuxedo and built like a bulldozer.

She watched the colors change in the sky. Dusk turned

toward night. The hues had softened into lavender, gloaming blue and a soft touch of green in the horizon. The sound of the live band, boots slapping the dance floor and hands clapping split the quiet of the landscape with lively abandon.

"Why aren't you dancing?"

Kaya looked around at her sister, Naleen. Older by two years, Naleen wore her long black hair to one side of her neck in a coiled side bun with a pretty, braided headband. She was several inches taller than Kaya. Her frame was curvy to Kaya's muscly one and she wore a tea-length strapless party dress in navy. "You used to love to dance," Naleen added, holding out her hand.

Kaya tipped the champagne glass to her sister's fingers and watched her drink. "Why is Mom here?" she asked.

Naleen raised a fashionably full brow as she lowered the glass and handed it back. "She was Santiago's nurse when he was transferred to the mental facility and stayed in touch with Paloma and Wolfe through the years."

Kaya raised her chin. "Ah."

"Is that why you're hiding?"

"I'm not hiding," Kaya said, but the words were lost in the echo chamber of the glass as she took another drink.

Naleen's wide mouth curved. "If only the people of Fuego knew how their sheriff cowers at the sight of her four-foot-eleven mother."

"I'm not hiding," Kaya repeated because it sounded good and strong, and she wanted to mean it.

"You're going to have to speak to her," Naleen advised. "Preferably before she finds out you and Everett Eaton are—"

"What?" Kaya intercepted swiftly. "What do you know about Everett?"

"You're having some kind of fling with him and the whole town knows it," Naleen answered. She raised her hands. "No judgement. You and me—we've always had a type."

"What type?"

"The hard cowboy type," Naleen answered smoothly. "The long, tall, gritty kind of cowboy that gets under our skin and doesn't leave. Not until we've been bucked off."

"I don't know what you're talking about."

"Look who's in denial." Naleen sighed as the band slid into a slow song and the bride and groom took to the floor. "I keep thinking about Sawni. Do you think she'd be happy Wolfe moved on and found someone like Eveline?"

Kaya nodded. "If she's watching this, she's seen everything else. The way he and his family searched for her, the way he lost his stepmother and stepsister in the fire, the false accusations made against him, the time he did in jail because of it… After everything he's been through, he deserves a life with the woman he loves. Sawni would want nothing less."

Naleen thought about it. "She did want the best for people." Turning her focus back to Kaya, she added, "She wanted you to be happy, too. You have to know that's the reason she took the job at The RC Resort. So that you could continue with the rodeo."

Kaya shifted from one foot to the other and didn't meet her sister's stare. She watched the others dance. Grief and regret were close to the surface, still. She had thought there would be some resolution to them if Sawni was found. She'd been wrong. She still had to wrangle with them.

"How's your leg?" Naleen asked.

"It's better," Kaya said. "Still sore at times—especially

on days I hike. But I think physical therapy is starting to pay off."

"Good. It's a damn fine wedding, isn't it?"

"They're a damn fine match," Kaya replied, happy to be moving on from the previous subjects. "Nova's got her summer job. Everett says she's a natural cowhand."

Naleen's wistful expression morphed into a fast frown as she found her daughter slow dancing with Lucas Barnes. "I keep telling myself she'll grow out of it—that she'll be burned out by the end of summer. But she's as stubborn as desert weather and just as determined. I'm afraid there's no fighting her nature. Now I know how Mom felt when you ran away to be a trick rider."

Kaya made a noise as she eyed the hand Lucas had low on Nova's waist. She raised the champagne glass to point it out. "Do you think those two are doing it?"

Naleen stiffened. "She wouldn't. She's only sixteen— practically a baby."

"You were sixteen when you lost it to Ryan MacKay," Kaya reminded her. "Then married him before you were eighteen because you got pregnant."

Naleen's jaw tightened. "That's not nice, Kaya."

"It's true," Kaya said. "I was sixteen when I lost it, too. To a cowboy with no more sense between his ears than Lucas over there. Are you sensing a pattern here? Altaha women lose their minds around silly cowboys. Nova's never struck me as a traditional sort, but Lucas's hand is well south of the mark."

"I'll be back," Naleen said, marching off to break up the festivities. Kaya grinned, dangling the champagne glass between two fingers. She hated to throw Nova at her mother's mercy, but Kaya had needed something—anything—to divert Naleen's attention from her.

She heard a growl near her ear and turned around.

Everett caught her by the waist, holding her at arm's length so that he could drink her with his eyes. "That ain't no uniform."

Kaya glanced down at the black dress she'd tried on and dismissed the night of their first date. "Even the sheriff's got to mix it up a little." She glanced over his fancy duds and was forced to take a bracing breath. "Anybody ever tell you you clean up good, cattle baron?"

He didn't take his eyes off her to examine the dark suit jacket with boot stitch that fit the long plains of his shoulders to perfection. Three dogs milled around his legs.

"Aren't you going to introduce me to your posse?" she asked.

He patted his thigh. The one that answered immediately sat at his silent motion to do so then stared, alert and sharp, waiting for the next command. It was an Australian cattle dog. "This is Boaz. She's the leader." As he passed a gentle hand between Boaz's ears, he peered at Kaya. "I have a weakness for strong females."

She smiled softly. He snapped, bringing one of the others around. "Sit," he said until the second cattle dog did so. "This is Boomer. He's four. He likes to herd, like Boaz, and he likes to play."

"Hello, Boomer," Kaya said when the dog's head tilted her way. His tongue lolled out, charming her, and she reached down to pet him.

"This other one's Bones," Everett said, snapping until Bones wound around to his front and sat on his feet. "He's still a pup."

Kaya felt her brow knit as she studied Bones more closely. "Um, Everett?"

"He's learning, still," Everett went on, rubbing Bones's

scruff until the dog's left leg began to mill in circles. "His energy still overrides his decision-making. But he'll be a fine cattle dog in the future, like the others."

"Everett," she said again. When his gaze fixed to hers, she pointed to Bones. "You realize that's a coyote."

Everett quickly cupped Bones's ears under his hands. "He doesn't know that."

She rolled her eyes. "Come on."

"He's not all coyote," Everett explained. "He was three weeks old when I found him in the sagebrush. His mother had been killed and his fellow pups had been eaten, most likely by Tombstone. They were in his territory. I didn't think he'd make it."

"But he did," she considered, sizing Bones up. "Does he yip at the moon?"

"Sometimes," Everett said. He winked. "But then again, so do I."

She pressed her lips together to stop herself from laughing. "And how do I know you're not part coyote?"

He chuckled. "You don't, Sheriff Sweetheart."

She shook her head. In Apache myth, Coyote was often depicted as either the villain or the savior. Kaya didn't think she could attribute either of those labels to Everett. After all they'd been through, she had a pretty good feeling he wasn't going to be the villain in her story.

As for *savior*… Kaya had done plenty of saving herself through the years. And Everett Eaton was hardly a knight in shining armor.

In some legends, it was Coyote who brought light to the world.

And Everett sure did light a fire in her.

When he stepped close again, easing her into his embrace, his eyes traced the seam of her lips and her cheekbones before meeting her assessing gaze. "You've got the night off."

"I do," she admitted. Her stomach clutched. His stare spread excitement in every vicinity.

He nodded. "I plan on making the most of it."

Her pulse rate doubled. They hadn't spent the night together since the evening after his arrest. Since, she'd been unable to ignore the fact that she no longer enjoyed going to bed alone.

"I'd like to dance with you, Kaya," he said. "I asked you once and you were hurting. Is your leg well enough to let me spin you around the dance floor a dozen times?"

He'd had her at the sound of her name. She slipped her hand into his outstretched one.

She'd knocked a full-grown man out with her fist once. But her hand felt small in Everett's. It even felt like it might belong there.

Naleen was right, she thought as her stomach fluttered. "Spin me," she said simply and followed his lead to the dance floor.

"Are you behaving yourself?" Paloma hissed in his ear as the stars came blinking into existence.

Everett flinched. He thought he'd been alone at the buffet table. "Do I look like I'm stuffing crab legs down my pants?"

"I'm more worried about you spiking the punch bowl," she said with a lowered brow. "I heard your little liquor bottles clinking in your vest before the ceremony started."

"Somebody had to calm Coldero down," Everett noted. He picked up a carrot stick. "I've never seen a man sweat his bride showing up to the altar that much." He dragged the stick through the dip bowl and lifted it toward his mouth.

She knocked it out of his hand before he could shove it home. At his stunned look, she snapped, "Put it on a plate, *then* eat it. It's your sister's wedding. The least you can do is act civilized."

He took the plate she handed him and started to pile things on it, muttering, "Jesus God Almighty... I walked her down the aisle, didn't I? I handed her over to Coldero real nicely..."

"Because you know what's good for you," Paloma said, picking up a plate of her own. She used tongs to select a chicken leg from a platter. "The line goes to the left, Everett Templeton," she added when he tried to wind to the right.

"I want the chicken," he told her. When she refused to budge, he groaned. "I want the chicken, *please*."

She used the tongs again to select a breast from the platter. She set it neatly in the center of his plate. "There you are. Now keep the line moving."

"There's no one behind us," he griped. Before she could smack him again, he picked up the serving fork next to the carrots and herded more than necessary onto his plate.

"There's someone you have to meet."

"I don't want to talk to people. I want to dance." He grinned. "I'm taking Kaya onto the dance floor again, soon as I'm done." They had fallen into step together seamlessly. The crowd had split and made room as Everett had found out again how she could answer him move for move and even show him up.

"You should be fixing her a plate, too," Paloma suggested. "The way you two carry on out there, she's going to need it."

"She's already eaten," he replied. He caught Paloma's knowing look. "What?"

"I found a pair of black panties in the upstairs ficus."

He froze, trying hard to look innocent. "They're Eveline's."

"Eveline throws her panties around her and Wolfe's place now," she said, stalking him to the end of the buffet table.

"Luella's then."

"Luella and Ellis moved into the cabin behind the bunkhouse with the girls a month ago," she reminded him, keeping pace easily as he rounded the table to the other side.

He grabbed a roll quickly, fumbling it when it burned him. He caught it, flipped it onto his plate and searched for napkins.

They were behind her. He'd missed them. Cursing, he planted his feet. "I'm thirty-eight years old. I can do what I want with who I want in my own house."

"I'll take it from here, Ms. Coldero."

Paloma subsided, going so far as to smile at the woman who'd decided to intrude. "I warmed him up for you, Darcia. Everett, have you met Ms. Altaha?"

Everett glanced from one woman to the other. The new one had silver-tinged hair. She was less than five feet tall, in his estimation. But her set mouth could raise the hair on a dog's back. Her dark eyes bore into him. He could see her Native heritage in her pronounced cheekbones and her dark skin tone.

The words *It's a trap* flagged across the windscreen of his consciousness. "Altaha," he repeated. "As in…"

"Kaya and Naleen's mother," Paloma supplied helpfully. She smiled as she veered around him. Patting him on the lapel of his Western-cut jacket, she lowered her voice and muttered, "Stand up straight and take it like a man, *mijo*."

Everett cleared his throat as she cleared off, leaving him alone with Kaya's mother. He turned his head on his neck to ease the tension. "It's nice to meet you, ma'am."

She had a stare a mile wide, he discovered when she didn't break it. Everett started to itch around the collar.

"So," Darcia Altaha said, "you're the man who's currently screwing my daughter."

Everett nearly swallowed his tongue. "Ah…not currently. I mean, not right at this second." He cleared his throat louder this time when she only narrowed her eyes.

"I'm no stranger to my daughter's single behavior," Darcia informed him. "She sleeps with men. Sometimes she enjoys them. Sometimes she finds them lacking."

He tried to think of something safe to say and found a minefield instead. "Uh…"

"It seems you're one of the ones she enjoys," Darcia revealed. "You must be very impressive, Mr. Eaton."

"Well, I think—"

Her chin lowered. "You shouldn't finish that thought."

He nodded quickly. "You're right, ma'am. I shouldn't."

"Good man," she said approvingly. "Kaya seems to be enjoying you more than the others."

Everett kept his mouth studiously shut. He was sweating as much as Coldero had before the wedding. If this kept up, he was going to need a change of clothes.

"My youngest daughter, Mr. Eaton," Darcia continued, taking several slow strides toward him, "does not do what she is told. As a child, she was next to impossible."

He felt the beginnings of a treacherous smile warming his face. "Is that right?"

"Kaya is responsible for every gray hair on my head." Her eyes widened for emphasis. "Do you see my head, Mr. Eaton?"

His mouth opened, closed, opened again. "I…think it's very nice."

"It is *covered* in gray."

He thought quickly. "She has a unique effect on people."

"You like to delegate," Darcia said.

He lifted a shoulder. "Sure."

"You're the boss," she went on. "The 'chief,' I believe."

He shook his head. "It's just a title."

"Yes," Darcia granted, "but you are a man accustomed to giving orders and having them followed to the letter."

"Yes, ma'am."

She nodded. "So heed what I tell you. Kaya will not be told what to do. She will not be ordered. She will not follow where others lead. No one delegates to Kaya. She will leave your bed at all hours of the night to put herself in danger, all in the name of law and order. She won't change or be tamed. The moment you try, she will run. This you must know before getting in too deep with my daughter."

He waited for more. When it didn't come, he wet his throat. "Ms. Altaha…"

"You will call me Darcia."

"I will?" When she pursed her lips, he decided, "I will. You can call me Everett, if you like."

"Fine," she granted.

"Your daughter," he said carefully, "is the single most amazing woman I've ever met in my life."

Her arms laced over the front of the beaded, forest green bodice of her dress. "Go on."

"She's powerful," he stated. "Some people may feel threatened by that in a woman, but I find it extremely attractive. She's an exceptional police officer and a far better sheriff than that last one we had here in Fuego. As a friend, you should know she saved my life. As a companion, she's everything a man could want and more."

"Are you everything a woman could want, Everett?" she challenged.

"I hope so, Mrs…er, Darcia. What's more, I hope I'm everything Kaya wants because I'm hers."

He heard it the same time she did. He heard the confession ring with truth. He let out an unsteady breath. "Well. There it is."

Darcia's hand was cool as it twined around his wrist. "It's all right, Everett."

He looked at her, trying to fathom the satisfaction on her face. "How'd you do that?"

"Where do you think my daughter got her interrogation skills?" she asked. "Certainly not from her father."

He let out a breathless laugh. And kept laughing. He was still laughing when he spotted Kaya weaving fast through the crowd to get to them.

"Mom," she said. "Are you playing nice?"

"Of course I am," she said. She smiled at Everett. "If you'll excuse me, I have to go talk to my granddaughter's date."

Everett watched Darcia round the buffet table, still choking on laughter.

"Everett?" Kaya turned him to her. "Are you okay?"

He stopped laughing abruptly. "Your mother scares the hell out of me."

"She left you standing," Kaya considered with a shake of her head. "You must have made a good impression."

He needed a stiff drink. "How does a man survive any of you Altaha women?"

"I've yet to meet the man who does," she explained.

"Is that right?" he asked, measuring.

"Eat up, cattle baron," she said, raising herself to her toes. She brushed a kiss across his cheek. "You owe me a slow one."

I'm hers. He heard it again in his head. Caught between the urge to beeline for the open bar or to fall willingly into her arms like the besotted puppy he was, he trailed her to the dance floor, wishing he'd left the buffet well enough alone.

Chapter 15

Kaya noticed Everett didn't say much after they saw Eveline and Wolfe off. Wolfe had been cleared to leave the country and would be on a plane with his new wife bound for the Caribbean in a matter of hours.

It wasn't until they were gone and the guests had slowly trickled out that Everett grabbed her by the hand and led her into the house.

He didn't say anything as he took off his jacket and toed off his boots upstairs. Well aware that Paloma and other family members were downstairs, she kept quiet, too, as he removed her dress and took her to bed.

The sex wasn't urgent, as it had been before. It felt like something else entirely—not quite soft but crystalline. His rough hands gentled. His strokes were sure but slow. He left the lights off and the windows open so that the desert breeze made the curtains restless and moon beams grazed the sheets.

She didn't realize until after they had both stilled, having rocked each other to climax, that he'd given her something finer than sex—something deeper and far more devastating.

He'd made love to her.

She lay awake thinking about it long after she was sure

he had dozed off. His back was to the window. Moonlight cast his profile into distinction but not his face. She could hear the restful sound of his lungs working. Under her hands, the muscles around his ribs swelled and released, swelled and released in long, languid pulls.

Hesitant, her touch tracked the ladder of his rib cage to his sternum. She felt the little round knot of scar tissue.

She cursed inwardly. He hadn't been touching her. He'd been touching her heart. He'd touched her soul, for crying out loud. He'd looked at her as he'd ushered her over every peak—not watchful and thirsty like last time...

He'd looked at her as if *she'd* brought light to the world.

Everything downstairs had quieted down. In the distance, she could hear coyotes yip and cows low. If she listened closely enough, she could hear the world turn.

He'd split her world in two. He'd broken it like an egg. There was no cleaning up what he'd untapped.

She was done for. It wasn't a comfortable thought. Yet it was a fact and she had to find some way to live with it.

She was going to have to find a way to cope with the strong possibility that she was in love with him.

"What have you done, cattle baron?" she whispered even as she raised her hand into the hair on the back of his head and caressed. She found her lips nestling against the underside of his jaw.

The crack rang out, its report loud. A dog started to howl a split second before the raised pane of the window shattered. Even as Everett jerked awake, Kaya closed her arms around him and rolled as the second shot echoed.

The bullet sang into the wall over their heads as they hit the floor with a jolting thud. "Get down!" she shouted, her hand locked on a hunk of his hair, forcing his head low to the ground. "Stay down!"

The third shot hit the bed. She heard the impact and badly wished for her weapon. Looking around, she saw her beaded handbag where she'd dropped it. Her dress pooled over it.

"Stay," she instructed as she shifted away.

"Where are you going?" he asked, then cursed again as another shot shattered what remained of the glass pane.

"Do as I say, Everett!" She shimmied across the floor, grabbed the bag and took out her phone. She dialed and counted the rings before dispatch picked up. "This is Sheriff Altaha. Shots fired," she reported. "I repeat—shots fired at Eaton Edge. The main house is under fire. Send all available units to this location." She left the line open as she extracted her gun. She found the clip, inserted it in the empty chamber. Using her thumb, she removed the catch and crawled toward the far window.

"Kaya?"

"Stay," she ordered, easing her back against the wall. She stayed out of the slant of light that revealed patterns in the wood flooring. Peering out into the yard, she kept her head clear, in the shadows, both hands gripping her weapon. She worked to slow her breathing, hoping her pulse rate would follow. It raced, walloping her breastbone. Adrenaline surged through her.

She could hear Everett moving around the bed. Knowing he'd left cover did nothing to calm her. Before she could chastise him, another shot rang out, hitting the windows of the room next door to theirs. "Where are the girls?" she asked. "Isla and Ingrid. Where do they sleep?"

"Ellis's house—just over the hill," came his tense answer. He was closer now. "It's Paloma I'm worried about."

She winced as more shots rang out. "There are two shooters," she determined.

"Yeah," he said, listening. "Around the stables."

"Up high," she said. "Is there roof access in the stables?"

"Through Paloma's quarters." Everett made a noise in his throat when the shooting didn't stop. "Kaya. I need to get to her."

"You need to stay where you are," she said.

"The hands. They're all going to come running. Ellis, too. We can't wait for backup. We need to get out there and stop this before my people are killed."

"I don't have visibility," she admitted. "Keep your head down and hand me my dress."

What was worse than walking into a firefight was knowing that Kaya was, too. By the time they made themselves decent and had retrieved his weapon from the safe on the first floor, he realized he was going to have to let her leave the cover of the house.

Paloma greeted them at the door. She fell into Everett's arms.

He smelled her blood before he raised his hand to the one on top of her head. His fingers came away wet and warm. "Those sons of bitches," he hissed, helping her to a seated position on the floor.

"It's not bad," Paloma moaned. "They didn't shoot me. They just knocked me out."

"Put pressure on the wound," Kaya said, handing him a handkerchief.

He covered the gash and pressed. When Paloma gasped, he felt his blood run cold. "I'll kill 'em."

The gunfire hadn't let up. They were hitting the kitchen windows now.

"You go out there," Paloma said, "you're as good as dead. You can't put me through that, *mijo*."

"I'll come back," he promised.

"They've probably got night vision goggles," Kaya deduced as they left through the front of the house. "It's how they knew we were in the room upstairs."

"I shouldn't have left the window open," he realized. As they neared the corner of the house, both gripping their weapons in a two-handed hold, they tensed at the sound of running.

Kaya held up a hand and motioned him back against the wall. They waited a beat, listening.

The sound of a high-pitched whinny split the night a split second before a high-strung colt bolted past in a flurry of hooves. Another followed it at breakneck speed.

"They let the horses out," he growled.

She inched toward the corner, her weapon high. "I need backup to get here. There's light enough to see the roof of the stables, but without cover..."

"I need to get to the barn," he said. At the turn of her head, he went on. "I have to make sure the cattle are secure. Never mind the horses. If they release the herd and open the gates..."

She nodded away the rest. "You go that way. I'll look for a shot."

He gripped her shoulder. It was bare but for the single black strap of her dress. "You be careful, Sheriff Sweetheart."

"You, too," she said before she darted around the side of the house. Everett took off at a run, keeping to the shadows. He ran through the small grove of evenly spaced trees that produced fruit in summer. Grateful for their spring foliage and the cover it provided, he ran hell for leather toward the shape of the barn, hoping his long legs and speed would serve him well.

Someone ran into him headlong. "Hands up!" he yelled.

"It's me," Ellis reported. "What the hell's going on? Who's shooting?"

"Luella. The girls. Are they all right?"

"They're safe," Ellis assured him. "I had her take them into the cellar and lock the door from the inside."

"We need to check the barn," Everett barked. He could hear sirens in the distance. They were closing in. The gunfire still hadn't let up. He thought of Kaya and wanted to scream. "They let the horses go."

"I hear them," Ellis told him. "I can go around the cabins, get farther out of range and make my way around. The men should be over that way, too. They'll help."

"Don't do anything stupid," Everett said, even as he moved in the direction of the stables.

"Hang on, where're you going?" Ellis called after him.

"Kaya's out there," Everett said, pointing. "I gotta—"

Ellis waved off the rest. "Go, then! Go!"

Everett bolted, running toward gunfire. The lights of police vehicles lit the night as he broke free of the trees and crouched low, closing the distance between the grove and the house.

There were holes in the tents on the patio. They flapped, loose, and snapped in the breeze. He followed what he hoped was Kaya's path from table to table. He ducked underneath the empty buffet table. His gaze seized on the front of the house. It gaped at the windows. There was little glass left for the moonlight to bounce off.

There was fear riding underneath the beat of his blood. But anger swelled beneath it, all but incinerating. His father's house, his family's land…his woman.

Pressing his lips together, he eyed the distance between him and the open gate. There was nothing but the night between him and the truck parked on the other side of it.

He took a long, deep breath before taking off like a runner at the starting gun.

Kaya could smell animal. And not just the horses.

She found a decent position behind the water trough and near the fence in the first corral. She kept herself still as she searched the roofline. She ducked back down after counting one, two shapes against the hard slant of moonlight.

Bastards had chosen a three-quarter moon to do their bidding.

Breathing carefully, she eased her weapon around the side of the trough. She peered down the length of the barrel, aiming for the first figure...

The sound of a snort reached her ears. Her finger froze on the trigger as the hairs on the back of her neck stood on end.

She looked over her shoulder.

The bull was huge. Its head was low. She saw the glint of its horns. It struck one hoof against the ground. Dust rose in a plume.

It lowed at the sound of gunfire and shifted, restless. More scared and uncertain than anything, it was lost among the maze of open gates and fences. But Kaya knew she was the only threat it had been able to pick apart from the dark landscape.

Caught between the trough and the open corral, she had nothing but her Glock to stop it if it charged.

It pawed the ground again, bellowing.

"Walk away, big boy," she coaxed under her breath as she raised the weapon. "Just walk away..." She felt a bead of sweat roll from her hairline to her cheek.

A shout split the night. "Hey!" And another, longer. "Heeeeeey!"

Kaya and the bull looked out to pasture and saw the tall figure with arms spread. "No," she moaned. Then louder, "No, no!"

The bull charged Everett. Kaya didn't hesitate. Knowing the gunmen had heard the shout and had made Everett, she raised the gun over the edge of the trough, sighted and squeezed off a round, then another.

She saw the gunman crumple. The second ducked out of sight.

Lowering her head once more, she searched the corral for Everett and the bull. When she saw nothing but grass waving in the wind, she tried not to panic. Shouts of "Police!" and "Drop your weapons!" reached her. She wished for a radio so that she could communicate with her deputies.

Scanning the roofline, she couldn't locate the second figure.

He was on the move.

The stable doors yawned wide. She stood and propelled herself toward the opening.

A man's silhouette appeared in the doorway. She took him down on a running leap at the knees.

A shot went off from his gun before he clattered to the floor.

The man reached for his weapon, but she kicked it out of reach. She grappled with him, going right up against his cloud of day-old sweat. He was big, strong and fought well.

She was a hair quicker. She punched him in the teeth. She hit him harder in the solar plexus. The fist to the groin made him wither.

"Turn over," she instructed. "Put your hands behind your back. Do it!"

When Deputy Wyatt arrived with the cuffs, she had her hands locked around the suspect's wrists. "Second shooter's on the roof," she told him, taking the cuffs he removed from his belt. She secured the attacker's hands behind his back.

"On it," he said. Using a flashlight, he moved into the dark stables, radioing for Root to follow.

"Don't move," she told the gunman, patting his pockets. She found more ammo clips and a flashlight but no wallet or identification.

"Kaya."

She glanced up and found Everett. After picking up the shooter's weapon and unloading it, she stood. "You're okay."

His eyes raced over her. "You?"

"I'm all right," she said. "The others?"

"Ellis," he said in answer.

"He's down?" she asked, alarmed.

He shook his head. "He and the hands are securing the barn."

Relief washed over her. She took a moment to run her gaze across his face and torso a few times. He was dirty and mussed, his hair not at all neat without his hat. She wanted to shove him back a step with both hands. She wanted to gather him to her and hold on until all the little fears…all the what-might-have-beens ceased to exist. "Stupid," she pushed out because she couldn't stop seeing him out in the open waving his hands and shouting like an idiot. It had made her choke with fear. "You were *so stupid*, Everett."

His brows came together. He took a step toward her.

Deputy Root arrived. "Wyatt has the second gunman in

custody," he reported, panting from running. "Says he's got an ID."

"Paloma Coldero is injured inside the house," Kaya stated. "We need to get her checked out."

"An officer's with her now," Root informed them. "She's conscious. They called for a bus, just to be sure."

She helped the suspect to his feet. He had high shoulders and a long face. "You're under arrest. Might as well tell us who you are."

"Fat chance," he grunted, then spit on the ground at her feet.

When Everett whipped forward, Root stopped him. "Take it easy," the deputy cautioned.

"I know you," Everett said, pointing at the gunman. "I've seen you—out at The RC Resort. You work security for True Claymore."

Kaya pulled on the attacker's arm until he faced the moon. Root helped by shining a light in his eyes. Her lips parted. Everett was right. She'd seen the man with the mayor, too.

He was one of the goons who had replaced her roadside attacker from years ago.

"He sent you here, didn't he?" Everett asked, struggling against Root's restraining arm. "This is payback for what I did to his car."

"Don't know what you're talking about," the shooter grunted, lowering his head and closing his eyes because the light in them was too much.

Kaya turned to look back at the house. True Claymore wouldn't be reckless enough to order his men to do something as drastic as this, would he?

Or had the good mayor reached the end of his rope?

Chapter 16

The long drive to The RC Resort might have been scenic if not for the sick taste on Kaya's tongue. It was always with her when she made the trip to Claymore's homestead.

Next to her, Agent Rutland shrugged out of his sport coat and checked the weapon holstered on his belt. "What's the plan, Sheriff?"

She frowned as the ranch house came into view. It was resplendent against a barren desert backdrop. "You're letting my department take the lead on this?"

"As it was you Claymore's hired men nearly shot through an open window, that's fair, I'd say."

Kaya swallowed, tasted bile and lowered her head so the brim of her hat covered whatever emotions were riding high in her eyes. If she was emotional, she couldn't be clearheaded. And she needed to be clearheaded.

She'd sworn she would be the one to lock True Claymore up. She had evidence—enough that she'd been able to secure a warrant. She had the gunmen's confessions. They'd resisted questioning at first, but Rutland had looked at their banking records. A recent bonus of ten grand a piece from their employer had seemed timely.

Everett and Ellis had found the gunmen's horses a half mile away from the barn while rounding up the misplaced horses and few escaped cattle. Their saddlebags had been packed enough for a week's sojourn.

If Kaya and her team hadn't apprehended them, they would be in the wind at this point.

A breath filtered slowly through her nose as she slowed to make the turn under the arch welcoming them to The RC Resort & Spa. "He had to have known the shooting would lead back to him sooner than later. He'll be ready."

"You think he'll make a stand?" Rutland asked cautiously as she eased the sheriff's all-terrain vehicle to a stop in the parking lot. There were a dozen other cars.

Kaya frowned at the shuttle van. It wasn't the same model Claymore's goons had removed her in years ago. But it sickened her to see it, nonetheless. She unbuckled her seat belt and scanned the entrance to the house. "His wife's a lawyer. She normally talks him out of trouble. My bet is he'll hide behind her. If he's desperate enough to fight…" She heard more than saw the second police vehicle ease to a stop behind hers. "…we'll take him down."

"Sheriff," Rutland said before she could open the door.

She glanced. The lines of his face gave her pause.

He inclined his head. "We don't have proof he had anything to do with those bodies on the mountain."

"Not yet," she added.

"Be careful," he advised. "Don't make this personal. If he killed your friend, Mescal, we'll dig deeper. We'll find the truth."

How did she tell him that the anger she felt—the almost blind rage—wasn't about Sawni, for once? It was about Everett.

She hadn't been alone in the crosshairs. Everett's body had been between the open window and her. She'd learned not to think too long about what might have been if the gunmen hadn't missed that first shot.

The texture of the bullet wound on his sternum came to her clearly, as if she were touching it now. She opened the door to the vehicle. The taste in her mouth now burned in her throat. She planted her hand on her belt and waited for Root and Wyatt to join them. "We're here to bring in the mayor," she reminded them. "If you have any problem with that, I'd advise you to wait outside."

"We're with you, Sheriff," Wyatt vowed. To his right, Root nodded.

She scanned them and felt a swell of pride. As a deputy herself, she'd learned to work with them and trust them. As one of the people responsible for Sheriff Jones's fall from grace, she hadn't thought she'd earn their loyalty as sheriff—not right away.

They'd proven their loyalty a dozen times over the last few weeks. They were the best of men. "Follow my lead," she said quietly before heading them and Rutland to the big front doors. She ignored the old-fashioned bellpull that acted as doorbell and knocked in a series of raps. "Sheriff's department," she called clearly. When no one answered, she rapped again.

The sound of the latch grinding put Kaya on alert. She forced herself to relax, outwardly. As the door parted from the jamb, she felt Root tense next to her.

The round face of a housekeeper greeted them, her face riddled with confusion. "*Hola?*" she said haltingly.

Kaya responded in Spanish. "*Buen día.* We're looking for True Claymore. *Está él en casa?*"

She shook her head quickly. "*No, no está aquí.*"

Kaya peered over the housekeeper's shoulder. There

was no one in the foyer that she could discern. "Do you know where he is?"

The housekeeper hesitated for a brief second before shaking her head. "No."

Kaya scrutinized her. She looked worried. "What about Annette Claymore? Is she home?"

The woman bit her lip. She glanced over her shoulder, then shook her head.

Rutland shifted forward slightly. "We have a warrant. Open the door, ma'am, so we can search the premises."

At the housekeeper's knitted brow, Kaya quickly translated. Still, the woman didn't open. "*Por favor*," Kaya added. *Don't protect them. It's not worth it.*

Slowly, the housekeeper gave in. The door opened and she stepped back. Kaya swept in. She nodded to the left and Wyatt went to search the dining room and kitchen. With a motion, she sent Root to do the same in the common area and spa rooms.

"What's back there?" Rutland asked, approaching the back of the house.

"Office," she said grimly. Guests weren't allowed in that part of the house. But she'd gone there anyway once, looking for evidence linking the Claymores to Sawni's disappearance...

"I'll look there," Rutland said.

"I'll sweep the upstairs." She moved in that direction.

At the landing, she began checking doors. The guests that had checked in were out riding or walking the nearby nature trail or shopping in town. The rooms were empty. She located True and Annette's master suite. The fur rugs and grand four-poster bed put her ill at ease. Drawers on the bureau were open. The closet, too, was open with clothes on the floor. There was no sign of a struggle. The bathroom counter was empty.

Where were the creams? The soaps? The lotions?

Kaya frowned as she traced her steps back into the bedroom, across the bear rug. Glass doors opened onto an expansive balcony.

Her radio chirped as she unlatched them. "Sheriff?"

She parted the radio from her belt and brought it to her mouth. "Go ahead."

Rutland answered. "Office has been swept. The desk and file cabinet are empty. The safe is open. There's nothing left."

"He knew we were coming," she replied. From the balcony, she could see the Claymore spread. The little chapel off to the left. The barn used for weddings and dances. Stables to the right.

She could see Root striding off to search the latter. "Who tipped them off?" It was no secret the Claymores had friends in high places. Could it have been the judge? Worse, someone in Kaya's office? "We need to put out a BOLO on True Claymore. It looks like Annette may have left with him."

Root's voice carried through the channel. "Sheriff, you want to get down to the stables."

"Did you find something?" she asked, hurrying back through the parted glass doors.

"The mayor's horse is missing."

She pushed herself forward, leaving the suite. "His horse?"

"The groom said he left on horseback before daybreak," Root replied. "He said he didn't pack light."

"Damn," she uttered, breaking into a run on the stairs.

* * *

The manhunt for True Claymore was the biggest mounted search in Fuego County in five years. But then, it wasn't every day a mayor went missing.

Everett pulled back on the reins, urging Crazy Alice into a walk. "Whoa, girl," he murmured. "Whoa." He patted her neck before swinging to the ground. They'd been out since first light, searching the area north from the Edge to The RC Resort.

Most likely, Claymore would have headed east and there were a dozen or more riders searching the state park area for signs of the man and his horse.

Everett and his team had been mobilized in the southwest quarter of the search area. The border overlapped Eaton territory. His men were spread over the hilly, mountainous region that circled Ol' Whalebones.

Everett led Crazy Alice to the edge of the river. It was shallow at the foot of Mount Elder. As his horse drank, Everett took his canteen off his belt and did the same. The sun had been hot on his back and he'd found no indication that Claymore and his mount had come this way.

He'd been disappointed when Kaya had placed him in charge of the lower region. She knew how much he wanted Claymore's hide. Being the one to find him would have been more than satisfying.

But he was still raw enough—still furious enough— to hurt the mayor for his part in the Eaton House attack. Paloma was still in the hospital. The doctors had assured him it was just for observation purposes, but Everett's gut twisted at the implications. Eveline had come back early to sit by her bedside with Luella. Wolfe had joined the search. He'd been assigned to the team in the northeast quadrant, likely due to his superior tracking skills.

And he was levelheaded enough that he wouldn't throttle Claymore when he found him.

No. Wolfe would bring him in nice and easy. Everett twisted the lid back on the canteen and sniffed, scanning the sky. No birds of prey circled. A hawk kited high on a draft, peering beadily at him.

Crazy Alice lifted her head. She turned it downwind and stilled. Her ribs lifted as she took as exaggerated breath, smelling.

Everett heard her tail swish. Her head arched high and she sidestepped toward him. He laid his hand on her withers. "What is it, girl?" he whispered, stroking in soothing circles. Her breath had quickened. He could feel the tension in her muscles. "What do you smell?"

Sounds carried in valleys. Everett strained to hear over the burbling of the river on the rocks. He heard the chirp of a bird. Then whistling.

The fine hairs on the back of his arms rose. Just like that, his horse's tension was his own. He locked his legs to keep from sidestepping, too. Under the brim of his hat, he searched the slopes of Mount Elder, scanning the sagebrush and boulders.

An eerie scream broke the quiet. It reverberated off the cliffs. Crazy Alice jumped and whinnied.

He grabbed the reins. "Easy, girl," he said, trying to stay calm. His rifle was in the sheath on her saddle. His boots skimmed across the ground as she dragged him with her in retreat. "Easy, girl. Easy."

Her head bobbed. She jerked the reins, but she stilled long enough for him to remove his weapon.

Common sense told him to head in the opposite direction, farther upriver where Claymore lands bisected the Edge. That was where Crazy Alice would flee. She knew as well as Everett they were in the heart of Tombstone's territory.

He clambered up rockfall, trying to reach high ground. He found a position in the shadow of a ledge. The valley spread out beneath him. He didn't need his binoculars to see the lion or its prey.

The horse was down. It lay on its side near the point where rock met river. If it had made it to water, it had died shortly after. There was a pool of blood under its head but no discernable tears in its flank.

The big cat had positioned itself on the cliff on the other side of the water. It yowled and paced, restless. Everett reached into the flap of his shirt and lifted his binoculars. Close up, he saw the lean body lines and the grimacing face with one eye missing.

Everett forced himself to take a moment. Sweat ran from his hairline. He inhaled for a full four seconds. Then he pushed it out, letting his lungs empty. Tombstone was not the harbinger of death and despair Everett associated him with. He was a predator with greater longevity or luck than others in the wild. Sighting him wasn't detrimental to Everett's family, as he'd feared in the past.

That was what common sense said. His stomach cramped, however. The last time he'd seen Tombstone this close—this clearly—his mother and stepsister had come to a horrible end. In some twisted way, Everett had felt responsible.

If he hadn't volunteered to go into Tombstone's territory that day to check the Wapusa's swollen banks after a week's rain and flooding, a part of him was convinced there wouldn't have been a fire across town at Coldero Ridge and his mother and half sister would still be alive.

He hadn't been close to his mother, Josephine. They

hadn't even been on speaking terms when she died. But she was his mother, and that little girl he'd barely known, Angel, still haunted his dreams.

He had to slow down his exhalations until they were twice as long as his inhales, a technique he'd learned in therapy over the last year. He did this until his heart no longer felt like a racing hare. It helped to visualize himself calm. He dropped his shoulders. He couldn't close his eyes to imagine his body relaxing but he worked to forge that mental picture nonetheless and felt his focus sharpening.

No doubt Tombstone would smell his fear over the dead horse if Everett didn't get it well enough in hand.

He changed focus, shifting his view to the horse again. Through the binoculars, he saw no saddle or bags, but the description matched that of True Claymore's mount—the one he'd escaped with in the early hours of yesterday morning.

Everett lowered the binocs to take the radio from his belt. It was slippery in his hold. Mashing down the call button, he said quietly, "This is team three leader. Sheriff, do you copy?"

It took a moment for static to hiss, then he heard Kaya's voice. It steadied him. "Go ahead, team three."

"I've got a dead horse at the base of Mount Elder where it meets the river. Over."

Tombstone's yowling filled the radio silence before Kaya answered back. "Recently deceased?"

"Affirmative," he replied. "Tombstone got here first, but something's holding him up. He won't approach."

"Are you safe?"

He heard the thread of discord in her voice and lifted the radio to his mouth again. "I'm hiding out across the valley. He doesn't know I'm here."

"Hold your position," she told him. "I'll be there in twenty. Any sign of the suspect?"

"Negative," Everett said, searching the valley again. "If it is his horse, he took the saddle and bags."

"Copy. Everett?"

"Yeah?" he said, knowing this was an open channel.

"Shoot if you have to."

It sounded better than any profession of love he'd ever heard. "I'll see you in twenty, Sheriff. Over."

Everett secured the radio, checked his rifle and hunkered down to wait.

Tombstone's frenzied pacing stopped. He leaped from the ledge and down a series of boulders, head low, body tensed, picking up speed.

Everett braced himself as the cougar charged the corpse.

A shot rang out. Between the cliff walls, it was deafening. The lion doubled back, screaming its displeasure.

Another gunshot followed, then a third.

Tombstone retreated, disappearing in the bend of cliff walls and river rocks in full flight.

Everett stayed where he was, keeping his head down. He had another ten minutes before Kaya's arrival.

Someone was protecting the horse's body.

If it was indeed Claymore's horse…

Everett used the rifle's scope to comb every inch of the valley below.

He didn't spot the shooter. But he had no line of sight directly beneath his position where an outcropping offered a respite from the sun.

Cautiously, he straightened slowly to standing. He kept his rifle up, his finger near the trigger as he crept along the slope. He veered around the rockfall. Any loose rock would tumble and alert the shooter to his presence. On firmer ground, he made his way down.

The horse's eyes were locked in a vacant stare. They had gone cloudy. There was a gunshot wound on its crown. Everett scanned its legs and saw the break in the back left. He could smell the decay. With the sun beating down on it and the blood drying, he estimated the horse's time of death to have been sometime in the night.

The gunman's position was right underneath him. Everett inched forward, easing to ground level out of the cave's line of sight. He pressed his back to the mountain, gripping the rifle in hands that were steadier now that Tombstone had retreated. He swallowed once before calling out. "How's it going, Claymore?"

A pause. Then, "Goddamn it, Eaton."

"Toss out your weapon where I can see it," Everett advised. "Don't make me come in there. I want you to walk out. Nice and easy."

"That'd be a fine thing." True's voice was tight. "But I'm not walking anywhere. Goliath broke my damn leg when he fell on it."

Everett's brows lifted under his hatband. "What about Annette? Is she injured?"

"What are you talking about?" True barked. "Annette's not with me."

"Don't lie to me, True," Everett growled.

"I'm telling the truth. Last I saw her, she was screaming at me to man up, stay at the resort where she could protect me. Woman never understood anything. When you're licked, you're licked. That's what my daddy used to say. He left, too. When the Feds came to get him for tax evasion, he made his exodus. He disappeared on horseback. His mount wandered back to us a week later. Nobody ever found any sign of him. Authorities told me he was as good as dead, but he was as hard as iron by that point. Indestructible. He's living on some beach in Mexico to this day."

True was rambling. Everett's frown deepened. "Your weapon. Throw it out where I can see it."

"Ah, hell," True muttered. "What have I got to lose?"

Everett heard the rifle bolt as it unlocked. The cartridges clinked as True emptied the chamber. The slow repetition of the bolt clicking assured Everett that the man was checking the chamber to ensure it was empty. The gold cartridges flashed in the sunlight as he threw them onto the rocks of the riverbed where they bounced and laid still. The rifle followed with a clatter.

Everett eased away from the wall. "Show me your hands," he directed as he swung into the opening, muzzle forward.

True raised his palms obediently. They were empty.

Everett scanned him, kicking the rifle farther from the low opening of the cave. Everett bent over slightly and watched True wave insolently as he sagged against a boulder. His legs splayed in front of him. The left turned outward.

Everett narrowed his eyes. "You got yourself in a state."

"You don't say," True remarked.

"That there's a compound fracture," Everett said. "Must be in a lot of pain."

True's face was flushed like a beet. His breathing wasn't right. It was rapid and ragged. Still, he tilted his head and scanned Everett. "I thought you'd be happier."

"I'd have been happy to find you on your feet."

"You'd have preferred *The Good, the Bad and the Ugly* with me standing on one side of the street and you on the other," True said. He let out a wheezing laugh. "You and my old man have a lot in common. He used to tell me he shot a man in Reno. He said Johnny Cash wrote that song about him. 'Just to watch him die,' he would sing when he'd had too much."

"Why did you flee south?" Everett asked. "That was stupid."

"Was it?" True asked, squinting. "I thought everybody'd be looking in the other direction. State lands. Or farther. Jicarilla territory. Nobody'd expect me to go near that mountain over there."

Everett knew what mountain he was talking about. "Did you kill the boy and those women?"

"You'd like that, wouldn't you?"

"I'd like to see you drawn and quartered after what those men did to Paloma and Eaton House," Everett told him.

"Hey, at least my guys let you and the sheriff finish first," True said. "I wouldn't have been so generous. They're the superstitious sort—assume it's bad luck to interrupt a man while he's laying his pipe."

The muscles in Everett's jaw ground against bone. He saw the horse's saddle propped behind True. He saw the saddlebags. Despite the agony the mayor was in, if True kept running his mouth, Everett was liable to get trigger-happy.

Where are you, Kaya?

"You want to kill me," True guessed. "Take your shot."

Everett found his finger inside the trigger guard. He pressed his lips together. "I won't be the one who puts you out of your misery," he muttered through his teeth.

"Don't be washed up like your old man," True barked at him. "Come on, Eaton. Shoot me!"

"No," Everett barked back. An eye for an eye was fine.

He believed in such things. But before True had been his enemy, he'd been Kaya's.

He wouldn't be the one to kill Kaya's justice. He couldn't.

The sounds of horses reached his ears. He looked around and saw Ghost slowing to cross the river. He and Kaya were leading Crazy Alice on a lead rope.

"Did you lose this?" she called as the horses' legs splashed across the Wapusa.

"I got him," Everett said and watched her shoulders go high.

Kaya nickered to Ghost, bringing him to a stop on the shore. She dismounted. "Tombstone?"

"He ran off," Everett told her. "I got *him*."

She closed the distance. Peering into the cave, she stilled.

True grimaced at her. "Howdy, Sheriff."

She didn't breathe. Everett fought the urge to touch her. "What do you want to do?"

Her gaze crawled back to his. "You didn't kill him."

He ignored the surprise.

Her lips seamed and for a brief flash her dark eyes deepened.

He eyed her mouth. "He's yours."

She blinked several times. "I need to call the chopper. He needs treatment. I have a first aid kit on my saddle…"

He lowered the rifle. "I'll get it."

She grabbed him as he started moving. "Everett," she whispered. When he stopped, she said, "Thank you."

"Later," he promised then moved off to retrieve her kit.

Chapter 17

With True Claymore in the hospital, Rutland and Kaya were unable to question him until he was out of sedation.

Annette Claymore hadn't been seen in over twenty-four hours. Part of her wardrobe had been removed from the master suite closet at The RC Resort. Her suitcase was missing as well as much of her jewelry.

Other than several thousand dollars in cash, they hadn't found the remaining contents of the office safe on True Claymore or in his saddlebags. Their housekeeper had reported that she had seen stacks of cash in the safe while cleaning.

Annette had taken her own exodus. Hers didn't have anything to do with Western glory, like True's. Kaya had a feeling her idea of escape was far more comfortable than riding off into the sunset.

"She doesn't have family in Fuego," Kaya explained to Rutland as she parked in front of Huck Claymore's house. "She's from Colorado and still has family there. But she's smart. She knows better than to go to the first place any investigator would look."

"If that tracks," Rutland said as they alighted from her sheriff's vehicle, "why would she come here?"

"She and Huck are close, from what I understand," Kaya

said, leading the way to the pretty two-story house on Fourth Street where the reverend had resided since taking up the position in the church two blocks away. "He may know something."

Rutland knocked over a small, stone statuette of a praying angel on her knees. He cursed and stopped to right it, then continued to the door.

Kaya's knees locked. All she could see was the angel and the others in the garden of various sizes and expressions on their knees.

On her knees.

Sawni had died on her knees. So had Bethany. Miller Higgins, too, and the oldest woman who had yet to be identified.

She fought a shiver. Hearing Rutland's knock on the door, she moved to his side.

"You all right, Sheriff?" Rutland asked, brows gathered together.

"Fine," she said with a shake of her head. "Just…odd feeling, is all."

The door opened before he could respond. Huck Claymore appeared, a look of vague surprise on his face. "Sheriff Altaha," he greeted, buttoning the cuff of his plain, white collared shirt. It was wrinkled around the shoulders, Kaya noticed. She'd never seen him anything but perfectly pressed. Come to think of it, she'd never seen him outside his robes or his pressed suit. The shirt collar was open at his throat, as if he'd just started dressing. It was five o'clock in the afternoon. "What can I do for you?"

"I'm sorry to bother you, reverend," Kaya said evenly. "I'm sure you've heard about your brother."

He nodded quickly. "Yes. Most unfortunate."

"Unfortunate that he's injured?" Rutland questioned. "Or unfortunate that he was found?"

The reverend peered at him innocently. "Unfortunate that he felt it necessary to flee in the first place instead of taking responsibility for his crimes. I was just changing so that I could visit him at the hospital. My brother may be misguided. But even misguided men need counsel."

Kaya lifted her chin. "Of course. We won't take up too much of your time. You've heard also, I assume, that your sister-in-law, Annette, is still missing."

He stepped out of the house, closing the door behind him. Bowing his head, he gave a nod. "I have heard that, yes, and I'm concerned about her. Greatly concerned."

"Why?" Rutland asked. "By all accounts, it appears that she, too, tried to flee."

"Annette had nothing to do with what happened at Eaton House. Those were my brother's men. They answer to him, not her."

"Then why would she leave?" Rutland wanted to know.

"Perhaps she feared my brother," Huck weighed. "Perhaps he thinks she knows too much about his criminal affairs and she felt she had no choice but to disappear."

"Do you know something about his criminal history that we don't, reverend?" Rutland pressed.

Huck shook his head. "The only thing I have, Agent Rutland, are my suspicions."

"Can you tell us more about those?" Kaya asked.

He glanced over their heads at the street. There were children playing on the sidewalk, a couple walking a dog and several neighbors sitting on porches or puttering around their gardens. "Now isn't the time or place. My brother's expecting me."

"Has your brother ever mentioned the bodies on the mountain?" Rutland asked.

Huck blanched. His lips trembled slightly before he pressed them together. "I don't think so."

"May we search the premises?" Rutland asked, taking a step forward, crowding Huck into his own door.

"Why would you need to search my house?" Huck asked, holding his ground. He was a big man, nearly a head taller than Rutland.

"You and your sister-in-law have a close relationship," Rutland explained. "It seems she may have confided in you. You fear for her safety. It isn't a stretch to assume that you are concerned enough—that you care enough—to let her hide out here from her husband, if necessary."

"But I told you I haven't seen her." Huck looked to Kaya for help. "Sheriff, this is superfluous."

Kaya thought about it. *He closed the door when he came out onto the porch.* Her pulse quickened. Rutland was right. "It'll only take a moment, reverend. Then we'll be out of your hair."

Disappointment tracked across his strong features. His jaw firmed. He shook his head. "I'm sorry. Without a warrant, I cannot let you in. I'm well within my rights to say so."

Kaya took a beat, then nodded. "You are."

"We'll be back with that warrant," Rutland told him as he stepped back slowly. "Have a nice evening."

She waited until they were back inside the car. "He's hiding something."

Rutland buckled his seat belt. "I'd bet my salary Annette Claymore is inside that house."

"If he's that concerned about her safety," Kaya said, pulling away from the curb, "he'll have her moved before a warrant is secure." She waited until she'd safely steered around a clutch of boys dribbling and passing a basketball to one another on the street before she smacked the steering wheel with the heel of her hand. "He knows something about what happened on Ol' Whalebones. I knew there was a connection to the murders and the Claymores."

"And I told you to drop it." Rutland's hand curled into a fist as he brought it to his mouth. "I was wrong." He met her gaze as she pulled up to the stop sign. "I'm sorry, Kaya."

She gave a slight nod. "I'll need to call the judge—the same one that got us the warrant for True's arrest."

"Getting a warrant for a small-town mayor is one thing," Rutland weighed. "Getting one for a minister may be more difficult. Say we find her. We need to hold her. She either fears for her life in regard to her husband or…"

"Or she's hiding because she has information or she had some part in his wrongdoing," she finished. "We have to take Annette into either protective or police custody before she leaves New Mexico."

Everett sat at Paloma's bedside. She was sleeping soundly, but he couldn't unsee the bandage wrapped around her head or what the wound had looked like before EMTs had arrived at Eaton Edge the night of the attack.

She looked white against the sheets. His hand held the lower half of his face as he watched the regular peaks and valleys of her vitals on the screen on the far side of the bed.

Someone touched his shoulder. He looked around to see Luella. Her smile wavered, but she gave it nonetheless. She gave so few smiles that he knew the gesture was heartfelt.

Coming to his feet, he faced her. "She's sleeping. The

doctor says she can go home tomorrow. She's starting to give orders. I suspect they're eager to see the back of her."

"Her vitals are strong. She's doing well. The doctor's right to let her go home and rest where she's more comfortable."

Luella had been a trauma nurse at this hospital before false rumors of her wrongdoing had led to her firing. Everett knew they'd offered the job back to her after her exoneration at the start of the year, but she'd refused. She and Eveline had started Ollero Creek Rescue, instead.

He struggled to trust those in the medical profession and always had, but he trusted her to the bone. "So you're taking the late shift?"

"Yes," she said. "There's something you should know. Ellis told me not to tell you, but that feels wrong."

"What?" he asked, tensing automatically.

She lowered her voice. "True Claymore is being held on the floor beneath this one. He's under heavy guard but is no longer sedated and may even be transferred sometime tomorrow."

Everett took a long breath in through the nose. He rolled his shoulders.

"You can't go near him," she told him in no uncertain terms. "But I felt you had a right to know."

He nodded, then lifted his hand to her shoulder and squeezed. He looked at Paloma. "Take care of her 'til I get back."

"You know I will," she assured him. "But I can handle the morning's shift, too. If you're not going to work, you should see the girls. Have breakfast with them and Ellis. It'll be good for all of you."

He smiled. "Aside from Isla and Ingrid, you're the best

thing that ever happened to my brother. You're good for his girls, too. You're good for all of us."

Her eyes widened. "That may be the nicest thing you've ever said—to anyone."

He shifted from one foot to the other, uncomfortable. "I guess weddings make me sentimental. I'll get over it."

"I don't think it's the wedding that's changed you," she considered.

"Hmm," he muttered when he saw the knowing look on her face. "Would you be willing to take the fall for some black panties Paloma found in the upstairs ficus?"

"That depends," she considered. "What'll you owe me for it?"

He laughed, then quieted himself quickly when Paloma stirred. "Don't marry my brother. You're too good for him."

"It's too late for me," she told him. "And, from what I hear, maybe somebody else I know, too."

He thought of Kaya and released a heavy breath. "I'll get back to you on that, Lu."

"Everett?" she asked as he retreated. When he turned back, she added, "You told me not to wait too long to tell Ellis what I wanted. Don't wait too long to tell Kaya, either."

"I don't know what she wants," he admitted. It sounded plaintive and he regretted it instantly.

"Still," she cautioned, "take it from someone who knows. Life doesn't wait. And these things…they slip away if you're not careful."

He stared back at her mutely before he shifted toward the door again and left.

Kaya stepped off the elevator on the second floor of Fuego County Hospital. She nodded to the guard posted there. "Officer Pettry."

"Sheriff," the young cop returned.

"Everything okay here?" she asked.

"Quiet," he replied. "No activity other than Mr. Eaton arriving about half an hour ago."

"Eaton," she parroted. "Which one?"

"The older one," he said.

Her shoes slapped against the linoleum floor in rapid succession as she rounded the corner to the corridor where Claymore's recovery room was located. She spotted the second officer, Logan, on the door and Everett leaning against the opposite whitewashed wall. As she closed in, Logan glanced over. At her questioning brow, he nodded slightly to show nothing was amiss.

Breathing a little easier, Kaya slowed. "Officer Logan," she said and watched Everett flinch out of the corner of her eye. "Anything to report?"

"Everything's good here, Sheriff Altaha," Logan replied diligently. "Though I hear the mayor's in a good deal of pain."

"Thank you for taking the late shift," she told him before pivoting to face the man against the wall. At the sight of his heavy eyes, she tilted her head. "Everett. What are you doing here?"

He glanced over her head at Logan. His jaw hardened a bit before his eyes returned to her face, weary. "I was visiting Paloma."

"Did you get lost?" she asked, letting amusement ease the question.

Perhaps he was too tired because emotions filed across the windows of his eyes and her heart stumbled in reaction. When his mouth remained stubbornly closed, she turned back to Logan. "Five minute break?" she asked. "I can man the door."

Logan nodded. "Thank you, sir."

She waited until he'd rounded the corner and she and Everett were by themselves in the corridor. "What's wrong, cattle baron?" she asked.

He took a breath to gather himself, unable to meet her eye now. "Since I took over the Edge last summer, I've nearly lost my sister to a madman. We've had a holdup at headquarters. One sheriff turned against us. We've found four bodies on the mountain. My men have been investigated and scrutinized, I've been suspected of murder, my brother-in-law was booked for it, two gunmen attacked Eaton House and the woman I'd call Mom if she'd let me is in the hospital. It hasn't been a year, and that's what's happened on my watch."

Kaya's lips parted as she watched the agony bleed through everything else. She shook her head quickly. "There's been a wedding at Eaton House. An incredible wedding. And there will be another soon. Two new beginnings. Eveline and Wolfe will start a family before the end of the year, from what I'm told. And through all of that, your family and your men haven't gone anywhere. They're more loyal to you than ever. Every single one of them vouched for you when Rutland investigated. Did you know that? And Paloma's going to be okay, Everett. She's okay. You are not responsible for all the negative things that have happened."

"I'm head of the family," he stated. "I'm chief of operations. Of course it's my responsibility."

"You carry too much on yourself," she accused. "Your father did that, too. He bore too much and died too soon. And don't you dare try to tell me one had nothing to do with the other."

Everett didn't say anything. His eyes circled her face instead, thoughtful even if his mouth was grim.

She couldn't help herself. She touched him while they were alone in the corridor, just them two. Sliding her hands from his elbows to his shoulders, she used her thumbs to massage where tension had sunk down deep. His chest lifted with his chin and his dark eyelashes closed halfway. His brow knitted and she could see everything he carried—every burden and worry.

She shook her head. "What is it you're afraid of?"

It took him a moment to answer. His eyes had closed completely. "I can't lose anyone else. I don't have what it takes."

A strong man admitting he wasn't strong enough was a powerful thing. She pulled him into her embrace, wrapping him tight until his face was in her hair, his front pressed to hers and her hands spread across the long, warm line of his back. "It's okay," she whispered, as compelled by the embrace as she was. With his arms circling her waist and the enduring chord of strength humming beneath his skin, she felt small and soft but also like she could take on ten men.

Together, they could take on the world. The certainty was scary and thrilling. It called to the person she was underneath the sheriff's uniform—the person he'd recognized from the moment all this had started between them.

She wavered, letting her palms come up to meet his shoulders again. "I have to question True now that he's awake."

He turned his face away. "I've got to get back."

She let him back away and hated the distance. What she wouldn't give to take him home to her own bed. "You should get some rest before work. There's still time before dawn."

"I'll keep, sweetheart," he said as he headed down the corridor, his hat brim low.

She watched him go and felt her brows arch. *Take care of yourself, cattle baron. Someone loves you.*

If she weren't such a coward, she'd shout it at his back. She'd known she loved him when she'd found True Claymore alive. Everett had wanted revenge. He believed in Old Western justice. He'd proved that many times. The mayor had Paloma's blood on his hands and Everett had needed vendetta for it.

But he'd handed True over to her, unharmed—a gift she'd never forget.

Pushing through the door to Claymore's room, she gauged the man's condition. His leg was bound in a heavy cast. He'd come out of surgery with no complications though his road to recovery wouldn't be short or easy.

How the mighty do fall, she mused at the sight of his baby blue hospital johnny and the crepey skin under his eyes that made him look fragile. His eyes lit on her, alive with pain. "You here to take me to jail?" When she approached the bed wordlessly and pulled up a chair to sit, he reached for the call button. "Hang on. If you're going to interrogate me, I'm going to need another shot of morphine."

"I've got something to say," she told him. "There's no question you're going to jail. You ordered the hit on Eaton House, and we've got the evidence to back that up. But it was sloppy. In the years that I've known you, I've never known you to be sloppy."

He spread his hands as he lifted them from the bedcovers. "What can I say? I finally snapped."

"Why?" she asked pointedly. "It wasn't because Everett Eaton dented your fender. The attacks are disproportionate. Something bigger pushed you to order your men to attack Eaton House. What was it?"

"I need my wife."

"Your wife's missing," she said, her voice reaching for the ceiling now. "Your brother claims it's because she's hiding out from you."

True frowned. "Huck told you that?"

She waited, watching.

True shook his head. "Annette. She's never been afraid of me. Hell, the only person any of us has ever been afraid of was…"

When he trailed off, she had to stop herself from leaning forward. "Yes?"

He looked toward the window. The blinds were shut tight. He shook his head again. "Annette's not afraid of me. I've never done anything to make her afraid."

"But someone else has," she guessed. "Who?"

True's lips thinned, and his eyes wavered with pain or guilt or grief. It was difficult to tell. "You think I killed those women and that boy. The ones on the mountain. You think I'm capable."

She found that she could be truthful. "I do."

"Why?" he asked, his face turning back to hers. "What have I done, Sheriff, to make you believe I'm the monster?"

She needed to break him. And she'd held out for so long. She could hardly breathe as she muttered, "Because even you shouldn't mess around with 'little rez girls.'"

He stared for a full minute. She saw the realization hit. Then the implications. His gaze raced over her, as if seeing her for the first time.

She didn't look away. It was satisfying—so satisfying—when she saw the fear sink in. He was afraid of her, of what she'd experienced. What she knew and had always known about him. "Tell me," she demanded. "Tell me why you had Sawni Mescal killed. I'd like to know that first. Then you can tell me about the others."

Air hissed through his teeth as he braced them shut. He closed his eyes. "I didn't kill her. I didn't kill any of them."

"Not by your hand," she said. "But you gave the order."

"No," he said, shaking his head frantically now.

"True." Kaya stood up. She gripped the raised railing of the bed that caged him in. "Annette's not here for you to hide behind. There's no hiding. Not anymore. You're going to be booked. If you tell me how it all went down—if you tell me the truth—the judge will soften the sentence. You know that."

"I know that!" he shouted. "Damn it, you don't think I know that? But I'm trying to tell you! I didn't kill them! I wasn't the one who gave the order!"

She narrowed her eyes. "If it wasn't you, then who did?"

He took a fortifying breath. "For you to know that, you have to know who my father was and what he did."

"Your father's been dead a long time, True. You can't hide behind him, either."

"My father died the same year Bethany Merchant did," he added. "He was alive for her death and the first's."

"Who was she?" Kaya asked, needing the identity of the first woman. "Who was the first victim?"

"My stepmother." He seemed to wrench the truth out of himself. "Or, the woman who was going to be my stepmother. She and my father were engaged. Her name was Melissa Beaton. She was twenty-two years younger than him."

"He had his fiancée killed?" Kaya asked. "Why?"

"I didn't know how or why until later. I didn't know until Huck told me…"

"Huck knew?"

He didn't so much look at her as through her. "Of course Huck knew. He was the one who did it—who my father ordered to kill her."

Kaya's mouth gaped. She closed it. "You're saying your brother, the reverend, killed the first victim, Melissa Beaton?"

"I'm saying," True said, rounding the words out slowly, "that you found those four bodies on the mountain because Huck killed them there. Because my father programmed him to do so."

Chapter 18

*P*rogrammed?

Kaya tried to make sense of what True was saying and wondered if he was speaking nonsense. "Your father couldn't have ordered Huck to kill all four of them. He was dead before Sawni Mescal worked at The RC Resort. Long before Miller Higgins went hiking on Ol' Whalebones."

"My father didn't fight in Vietnam. Do you know what he did instead, Sheriff?" True asked.

"No."

"He was part of a training initiative for special forces," he said. "It was experimental. The theory was that a man could be trained to kill on command. Like Pavlov. If a dog can be programmed to salivate at the sound of a bell, then a man can be trained to execute a command—no matter how ruthless—at the sound of a 'kill word,' as he called it. After the war was lost, he was sent home to New Mexico. He had orders never to talk about or reveal what he did before he got there. He disobeyed orders. Not only that, he kept the program going. He knew Fuego County was rough country. 'Lawless,' as he used to say. He needed a soldier to do his bidding. Huck was born first. If he hadn't been, it would have been me. From the time he could walk, my father started programming him to kill."

The information was hard to take in. Kaya stepped back from the bed and moved away to roam the section of floor between the door and the window. She roved back to the foot of the bed and stopped. "So your father gave Huck the word to kill Melissa Beaton."

"Yes," True said, unable to meet her eye.

"How old was Huck when this happened?"

True's bottom lip shook once, then stopped. "Twelve. Just twelve."

"Why would your father want Melissa killed?" Kaya wondered.

"He said it was because she strayed," True revealed. "I always thought it was because he needed to see if his programming had worked. It's not like he loved her or needed her. My father wasn't motivated by those things. He was motivated by anger and greed. Growing up at RC was like the worst episode of *Survivor* you've ever seen. He made sure I knew what he could make Huck do. It didn't matter how much my brother loved me. If my father gave the word, Huck would kill me—without even thinking, he'd kill me. I couldn't run away and I sure as hell couldn't tell anyone."

"Why is there no record of this?" she asked. "Someone must've noticed a woman was missing from your ranch."

"People who worked there looked the other way," he revealed. "My father bought their silence."

"She didn't have family?" she asked. "Friends? Someone who would have asked questions when she disappeared?"

"She was a stripper from San Antonio. We thought somebody might come looking for her. Nobody ever showed up."

"What about Bethany Merchant?" Kaya asked. "And why did so much time go by between the killings?"

"Huck got away," True said. "Killing Melissa destroyed him. He left school, started drinking. Then he ran off and got a job as a ranch hand somewhere in East Texas."

"Why did he come back?" Kaya asked.

"My father's men found him," True explained. "They dragged him back. He paid for it. Believe me. My father made him pay. He took his pound of flesh. He made Huck bleed."

A shiver went up Kaya's spine. She went to the window again. "This was when?"

"About six months before Bethany Merchant turned up missing," True said grimly.

"Why did your father order Huck to kill Bethany?" she asked. "She was just a girl."

"She wasn't just a girl," True said resentfully. "That son of a bitch made Huck kill her because I loved her. Because I got her pregnant."

When Kaya stared, True nodded. "You know I'm telling the truth now, don't you? The ME would have told you she was a couple months pregnant when she died. The baby was mine. She was hung up on Everett Eaton, but I loved her. I would have gone anywhere with her if she'd have asked me."

"She didn't." Kaya put the pieces together. "She asked him."

"She asked Eaton, and it shattered my heart," True said. "She cornered him at the rodeo because she wanted to meet him at the motel that night she disappeared. She was going to tell him there—that she was pregnant, that the baby was his and he was trapped. He would've had to go east with her to college the way she wanted him to. But Huck met her at the motel instead. My father found out about the baby. After she was gone and I saw how broken Huck was again, I knew he'd given the order. She died because he couldn't abide his line being plagued by the potential of a bastard."

Kaya didn't know if she could hear any more. But she had to. She had to know everything. "Legal records show the first land dispute between your family and the Eatons was around this time," she noted.

"The lines between the RC and Eaton Edge are fuzzy," he explained, "at least when you're out there in the mountains. My father thought the mountain was on our side. After Bethany died, he realized he was wrong. He didn't like lawyers, but he hired one to file a claim before his death."

"Sawni Mescal." She forced the name out. "I need to know why Sawni Mescal was killed. If your father was dead, who was controlling Huck if not you?"

At this point, True raised a hand to his brow. He lowered his head, looking broken himself.

"True," she said gently. He may have kept his family's secrets. But it had haunted him every bit as much as Sawni's disappearance had haunted her. "Please."

He sniffed and lifted his head again. His face had turned red. The words quavered slightly when he spoke again. "I, uh… I met Annette, at college. She was prelaw, from a good family. I didn't want to bring her home. I didn't want her to know what…who I came from. But Dad was dead and I thought maybe everything died with him. Everything but Huck. So I took her home. And she and Huck… They became close. Closer than I expected. I didn't know he'd told her. Not until after the rez girl… She said her name was Kaya."

"You know her name." The response was punchy, but she was no longer in control. She was beyond it.

"Sawni Mescal worked for us for a while without incident," True said. "It was summertime. That's why we needed the extra help. Annette and I had a few months off school and her, me and Huck... We spent it on the ranch. We talked about what it was, what it could be. For the first time, I saw it as something to be redeemed. Something that Huck and I could be proud of. Together, we could make the RC something special. Annette and I even talked about getting married, which thrilled me to pieces. I thought if she and I got married, Huck and I could start over. We could forget everything that happened before—just sweep it under the rug and start clean. But then Annette started to think something was off about Sawni."

"What exactly?"

"Annette thought Sawni wanted Huck," True said. "The girl and Huck were friendly. I didn't see anything deeper than that. There was an age difference, and Huck was friendly with everyone. The girl kept to herself, though, and didn't respond much to Annette's questioning. Annette felt protective of Huck. She seemed jealous, even. I tried not to dwell on it. If she was jealous, it was because she loved him as much or more than she loved me, and after everything that happened with Bethany and Everett Eaton, I couldn't let my mind go there. There were too many ghosts. So I let it be. For weeks. And her hatred toward Sawni festered and whatever she felt for Huck... She became *possessive*. I didn't know until after the girl disappeared and everyone started looking for her that Huck had told Annette everything—about our father, about him, Melissa and Bethany. And she was angry enough...obsessed enough...to use my father's kill code—the one Huck had trusted her with—to snuff Sawni out. Like she was nothing. Dust in the frickin' wind."

Kaya breathed through her nose. Her eyes burned. "So you *married her*, True?"

True turned his eyes down to the hands twisted in his lap. "She knew our secrets. There was no getting out of it at that point. And once she saw how much it destroyed Huck again, she was sorry. She used the trust fund from her parents to send him to a specialist. Someone we could trust. She paid for his therapy. She paid for him to go to some monastery in California where you're forbidden to speak. It was supposed to be healing and he did heal, somewhat.

"When he was done there, he wanted to go to seminary school. He wanted his slate wiped clean. He wanted to be cleansed. The only way he felt he could do that was to become a shepherd of God. So she paid his way. Anything he needed, she sponsored him—on one condition. If he became a minister, he had to return to Fuego. After everything, she felt we had to keep an eye on him. If he'd told her everything, he'd tell anyone else he felt close to. He could have married, Sheriff. Started a family. Started over, finally. But Annette… She couldn't let that happen. If he loved her enough to spill his guts, he'd do it all again for another woman."

"Who kept Sawni's diary and why?" she asked.

"That was Annette. I told her it was foolhardy. Dad burned everything of Melissa's. He didn't take anything from Bethany, either, when she died. He didn't believe in leaving traces. Like I said, though, Annette was obsessed with the Mescal girl. She kept everything in the girl's bag."

"Was it her, too, who turned it in?" Kaya asked.

"Yes," True answered. "She had a row with Huck about it. She showed us the pages she'd torn out—the ones that mentioned her and Huck and me. It was the only thing belonging to Sawni she ever burned."

"What was the point in turning in the diary to begin with?" Kaya asked.

"She thought you and the FBI were sniffing too close in our direction. She got paranoid. She knew Wolfe was mentioned in the pages she left in the diary. She thought you'd start looking his way instead. It worked, for a time."

Kaya spread her feet apart and wrapped her arms around herself. "Tell me about Miller Higgins."

"Higgins was an accident," True said regrettably. "Despite Annette's warnings, Huck started spending time with a woman he met in Taos. They became close. Too close, to Annette's thinking. When he wouldn't listen to her and let the woman go, she took him to the mountain as a reminder why he couldn't be with anyone. They got into a heated argument. Higgins heard everything. Too much. Annette had Huck catch him…"

"She gave the kill order again," Kaya said with an unbelieving shake of her head.

"It was too much," True moaned. "And then the bodies were found, and I knew if any of the three of us made a mistake…a single mistake…you'd know. The Feds arrived and we started to scramble. I started to unravel. Huck talked about leaving, disappearing again, taking the Taos woman with him. Annette wouldn't let him go. I couldn't ignore how much it all hurt—how much she'd come to love him when it was supposed to be me. If she was going to be obsessed with anyone, it should've been me. All my spite and anger came to a head when Eaton did what he did at the festival. Finally, I had somebody I could pin all my frustrations on without hurting anyone I loved."

"If you hadn't ordered the hit," Kaya told him, "you'd still be at The RC Resort. And your secrets would still be yours."

True shook his head. "And none of us… We'd never be free. We'd carry it on our backs for the rest of our lives. To hell with what my wife wants anymore. I can't live like this anymore. And my brother can't, either. His spirit has been traded away by others for too long. If I want him to remain the man he is—the one he should've been—I can't let this go on. If I've got to do time to save him, you can be damn sure I can live with that. My father's sins—his ghost—have been alive in this world too long."

"I need to find Annette," Kaya said. "Agent Rutland and I think she is—or was—hiding out at Huck's house. Do you think that's where she would have gone?"

He hesitated. Then he passed his hand under his nose. "She'd have gone there. But enough time's passed that she's probably up on the mountain or on her way there now."

"The mountain," Kaya repeated. "Whalebones?"

He nodded. "That's where she told me to hide it before I split town. She left me enough to get to Mexico and told me to hide the rest."

"Hide what, True?" she pressed.

"The money," he said. "My father's money. Everything the Feds came looking for when he took his exodus. We saved it for the day we'd need it to do the same. I hid her and Huck's cut on the mountain where the bodies were found, as she told me. If that damned cougar hadn't startled us, my horse wouldn't have broken his leg or mine. Secrets would still be secrets. We would've gotten away with everything. Everything except our souls."

Chapter 19

Everett had Huck Claymore in his sights. The reverend had no idea. Still, Everett kept his finger outside the trigger guard as he followed Huck and Annette's progress on the trailhead of Ol' Whalebones.

As soon as Everett had returned to Eaton House from the hospital in the early hours before dawn, Kaya had called. She was mobilizing the mounted search again. There would be another manhunt—this time for True Claymore's brother and wife. And the most likely place they would be found was the mountain.

The other members of the search party would take time to get into position, but Everett, Ellis and their men were closest.

If you find them, I need you not to engage. Call in your coordinates and wait.

Waiting didn't sit well knowing he was looking at the man who'd killed four people and the woman who had ordered him to do so.

If Annette's with him, Huck Claymore is expected to be armed and extremely dangerous. Do not engage, Everett.

Everett didn't understand Annette's hold on the reverend. But he had understood the urgency in Kaya's voice—the fear behind it.

Something about these two had her spooked. His promise to Kaya was the only thing tethering him from stopping them before they reached the summit. Once they did, they would be out of Everett's line of sight.

"Should we follow them?" Javier asked at his right shoulder.

Ellis, on Everett's left, made a discouraging noise. "Orders are we hang back."

"We'll lose them on the ridge," Javier reasoned. "We could find another position…"

"Sheriff Altaha told us not to approach," Ellis told him. "Right?"

Everett frowned. Annette and Huck were gaining ground too quickly.

"Everett?"

Everett lifted his head, staring across the muzzle into the distance. "You two wait here. I need to get closer."

Ellis gripped him. "What?"

"If they escape on my watch, I'm the one who has to live with it."

"What do I tell her when she gets here?" Ellis asked, not having to say her name for Everett to know who he spoke of.

"She knows I'm a man of my word," Everett returned before he left the small circle of boulders where the trio had been hiding. "Tell her I've got her back."

Kaya couldn't hail Everett on the radio. She didn't enjoy not knowing where he was or what he was planning to do.

He told me to tell you he's got your back, Ellis had said when she'd located him and Javier in the canyon below.

She and Rutland picked their way over rocks as they approached the place True Claymore had described—close to where the four victims had been found over the edge of the cliff. Root and Wyatt weren't far behind. She raised her hand when she heard amplified voices on the wind. Her team slowed. No one had eyes on Huck or Annette anymore. In the canyon below, Ellis and Javier had lost sight of them close to a half hour ago.

"That's Annette," she muttered to Rutland, recognizing the voice if not the harsh tone reverberating off the rocks around them. She glanced back at Root and Wyatt. "Silence your radios. We don't want to alert them."

They obeyed and Kaya reached down to twist the dial on the radio on her belt, muting it.

Rutland leaned toward her. "If they see us coming, you realize Annette could go ahead with the kill code."

"Huck is used to enacting it against a single person," she said. "He never shoots them on the spot. He gets them into position, executes them all with the same shot to the back of the head. He's never faced anyone that was trained in combat, much less four. Root and Wyatt approach from the north, us to the south. Unless you'd rather hang back."

He shook his head, his standard issue already braced between his hands. "I'm with you, Sheriff."

She nodded, then gave the motion for the four of them to spread out.

Everett lay belly-down on the canyon wall, barely breathing. The wind was against him. Any shot he took, he would have to take it into account.

He was alone across the wide gap between the top of the canyon and Ol' Whalebones. The river ran between, its rush audible even at this height. He could see the ledge where Huck and Annette had hidden the bodies. He could see the pair arguing on the cliff edge above it.

His finger tensed near the trigger when he saw Kaya

creeping toward them from the south, Rutland closing on her six.

The shovel in Huck's hand waved as he gestured wildly. There was a mound of dirt at his feet. Annette didn't cower. She grabbed him by the shirt, pushing, inching him back toward the ledge.

Kaya's crouching walk quickened, her feet moving swiftly across the ground, her pistol in a two-handed hold. Rutland followed. When she stood, the wind carried her terse command to *freeze*. Annette pivoted. Huck dropped the shovel. Everything inside Everett did freeze as he watched it tumble end over end over the cliff's edge and fell in a silent arc to the water below.

Kaya watched Root and Wyatt crowd Annette and Huck from the north side. She was aware of the wind teasing her hair and the brim of her hat. She was more aware of the long plunge down the cliff wall to her left. She felt more than heard Rutland behind her. Her eyes moved over Huck's face, trying to gauge his expression.

The debate between him and Annette had reached screaming pitch by the time Kaya had given the order. She'd seen Annette nearly shove Huck off the cliff's edge and had decided to move in.

"Sheriff Altaha," Annette said. Flushed, she was not the polished mayor's wife people in Fuego knew her to be. She swallowed, reaching down to straighten the sand-colored vest she wore over her front. "This is a surprise."

"Show us your hands!" Rutland shouted when Huck's began to reach around his back.

Kaya stiffened even as Huck's hand lifted into the air along with the other. He looked miserable, she thought briefly. He stepped a hair closer to Annette, his toes inching over the edge of the hole they had dug. "You're both under arrest."

"For what?" Annette challenged.

"Huck for the murders of Melissa Beaton, Bethany Merchant, Sawni Mescal and Miller Higgins," Kaya informed her. "You'll be charged in the deaths of Mescal and Higgins."

Annette's eyes widened. "Those are serious charges, Sheriff. Are you sure you have the right people?"

"I have your husband True Claymore's detailed statement," Kaya replied and saw Huck waver like a blade of grass over his feet.

"True says we did this?" Annette laughed. "That's ridiculous. He'll say anything at this point to get himself out of trouble. He's accustomed to talking his way out of sticky situations."

"A search and seizure of Huck's residence turned over Miller Higgins's cell phone. If True's guilty, then what are you two doing at the murder scene? Why are the horses we found at the foot of the mountain packed with a week's worth of rations?"

Annette's mouth fumbled.

Kaya lowered her chin. "Come forward quietly so that we can bring you both in for questioning. Resisting arrest won't work well for you if you're innocent. You're a criminal attorney, Annette. You know this."

Huck's feet shuffled forward, but Annette's arm snapped up to block him. "No."

"Annette." His fingers closed around her wrist in a gentle bracelet. "It's over."

"No!" she shouted. "Not like this! I will *not* see you rot in prison for this!"

"You won't see it," he assured her. His front buffered against her back and his other hand came up to meet the line of her shoulders. "I'm tired, Annette. I can't do this anymore."

Her gaze fused to his. "You can't live with me anymore, Huck? Is that what you mean?"

His shoulders lifted and his expression grew helpless. When he lowered them, his posture caved. "I'm sorry," he whispered.

Annette nodded slowly, jaw flexing. "You won't have to." In a lightning move, she reached around his waist.

"Don't!" Kaya yelled when Annette's grip closed over the butt of Huck's gun. She pushed herself forward. "Hold it!"

Annette threw her shoulder into Huck's chest.

His heel caught on the mound of earth. His hands windmilled as he tipped over the ledge and fell into the open air.

Annette whirled, her gun hand trained on Kaya. "Tell them to get back!" she cried, pointing at the deputies behind her. "Tell them or I'll shoot!"

Kaya lifted her chin to Wyatt. He and Root shuffled backward. "Any chance you had of talking yourself out of murder charges is gone. You realize that, don't you?"

"Not if you let me go," Annette told her.

"You pushed him off the cliff." Kaya shook her head. "Why did you have to kill him?"

"I gave him the easy way out," Annette stated. "He couldn't have sat in a cell for the rest of his life thinking about all the things he's done. He's not built for that. Yeah, he killed those people. But he isn't a killer. He never would've hurt anyone—"

"If not for his father," Kaya finished. "If not for you."

"This doesn't have to end badly," Annette argued. "Huck's gone. He can't hurt anyone anymore. Just back off and stay back and you'll never see me again. I'll leave what's in that hole for all of you."

Kaya's eyes jumped from Annette's right eye to her left and back. "I can't do that."

Annette tilted her head slightly. The sheen over her eyes caught the light. Kaya saw the grief and guilt wash over her about what she had done to Huck.

Kaya lifted one hand from her weapon to motion Rutland back.

"No!" he hissed.

"Just do it," she shot back before repositioning her hands on the Glock when the rocks under Rutland's feet crunched under his careful retreat.

"That's typical," Annette muttered. "My husband disappointed me. Even Huck disappointed me in the end. Now you. I expected more of Fuego's first woman sheriff."

Kaya wasn't going to be like the reverend. She wasn't going to apologize. "I don't think Huck disappointed you. I think he did everything you ever told him to."

Annette's voice broke. "Except run away with me."

"He has run," Kaya told him. "In the past, he ran to get away from all of this. But it followed him. He knew if he ran again, he'd never be free of it. And neither would you."

"The truth wouldn't have set him free, either!" Annette cried. "Don't you understand? That's why he had to die!"

Kaya nodded. "I know what it is to love someone—to love all of him—the good side of him and the bad. I know what it is to live without someone you love—to feel responsible for what happened to them. It tears at the very fabric of who you are."

Tears tracked down Annette's cheeks. "Lower your weapon, Kaya. Please…just lower the gun."

"In order for me to do that, you have to lower yours first," Kaya said evenly.

Annette shifted onto her back foot. The gun lowered by a hair.

"Slow," Kaya murmured, watching Annette's gun turn sideways and her knees bend. She edged forward. "That's it, Annette. Nice and slow."

The gun came to rest on the rocks between them. "Now you," Annette said.

"Step back," Kaya advised. As Annette did so, Kaya released one hand from her weapon. She set it on the ground. Stepping over them, she reached for her cuffs.

Annette backed away, skittish. "You didn't say you were going to restrain me."

"It's procedure," Kaya reminded her. She stepped forward again. When Annette retreated toward the ledge, she stopped, holding up both hands. She didn't know if Annette was desperate enough to follow Huck over the cliff. "All right, look. If you promise not to resist, we can walk out of here together. No restraints."

"Until we get to the bottom of the mountain?" Annette said with narrowed eyes.

Kaya measured her and realized she had no intention of making it all the way to the bottom of the mountain. Not without running. "Yes," she lied.

Annette stilled. She let Kaya close the distance.

Kaya took hold of her arm. "Come on," she said, nodding in the direction she had come.

Annette twisted, attempting to break the hold. She forced Kaya back a long step.

Kaya caught her breath. She felt open air behind her. Annette drove an elbow into her gut. Kaya felt her heels slide back over the ledge.

On the wind, she thought she heard the sound of her name.

* * *

Everett didn't have a clear shot. He hadn't had one since Kaya laid down her weapon and crossed to Annette.

He watched helplessly as Annette tried to drive Kaya back over the ridge. For a second, it looked like she would go over, crashing to the same ledge where Huck lay.

Kaya lunged, grabbing Annette as she did so and shoving her to the ground. She tried to restrain her.

Annette was fighting for her life, arms and legs flailing. She kicked, punched, bit. Her fist closed over a rock and swung it up to connect with Kaya's temple.

"Son of a bitch," Everett breathed as Kaya's head snapped back. Rutland and the deputies rushed to break up the fight. "Hurry up!" he yelled. Why had they left in the first place?

Kaya tried to overtake Annette by pinning her in a reverse hold, but Annette rolled out of it, away from the edge. She scrambled for something on the ground as Rutland lunged for her.

A shot echoed across the canyon and Rutland fell. Kaya had brought herself to her feet, grappling for the Taser on her belt. Annette pointed the gun at her.

Everett felt the trigger, placing Annette in the center of his scope. He remembered the wind at the last second, adjusted his aim.

The rifle kicked against his shoulder as he squeezed.

Kaya watched Annette slump in a limp sprawl on the rocks of the cliff edge. Her Taser was in her fist and her deputies were behind her. Rutland was still down.

Blood pooled beneath the line of Annette's throat. Her body had jerked sideways. Which meant the shot had come from the north…

Kaya looked wildly across the empty space of the canyon to the cliff side a hundred feet across.

She had to squint. The rock to the head had made her see stars and her vision double. She watched a figure and its carbon copy unfold from a sprawl on the flat top of the canyon. As he stood up, she recognized Everett's long lean form. He lifted his hand, waved.

Ellis's words came back to her.

Everett said to tell you he's got your back.

A sob worked against her throat, and she braced her hands on her knees as they loosened. Root grabbed her arms, preventing her slide to the rough ground, while Wyatt sailed by to check Rutland's condition.

As Root asked if she was okay, Kaya's gaze fell on Annette. For a second, she thought their eyes locked. It took a delayed second for her to realize the other woman was dead. She had tried to kill Kaya. And Everett had been quicker.

She looked across the canyon again and saw that Everett had picked up his rifle and was running for the sloping side of the cliff face he'd somehow shimmied up to get to his position. Shrill ringing pierced her ears. Blinking, she struggled to stay conscious—at least until she had a chance to kiss the cattle baron when he arrived.

Chapter 20

"True Claymore is in custody. Reverend Huck Claymore and Annette Claymore are both deceased. Agent Rutland is in surgery but is expected to recover. Sheriff Altaha was injured, but she is doing well and should be back at work next week…"

"He's doing fine," Naleen commented at Kaya's bedside. Deputy Root's face filled the screen of the television high on the wall opposite the hospital bed.

"He's doing great," Kaya granted. "But I still could've done the press conference."

"The doctor says you have to stay overnight," her mother, Darcia, said as she fussed around the room, straightening the curtains, adjusting the blinds. Turning the chairs so they were angled just so with the bed.

She was driving Kaya crazy. They both were.

Nova breezed in with a large grease-stained paper bag. "I brought reinforcements."

Kaya sat up in bed too quickly and winced when her head split open with pain. She saw little white lights and leaned back on her elbows. "Damn it!"

"You might be the world's worst patient," Naleen considered as she received the bag from her daughter and rattled the paper as she opened it.

Kaya's teeth ground at the noise. "Nova, get out. I'm about to say more bad words."

"You go ahead, Aunt Kaya," Nova invited. "After spring break at the Edge, I feel like I've got them all memorized. Did you know there are over fifty different ways to use the word fu—"

"Do you really think finishing that sentence will convince me to let you work there all summer?" Naleen questioned.

"Do you really think talking at this volume is making me any friendlier?" Kaya drawled.

The door opened again and two people walked into the room. Kaya's jaw came unhinged when she saw Sawni's mother and father.

Mrs. Mescal carried a vase full of flowers. She looked small and kindly behind them as she smiled hesitantly. "How's the patient?" she asked in her familiar quiet voice.

When Kaya remained speechless, Naleen stood up from her chair. "Indignant."

Mr. Mescal chuckled. He was not a tall man, but his presence had a habit of filling any room he was in. That effect had dimmed after Sawni's disappearance. Kaya had noticed that at the funeral as well. But his shoulders were back, and his smile was broad as he scanned the bandage on Kaya's temple. "The headache's to blame, I'm sure."

"It's the captivity," Kaya found herself saying. She glanced at Naleen. "Can you…"

Naleen patted her arm. "Nova and I will step out."

"Leave the bag," Kaya said, snatching it from her before Naleen could escape with it.

Darcia sat down in the chair closest to the window, signaling that she intended to stay. Kaya didn't have the words to tell her to leave, too.

Mrs. Mescal waited until Nova and Naleen closed the door before placing the vase on the bedside table.

Kaya reached out to touch a delicate spray of petals. "Lilies," she said. "For Sawni."

"Our Sawni did love lilies, didn't she?" Mrs. Mescal asked, tracing the shape of another. "The lilies are for her. The peach roses are for you."

Kaya met her eyes and noticed the veil of wet over her dark irises.

Mrs. Mescal turned the vase slightly, fidgeting. "Do you still like peach roses—or do you prefer something else now?"

"Peach roses are fine," Kaya said, her voice breaking up.

Mrs. Mescal's hand found hers. "I'm sorry we didn't keep in touch through the years. I'm afraid you might think it was because we blamed you for what happened. That wasn't the case. Not at all. Seeing you…reminded us of her. So we cut ties when we should have gathered. Nothing heals like community. You needed that as much as we did, and we denied you."

Kaya shook her head. "I denied myself."

"Nonetheless…" Mrs. Mescal patted her hand. "When I saw you at the memorial, you looked so guilty and ashamed—still, after all this time."

"I was afraid I disappointed you." She lifted her eyes to Mr. Mescal who stood now at the foot of the bed.

"Why would you disappoint us, Kaya?" he asked. "You've risen. You've made your people proud."

"You found her," Mrs. Mescal muttered. "You found our Sawni and brought her home. But even if you hadn't, you should know we're proud of you."

Kaya looked to her mother who sat quietly. Darcia nodded in quiet agreement and Kaya had to look away. "Thank you," she said. She reached up to swipe at tears. "Sawni used to get so mad because she'd cry at the drop of a hat and I didn't. Now look at me."

Mrs. Mescal released a sobbing laugh.

"We bend," Mr. Mescal stated, "so that life doesn't break us."

Kaya sighed at the wisdom. "I think I get that now."

Mrs. Mescal leaned down and pressed a kiss to the center of her brow. "Bless you, Kaya Altaha."

Kaya mimicked Mr. Mescal's wave and watched him and Sawni's mother file out. She raised both hands to her head as the door snicked closed. "Did you know they were coming?"

"I didn't," Darcia said, rising to smooth the covers over Kaya's legs. "But I'm happy that they did. You needed that. So did they. Our families have needed each other for some time. Maybe now things can go back to the way they were."

It would be bittersweet without Sawni there, but Kaya found herself wishing the same.

The door crashed open, knocking against the wall. Darcia jumped at the sudden noise and the man that charged into the room. "Are you all right?" Everett demanded to know when he found Kaya lying in the bed.

Her heart stuttered. The wash of her pulse made her head ache in time with it. Still, she hadn't seen Everett since the rescue chopper had arrived to transport Rutland to the hospital. He, Root and Wyatt had insisted she go, too. She cleared her throat and tried to sit up straighter against the pillows stacked behind her. "I'm fine. Why wouldn't I be?"

He swept an arm toward the door. "There's people crying out in the hall like there's somebody on their deathbed in here."

"No one's on their deathbed," Darcia assured him. Her tone dripped with both frustration and amusement. "You silly man."

"You're fine," he repeated, eyes drilling into Kaya, hands propped on his waist.

"Yes," she insisted. "The doctor wanted to keep me for observation through the night as a precaution."

"There's nothing wrong with you?" he stated in question.

She pressed her lips together because she was very close to smiling. "No."

He nodded faintly before he flicked a glance at her mother. "Darcia."

"Everett," Darcia volleyed back.

"Nice to see you again."

"Is it?" she asked mildly.

He shifted, uncomfortable.

Kaya took pity on him. It was nice to know she wasn't the only one who withered in her mother's presence. She lifted the bag from the bed. "Do you want a burger?"

"I could eat," he weighed. He looked around. "Do you have a drink?"

"I don't," she realized. "Nova forgot to grab one."

"What do you want?" he asked, sidestepping quickly to the door. "I'll get you something."

"A coke is fine," she replied.

He grabbed the handle of the door. "Darcia? Can I interest you?"

"You interest my daughter enough for both of us, thank you," Darcia retorted.

He grimaced, then pinned his gaze again to Kaya. "Do you need me to do anything else?"

She started to say no, then stopped. "I need to get out of here."

He lifted his chin and a mischievous grin lit his eyes, turning the corner of his mouth up in a crooked smile. "Oh, I'll get you out of here, Sheriff Sweetheart. Don't you worry."

Kaya didn't realize how wide her smile reached until she looked at Darcia. She shrank back into the bed. "What's with the look, Mom?" she asked bracingly.

Darcia's half-lidded stare was more incisive than usual. Her lips parted a moment before she spoke, as if she were weighing her words or whether to say them. "You've been waiting."

"For…" Kaya prompted.

"For redemption," Darcia said with a wag of her chin. "The Mescals have given it. You always had it, but it took them visiting here today for you to believe that."

"Okay," Kaya said, unsure.

"You've been waiting for something else," Darcia continued. "Something you've probably never been aware of. I've always found it so curious how Naleen could fall so fast and dive into relationships with hardly a second thought and you never could bring yourself to do so."

Kaya had to fight the urge to roll her eyes. She fought it hard. "Mom. Naleen and I are hardly the same person—"

"Very true," Darcia agreed. "But I know now—what you've been waiting for."

Kaya narrowed her eyes. "Care to clue me in?"

"You've been waiting for a warrior."

A laugh burst out of Kaya. "A warrior? How Apache princess of me," she said derisively.

Darcia looked at her until her amusement faded, and Kaya was left to contemplate the seriousness of her expression. "He's a warrior like you," Darcia continued. "You've never found your equal—until now." She stood. "If he's returning, I think I'll take a walk. He won't want me staring daggers at him while he mashes food into his hairy face."

"Why did you tell me all that if you don't like him?" Kaya wondered.

Darcia closed the flaps of her long sweater over her front. "I don't mind him. But you'll allow me to resent the man who's stolen the heart of my youngest daughter. You may be the sheriff of Fuego County, Kaya Altaha. But you are still my child." With a nod, she left the room, leaving Kaya to grapple with her thoughts.

Before daybreak, the kitchen at Eaton House stood silent and still. The rest of the house lay quiet, too. The boards over the windows blocked the faint stain over the mountains, buttes and cliffs that heralded another long day of working cattle. The windows would be replaced later in the week. Repairs were still going on at Eaton House, off and on, but it was slowly coming together again. Soon, the ambush would only be a bitter memory.

In the dark, Everett pulled on his boots. He didn't bother to button his shirt as he crossed to the counter and the cubby where Paloma kept the coffeepot. He took down mugs. Pouring the coffee, he left it strong and black and lifted the mugs by the handles. No sooner had he turned than he hitched at the sight of the figure hovering in the doorway.

"Jesus Holyfield Christ!" he exclaimed, touching the mugs safely down to the counter next to him as the liquid sloshed over the rims. He grabbed his heart like it was going places. "You can't do that to somebody who's had his chest opened up in the last ten months."

Paloma clicked her tongue, tying the belt of her quilted, scarlet robe as she entered the room she'd ruled for the last three decades. "You're jumpier than usual. Not that that's a wonder." She grabbed the hand towel draped across the handle of the oven and tossed it to him.

He dried the piping hot liquid that ran in between his fingers.

"She's upstairs," Paloma said, eyeing the pair of mugs.

He tossed the towel onto the counter. "She fought me tooth and nail about not letting her go home. But I couldn't sleep. Not without knowing she was okay."

"You stole her from the hospital sooner than doctors advised," Paloma reminded him.

"I did it because she asked me to," Everett responded. "I'd do anything..."

She lifted her chin knowingly when he trailed off. "You'd do anything for her," she said, laying it out for him.

He pressed one hand to the countertop. Paloma saw everything. She saw him better than most.

She sighed. "Oh, *mijo*—"

"What are you doing out of bed?" he intervened smoothly. "You shouldn't be up."

"I feel fine," she assured him. "I'd feel a sight better if you children would stop fussing over me and let me get back to my work."

"You don't need work," he argued. "You need rest."

She grabbed him by the open flaps of his shirt. "Look at me, Everett Templeton. Look *here*." When he obeyed, she widened her eyes. "I am fine. Paloma's fine. *You*, on the other hand, are a basket case."

He sneered. "Now you're just being mean."

"You're not blind," she said gravely. "Nor are you stupid. You know what it is to love someone. What it *means*."

"How do you know?" he asked, uneasy.

"You love your brother," she told him. "You love your sister, despite what you have to say about her. You loved your father more than any son has."

He frowned but couldn't argue.

"You love your men," she went on. "And you love me. We've had our spats. But you were my child long before Ellis and Eveline decided to be. You chose me first."

He dropped his gaze from hers. Yes, he'd chosen her. Like a lifeline, he'd reached. She'd answered. He wondered if she knew, by doing so, that she'd saved him. He shifted his feet and cleared his throat to block the emotions building in the back of his throat.

She waited until he stilled. Then she said, "I never thought the day would come when I would have to point out to you that you've chosen someone else."

"Yeah," he whispered because his voice was somehow lost. "Me neither."

"She's worthy of it," she told him. "She's worthy of your heart."

"That's not what I'm worried about," he admitted.

"What are you worried about, *mijo*?"

He shook his head restlessly. "I don't know if she wants it."

Paloma nodded, drawing a long breath. Lovingly, she gathered the flaps of his shirt together. "You watched your father get his heart broken. It broke when your mother left. It broke a little more when she married my brother, his friend. It broke when she had another child—someone else's. It broke every time he saw either one of them in town. They say people don't die of a broken heart, but in the end, there was no doctor in this world who could fix it, was there?"

Everett was unable to contemplate the lengths to which his father had suffered. "We buried him with it. Why did we do that? You don't bury a man with the gun that killed him."

"The heart defines the man," Paloma insisted. "The same heart loved you and your siblings with every beat. It forgave your mother and my brother. Every betrayal, big and small."

"He was a fool for that," Everett stated.

"He could have been bitter," Paloma spoke over him. "He could have gone off like a demon—like that Whip Decker—and killed them both for it. He could have shut out what remained of his family, given up your birthright and fled. He didn't do those things because he was no fool. He did them because his heart was strong."

"Why're we talking about him?" he asked. Talking about Hammond hurt. Would it never not hurt?

"Because now you're the one who has to decide how your heart defines you," Paloma asserted. "Starting with your woman upstairs." He opened his mouth, but she stopped him. "She's your woman, Everett. There's no denying it."

"I'm hers," he granted. "She hasn't told me yet whether she wants to be mine. Not in the long run. She hasn't told me whether she wants this life with me. And it was me that told her I wasn't easy to live with. She knows all too well that this life is hard."

"Life's hard with or without the person you need most in this world," Paloma explained. "What do you want?"

"I *know* what I want," he said through his teeth.

"Does she?"

He hesitated long enough for her to pounce. "Tell her," Paloma told him. "Tell her, *mijo*, so I don't have to watch you live the rest of your life with regret. Never mind your heart. Do you think mine could stand that?"

He ran his eyes over her face. A smile grew on his. "You like kicking my ass, don't you?"

"What do you think gets me out of bed every morning?" She laid her hands, one on top of the other, over the center of his chest. "Be a good man and try not to plague us both to death."

"No promises," he replied, then added "*Mami*" and watched her eyes grow damp. She drew him into her arms and, for once, he went quietly.

Kaya woke facedown in a bed that was not her own with her head about to implode. She rolled slowly to her back, reaching up to hold her head on her shoulders.

She felt like she'd been hit with a rock much bigger than the one that had concussed her.

Going back to sleep seemed like the safest option. If she slept through the headbanging, she wouldn't have to learn to live through it.

As she tried to slink back into the deep, empty chamber she'd just climbed out of, the aching in her head crescendoed and she realized there would be no respite until she took something for the pain.

Groaning, she dug her elbows into the flannel sheet and propped herself up part of the way. Her neck muscles screamed, and she wished for a hammer to knock herself out with.

A hand gripped her shoulder, preventing her from rising further. She angled her head back.

"Stay down," Everett instructed.

"I have things to do," she grumbled at him.

"Such as?" he asked, lifting a single brow.

"Where'd you put my phone?" she asked. "I have to call Root and Wyatt and check in…"

"Nope."

She sighed, dropping her chin to her chest because her head felt heavy. "Not this again. I'm sheriff. I have responsibilities…"

"Not today," he informed her. "Not tomorrow, either. For the next few days, you're not the sheriff."

She frowned. "I'm just your sweetheart?"

His hand slid from her shoulder as he stepped away. "No. You're Kaya. And that's enough."

She raised her hand to the back of her neck, trying her best to ignore the pancake-flippy feeling his words placed in her stomach. "Do I smell coffee?"

He thrust a mug into her face.

She grabbed it like a lifeline.

Everett piled pillows behind her. "Slow," he told her when she began to scoot back.

"I'm not an invalid," she informed him. Clutching the mug in both hands, she let the heat seep into her fingers and closed her eyes, breathing in the aroma. "That's nice."

"Drink," he said as he sat on the edge of the bed with his own mug. "It's been sitting for a minute."

She did and found the temperature to be just right. Scanning his profile, she swallowed and waited until the warmth spread to her belly. "How long have you been watching me sleep?"

He drank in answer.

"Hmm," she muttered thoughtfully. "Just so I know— how long do you plan on doing that?"

He lowered the coffee. His voice delved deep. "Until I'm certain you're going to keep waking up."

"I'm fine."

His eyes roved over the bandage on her temple and what she imagined were bruises starting to color her skin. "I nearly had to watch you go over a cliff and get shot again. You'll let me worry about you."

He'd come close to watching her die again. He'd saved her life—again.

She closed her eyes. "Thank you."

"It's just coffee."

"Not for that." She shook her head. "For having my back."

"Always," he said softly.

She looked away because it was too much. He was too much.

His mug clacked onto the bedside table. "I've got things to say to you."

She wasn't sure she was ready to hear them.

"Right now, though, you need something to eat. You can't take those pain meds the doctor sent you home with on an empty stomach. Paloma was making you a plate when I left the kitchen. I'll go see if it's ready. When you've taken something, you can go back to sleep and rest some more."

As he moved to the door, she wanted to call him back but saw the stubborn line of his shoulders and forced herself to stop. When he closed the door, she slunk back down into the covers and pulled them over her head, overwhelmed by all that was inside her.

Kaya could only take so much coddling. On the second day, by the afternoon, she was out of bed and wouldn't hear refusal from Everett, Paloma or Luella—who Everett had brought in to do regular checks on Kaya as a nurse.

That evening, close to sundown, she ventured out onto

the patio, settled into one of the wooden Adirondack chairs and wouldn't hear a word spoken from any of them about returning indoors until the bugs started to bite and the cool night air began to nip.

Upstairs, Paloma drew her a hot bath. Soaking felt divine. Parts of Kaya ached from the skirmish with Annette—not just her head. She didn't mind so much when Paloma lingered nearby, as if she were afraid Kaya would drown if she left the room. She even helped Kaya wash her hair without getting the bandage on her temple wet.

"Thank you," Kaya murmured as Paloma helped her dry and dress.

"It's no trouble," Paloma replied. She handed Kaya a fresh stack of clothes. "Your sister brought these for you."

"It *is* trouble," Kaya argued. "You've all gone to way too much trouble—"

"Kaya Altaha," Paloma snapped, "out there you may be the sheriff and you may have to care for everyone else. But under this roof, you are in our care. It's my duty to care for Hammond's children, his grandchildren and the ones they choose and that pleases me. You've done enough. Our troubles are over because of all you have done. All we ask is that you let us take care of you now. *Por favor.*"

Kaya held the knot under her collarbone that kept the towel closed around her and the clothes Paloma had given her with the other hand. "*Si, señora,*" she murmured.

A smile touched Paloma's eyes but not her mouth. Reaching up, she brushed the hair back from Kaya's face. "*Buen.*"

Kaya responded by taking her hand. "Paloma?"

"What is it, *niña*?"

"Does it take as much strength as I think it does?"

"To do what?"

"To…" Kaya pressed her lips together. Then she closed her eyes and made them part again. "To love him the way that you do…for as long as you have…"

Paloma blinked in surprise. "It takes strength to love anybody." When Kaya bit her lip, she straightened her shoulders. "But he isn't just anybody. Is he?"

Kaya shook her head silently. She felt open and tried to make her expression unreadable.

Paloma squeezed her hand. "I have loved him—even when I thought he would never change. But he has changed. Do you know why?"

"No," Kaya replied.

"Then you are blind," Paloma said simply.

Kaya searched the woman's face. She started to shake her head again, then stopped when Paloma eyed her in warning. She released a breath. "I haven't changed him."

"He did some of the work himself," Paloma admitted. "He was forced to open himself—to grief. To acceptance. That is how love found him. But we do not love him because he has changed."

Kaya thought about it. "No," she stated.

Paloma nodded. "That is how you know it is strong. That is how you know this has what it takes. Do you think he is strong enough to be your man—through everything, good and bad?"

"I do," she realized with no hesitation. She could see it—him and her, through thick and thin, together. She heard herself gasp. That was the answer, wasn't it? To all her questions. "Do you do this every day?"

"What?"

"Change people's lives," Kaya said softly. She jumped a bit when Paloma laughed in a loud, genuine burst. Then she laughed at herself and pressed her fingers to the center of her brow. "I'm sorry. I'm a mess."

"If this is you at your lowest, Kaya, may I just say," Paloma said, "you handle yourself with more dignity and strength than anyone in this house before you."

"Never meet me when I'm sick or hungry," Kaya asked and laughed much more easily with Paloma the second time.

Everett had finally gone from watching her sleep to sleeping beside her. The bags under his eyes had started to pop. He'd come to need rest as much as he said she did.

Kaya found herself sleepless. The pain had slunk back to an irritating level. She was no longer buried by it. She hoped tomorrow it would be mild enough that she could manage a trip into town. The desire to speak with her deputies had only escalated. She'd checked with the hospital to hear Rutland's status. Surgery had gone well, and he was recovering.

The fallout for Fuego would be long. The mayor was facing charges. The reverend had killed four people, at the behest of his father and sister-in-law. He and Annette Claymore were dead.

Kaya had to get back on patrol, if only to show the people of Fuego some measure of assurance.

She just had to get past the big tough cattleman first.

He looked soft when he slept. His breath whispered across her face. She lifted her fingertips to feather across his lips. They parted at the motion and she licked her lips to stop from kissing his. *Let him sleep*, she told herself, despite the need. It kindled, insistent.

She knew what flowered with it. She knew what she felt beyond need and want. And she knew how loud that voice screamed whenever he looked at her. Like she was still on that pedestal he'd put her on at the beginning of all this. It didn't matter how broken or bruised she was. He looked at her, and she believed—in herself. In him. Everything.

True to routine, Everett stirred near dawn. He raised one arm over his head and opened his eyes to find her sitting up in bed.

"Thirsty?" she asked.

"You have no idea."

He sat up slowly, letting the sheet fall to his waist and he took the drink she handed him. Together, they drank in silence.

He judged her constitution. "You're stronger today."

"I think so," she said. When he raised one knee and drank again, she bit her lip. "You said you had things to say to me."

"When you're ready."

She waited until he'd finished his coffee before she admitted, "I think I'm ready to hear them."

"Better be sure, Sheriff Sweetheart," he warned.

"I'm sheriff again, it seems," she observed.

When she didn't break eye contact, he took the mug from her. "You think you can handle getting dressed?"

"Why?" she asked as he got out of bed.

"Because we're going for a ride."

The horses shambled. He wouldn't hear of them going faster.

"We could've walked faster than this," Kaya informed him.

"If you'd stop complaining for a few seconds at a time, we could do something crazy like enjoy the sunrise," he stated.

She didn't so much settle into silence as bristle at it. The light coming into the world did draw her gaze, however, and hold it. Day broke the grip of grim night, painting Eaton Edge and its river, hills and mountains in nature's watercolors, one after the other, until the sun's golden fingers grasped for its first hold of the sky.

Kaya had no words, so she let Everett and Crazy Alice lead her and Elsie, the gentle, sweet Haflinger he'd put her on, down a dirt trail a mile to the west of Eaton House, past Paloma's vegetable garden, past the orchard with its neat rows of trees, beyond the bunkhouse where the hands were beginning to stir and the cabin Ellis and Luella shared with the girls… They rode until the buildings were far behind them.

Finally, when the sun had rounded over the top of Ol' Whalebones, Everett tugged on the reins to bring Crazy Alice to a halt. Kaya did the same. "Where are we?" she asked, frowning at the ponderosa pines surrounding both sides of the trail.

He walked around Crazy Alice to grab Elsie's bridle and ran a hand over her long neck. "Attagirl," he murmured. Then he reached out a hand for Kaya's.

She ignored it. She'd gotten on the horse without his help. She could get off it, too. To prove it, she nudged her right toes out of the stirrups and swung her leg over Elsie's back. Gripping the horn, she lowered smoothly to the ground.

The change in altitude made her head spin. She stumbled as she brought her other leg down.

He caught her, gripping her upper arm. He cupped the back of her shoulders to keep her off the ground. "You said you were ready," he said near her ear.

"Stand me back up," she instructed, gritting her teeth. "I'm ready, damn it."

He made a noise in his throat but helped her steady herself. After several long seconds in which he watched for signs of weakness, he asked, "You good?"

She jerked a nod. He didn't let go of her arm, she noted, as they walked off the trail and into the trees. "Where are we?" she asked again.

Winding his way through the long shadows of the ponderosas, he hooked a right and guided her into an open glade.

The headstone gave her pause. It was centered in the safety of the dell. She opened her mouth to say something, then stopped because Everett released her and moved closer to the stone.

She watched as he crouched in front of it and tugged weeds from its base, then tossed them away before standing again. "This is where we buried him."

Kaya walked around the stone to stand at his side. It rose out of the ground to the height of her shoulders, coming to a point. The shape of a ten-gallon hat was etched just beneath the crest, followed by the name "HAMMOND WAYNE EATON" and the dates that marked his birth and death. The words "LOVING FATHER, GRANDFATHER & FRIEND" were carved in the center.

She read the words by Virgil inscribed in small italics below. "'May the countryside and the gliding valley streams content me.'" It felt sweet and so sad. She twined her fingers through Everett's and felt his hold tighten.

"He stands alone here," he muttered.

The breeze rustled the leaves. A hawk called from the distance. Otherwise, there was nothing here but the stone.

It felt lonely. She made sure her eyes were clear as she raised them to his. "Why are we here?"

"Because that's not what I want." He paced away. Tracing an unseen path around the glade, he lowered his hat with one hand to drag the other through his thick hair once, twice and again, mussing the waves thoroughly.

When he ceased the restless roving, he faced her, planting his feet. "Until he died, I didn't give dying alone a thought. Then something happened." He pointed in accusation. "You."

Her lips parted, but he spoke again before she could. "I don't need much in this life. I never needed to be the boss or the man everybody looks to when the day's starting. Before last summer, all I wanted was to know that my family was going to be okay—that we'd survive because life keeps swinging at us. I thought that was all I needed. All I'd ever need."

Her pulse was high, she realized, when he paused. She was starting to feel heady again. There was nothing to grab but the headstone so she crossed her arms over her chest. "Until me?" she asked.

"You're damn right until you," he muttered, holding his hat in two hands.

She watched him bend the brim, misshape it. "Why does that bother you so much?"

He stopped and quashed the hat over his head again. Planting his hands on his hips, he looked at her long under the shadow of it. "Because I need you to marry me."

Kaya realized after half a minute that she was gawking at him. She looked around—at the circle of trees, the empty glade—and shook her head. "You're proposing."

He made a face. "The hell did you think I was doing?"

She held up a hand, trying to get a grip on the situation. "You're…proposing to me…in a graveyard." And she started to laugh.

She laughed herself silly. She laughed until it hurt and she was bent over double, her hands on her knees, eyes tearing. "Oh, Christ," she hooted, swiping the back of her hand over them. She raised herself back up to standing, throwing her head back to peer at the sky. "That's good stuff."

"You 'bout done, sweetheart?"

She saw the deep-riddled scowl on his face and sighed at him. "Oh, I'm done. Believe you me."

He smacked his lips together unsatisfactorily. "Fine." He turned sharply on his heel and walked away.

She tailed him. "Wait a minute. Where're you going?"

"I know when I'm licked," he tossed over his shoulder.

She sprinted to catch up and grabbed her head when it protested. "Stop, please!"

He whirled back around just as fast as he'd left. "Look, I'll get on my knees."

"Everett—"

"Is that what you want, Kaya? You want me on my knees for you?"

"No!" she shouted when he started to kneel. "Get up!" Grabbing him by the shoulders, she yanked until he straightened to his full height again. She hissed when her head sang an aching tune.

He cradled the side of her head gently.

Who knew he could be so gentle? Yet another reason she loved him. "I don't want you to kneel for me," she told him. "Life's brought you to your knees one too many times before." Before he could open his mouth, she clapped her hand over it to make sure he listened for once. "And my answer isn't no. It was never no. It's yes."

As she lowered her hand, he blurted, "Yes?"

"Unequivocally yes," Kaya breathed and beamed at his utter confusion. "It may kill us both, but I'll be your wife." She framed his face in her hands and stroked his bearded cheeks. "You won't have to walk this world alone anymore—or the next one."

He lost his breath. His hands met either side of her jaw and he lowered his brow to hers. "It's a yes."

"Yes." She would've closed her eyes if he had. But understanding started to gleam there and she saw relief riding behind it. She threw her arms around him and buried her face in his shoulder. "I told you, didn't I—that I was your woman?"

"Christ," he breathed in disbelief. "Mine."

"I didn't think I was strong enough," she admitted.

"You're the strongest person I've ever known," he said. "I'm in love with you—and have been for a while. Sorry it's taken me so long to say it. I guess I wasn't strong enough, either. You make me stronger."

She sighed, taking a moment to savor it all. He loved her. He wanted to be with her, always. "I love you, too." She swallowed. "I love you so much, I'm overwhelmed by it. You're not walking away, and neither am I. This is it."

He nodded. "This is it," he whispered in agreement.

"I'm in, Everett—all in. Do you see that?"

"I see you," he assured her. He swayed with her over the grass. His arms gathered her against his chest. "I see us." He touched a kiss to her cheek, then the high point of her brow and her other cheek. He grinned and she felt his happiness and her own radiating through her. "To the very end."

In the quiet glade, in the shadow of the trees, she felt Everett's warmth and for the first time in her life, she knew something beyond life's uncertainty. She was certain they would be together. She was certain they would love each other truly, uncompromisingly.

To the very end.

* * * * *